Praise for Sharon Ward

Sharon Ward's IN DEEP is a stellar, pulse-pounding debut novel featuring a female underwater photographer. A heady mix of underwater adventure, mystery, and romance.

— Hallie Ephron, New York Times bestselling author

Pack your SCUBA fins for a wild trip to the Cayman Islands. *In Deep* delivers on twists and turns while introducing a phenomenal new protagonist in underwater photographer Fin Fleming, tough, perceptive and fearless.

— Edwin Hill, author of *The Secrets We Share*

How much did I love In Deep? Let me count the ways. Fin Fleming, underwater photographer, is a courageous yet vulnerable protagonist I want to sip Margaritas with. The Cayman Islands are exotic and alluring, yet tinged with danger. The underwater scenes and SCUBA diving details are rendered in stunning detail. Wrap that all into a thrilling mystery and you'll be left as breathless as - well, no spoilers here. You must read it to find out!

— C. Michele Dorsey, Author of the Sabrina Salter Mysteries: No Virgin Island, Permanent Sunset, and Tropical Depression

Breathtaking on two levels, Sharon Ward's debut novel IN DEEP will captivate experienced divers as well as those who've only dreamed of exploring the beauty beneath the sea. The underwater world off the Cayman Islands is stunningly rendered, and the complex mystery involving underwater photographer Fin Fleming, especially the electrifying dive scenes, will have readers holding their breath. Brava!

— Brenda Buchanan Author of the Joe Gale Mystery Series

In Deep is a smart and original story that sucks you in from page one. Edge-of-your-seat suspense, a hauntingly realistic villain, and a jaw-dropping twist make this pacy read unputdownable until the very last word.

— Stephanie Scott-Snyder, Author of When Women Offend: Crime and the Female Perpetrator

Sea Monsters

Sea Monsters

The Fin Fleming Scuba Diving Mystery Series

Book 8

Sharon Ward

Covers by Cover2Book.com

ISBN eBook: 978-1-958478-26-4

ISBN Trade Paper: 978-1-958478-27-1

ISBN Hard Cover: 978-1-958478-28-8

Printed in USA

First Edition

Taylor and Milan, Brave Souls

And Jack, who continues to be the best husband in the universe.

ALONZO

Chapter 1
Alonzo

ALONZO HAD no reason to be nervous. Everybody knew he had full rights to be diving here—now or any other time he wanted. Even so, he looked around, making sure he was alone and that nobody was watching his dive preparations.

But he was nervous because this dive was different.

He was aware that the difference was all inside his own head. He hadn't told anyone about his suspicions, and of course, nobody could read his mind. But still he felt that little spark of fear, making his hands tremble and his breath come faster.

He took a couple of gentle, deep breaths to slow down his heart rate and to control his air consumption. The dive would be deep, so he'd need to take as many tanks as he could carry to make sure he'd have enough time to take a good look around the site. He wanted as much dive time as possible to see if he could find proof that his suspicions were true.

This tiny island had been in his family for generations, and the entire family had always worked hard to make it prosperous and healthy. Then his father died—or at least, they'd assumed he was dead. He'd gone out in his boat one day and never returned.

After what he'd deemed a 'suitable' interval, his older brother Miguel had petitioned the court to declare his father dead. As soon as the judge granted the petition, Miguel had sold the family's island to a construction company, Kraken Industries and Resorts.

The company had said they wanted to build a unique luxury resort on the island, one with several lavish underwater glass walled suites and viewing rooms as well as all the usual topside hotel amenities. They'd sworn they would abide by environmentally safe building practices and do nothing to harm the island or the surrounding waters. But now they were two years into the project, and they'd made very little progress on the land-based part of the resort.

They'd also promised Miguel that Mama could live rent free on the island for the rest of her life, but Alonzo knew she was increasingly unhappy staying there. Her favorite goat was ill again, and her prized chickens had also grown sickly. Her best pig had died while trying to give birth to a malformed piglet that was already dead. After that, Mama had crossed herself and retreated to her back porch where she couldn't see the destruction of her now despoiled island home.

And another thing. Lately Alonzo had noticed dead fish and birds washing up on the once pristine sandy beaches. The formerly pure white sand was now a grimy, gritty, grey. The fresh water from the spring in the island's center, once deliciously pure, now tasted rank and oily.

He knew there was something wrong.

Really wrong.

He'd applied for a job with the construction company, and to his surprise, they'd hired him right away to work in the office. He kept a sharp eye open for anything that seemed out of place, but he didn't see anything in the records that might account for the environmental changes.

That's when he'd decided to ask for a transfer to the underwater construction crew. Maybe the problem was happening underwater, out of sight. It'd been hard to bide his time until he'd earned the trust of the top managers, but he thought for sure he had it now.

He'd made the transfer months ago, and until this week they still hadn't allowed him to join the team actually working on the project. Instead, day after day, they'd assigned him to surface support.

Every. Single. Day.

It was time to up his investigation.

Hence, today's solo dive.

The sun had barely been up when he'd lugged his tanks and his gear over to the wooden platform the company's divers used each day when they set off to work underwater. He planned to carry multiple tanks he could use depending on his depth, how long his dive lasted, and what he encountered while he was down there.

Because he didn't know what he might find during the dive, he had several different kinds of breathing gas with him. He'd thought of everything.

He had a tank of Trimix—a mixture of helium, oxygen, and nitrogen that would allow him to extend his bottom time and could help protect him from decompression sickness in case he had to go deep. He had a Nitrox tank to allow him to extend his dive time when he was above ninety feet, and two tanks of regular air on a double backplate.

In addition, he had a small spare air tank in the pocket of his BCD—his buoyancy control device that helped him stay at a specific depth underwater or to relax and float on the surface without having to kick or swim. He was well prepared.

The gear was heavy, weighing close to 350 or 400 pounds, so he dropped the Trimix and Nitrox tanks over the edge of the platform attached to a line. He'd attach them to his side harnesses once he was underwater where their weight would be more manageable. He leaned over and put his hand on the side of a nearby cart for balance while he slipped his feet into his full-foot fins. Then he pulled on his mask and stepped into the water.

As soon as he'd attached his supplementary tanks, he began his descent. He looked around with puzzled sorrow, remembering that in years past, the underwater visibility had stretched out to two or three hundred feet horizontally through water as clear as glass. But now, the ocean water was full of greyish silt, and he could only see about fifteen feet in any direction.

He thought maybe the water would clear up as he descended and left the construction detritus behind, so he swam down quickly, pausing only to clear his ears. After a minute, he was well below sixty feet, but visibility hadn't gotten any better.

A trickle of water leaked into his mask from the space under his nose where his mustache made it impossible to get a tight seal. The water was cool, but still it felt like his skin was burning where the water touched it. He opened his mouth in shock at the burn, and water seeped in around his regulator. That burned too, and the water tasted awful. He removed his regulator so he could cough and spit to get rid of the nasty water. He purged the regulator and replaced his mouthpiece before continuing his descent.

When he neared the bottom of the wall, he swam around the base of the island, which had been formed by volcanic activity eons ago. He knew the entire area well. After all, he'd been born on the island and he'd been diving here since he was a child.

He neared an area where his father had always told him not to dive. Papa had said sea monsters lived there, and that Miguel and Alonzo should always stay as far away as possible. But later, shortly before he'd disappeared, Papa had taken Miguel diving there. Neither ever told Alonzo what they saw, but before he left the island Miguel had said there were so many monsters down below that he'd never again in his life have to worry about money.

Alonzo wasn't sure what he meant by that, except if it was true about the money, then why had Miguel sold the island?

Alonzo swam past some metal debris left by the construction crew, and then passed a small conical contraption that thrummed with a low and unpleasant noise that made him dizzy. He kept going until he swung around a large coral formation deeply shadowed by the shelf of the massive pinnacle overhanging it. He fished a small underwater flashlight out of his BCD pocket and flicked it on so he could check out the area. He immediately noticed something he'd never seen before.

It looked like the mouth of a small cave. How could a cave have suddenly appeared? He desperately wanted to see what was inside, but the cave entrance was too small for him to enter while wearing all those bulky tanks, so he detached the two tanks from his side mounts to streamline his profile enough to squeeze through the entrance.

He was excited by his find. Could this cave be where the monsters his father had talked about lived? And what kind of monsters had he meant?

There was only one way to find out. Holding his flashlight ahead of him to light his way, he swam bravely into the mouth of the cave.

Alonzo had too much experience as a diver to go deeply into the cave without ropes or a reel, and his light was much too feeble to illuminate the entire cave from the entrance. He was wildly curious to see the cavern's interior, so even though it wasn't a good practice, he opted to go further inside, even without the proper safety equipment.

He promised himself that no matter what he saw, he wouldn't go into the cave very far on this first dive. He could always come back another time with the necessary cave diving safety equipment so he could explore the cave more fully. To be even safer on this first exploration, he decided he'd turn around when he still had well over half his breathing gases in his tanks.

He knew that by keeping the main wall on his left side as he penetrated the cavern, he could easily find his way back to the entry point by turning around so the wall was on his right when he wanted to exit.

He just couldn't go more than arm's length from the cavern's wall. No exploration on branching routes. No trips across the cavern's center. He swore to himself that no matter what he saw inside, he'd stay close to the cave's wall so he wouldn't get lost or disoriented.

He swam ahead slowly, pausing after every kick to shine his light around the cavern to see what was there. He'd gone in far enough so that he could no longer see the cave's entrance when he turned around to look for it. He strained his eyes, searching for the exit when a glint in the feeble beam of his flashlight caught his eye.

He stared. The object looked like it was made of shiny yellow metal, and at first he thought it was a giant squid with big eyes and long tentacles. The he realized it was a kraken statue. Whatever it was, it looked valuable, but why would anyone hide such a valuable object here?

Curious and excited, he forgot about his promise to stay close to the wall. He swam quickly over to investigate his find.

Nestled next to a large clump of coral, there was indeed a golden sea monster figurine. In fact, there were dozens of them, along with gold coins and several pieces of gold jewelry. He touched the kraken gently, almost reverently. He put the golden kraken in his BCD pocket to take back with him, then he reached out with one finger and caressed the scales on the back of a tiny seahorse dressed in jeweled armor.

These statues were so beautiful, and there were so many of them. And if they were real gold, he finally understood why Miquel had said he'd never have to worry about money again.

He tamped down his rage at his brother and his father, who'd been sitting on this trove of potential wealth while his poor mother had worked so hard her whole life, tending the livestock, cooking, and cleaning up after them. They could have easily given her a life of ease, but they'd chosen not to. What sense did it make to hoard a treasure while his sweet mother worked herself half to death? He shook his head at their stupidity and selfishness.

He stuffed a few more of the figurines and a gold ring set with a large pearl into the inner pocket of his BCD before realizing it was past time to head for the surface. His air was already running low, well past the turn-around point he'd promised himself.

He'd forgotten about cave diving safety procedures, and he'd turned around several times as he examined the treasure. Now, without the wall to guide him on his way out, Alonzo was confused and disoriented. He swam quickly in the direction where he thought the mouth of the cave was, but soon bumped into a wall. He turned around, swinging his flashlight to see if he could catch a glimmer of light from outside the cave. His heart was pounding and his mouth was dry. He'd been so stupid.

Stupid, and just as greedy as his father and his brother.

He took a deep breath to control his panic. There. Was that spot ahead just a little bit lighter, the faint glow showing the way back to open water? Maybe he was fooling himself, but it didn't matter either way. He had to get out of the cave, and with no idea which way was out, this direction was as good as any.

After a few kicks he breathed a sigh of relief. The glow was getting brighter. He'd chosen his direction well.

A couple more kicks, and he exited the cave. He spared a quick glance for the buzzing mechanical cones he'd seen earlier, although he still had no idea what they were. He started to ascend, turning to swim back along the vertical wall as he rose.

He hadn't gone more than a few kicks when he felt a blinding pain in his head and across his back. He gasped in shock, and his regulator flew out of his mouth. The impact pushed him down to a shelf of rock that jutted out below him. As he landed on the shelf, a heavy metal plate settled across his back, pinning him to the rocks. The weight held his entire body, including his neck and shoulders, immobilized. No matter how he pushed and squirmed, he couldn't dislodge the heavy plate. He stretched out his right arm to try to recover his regulator, but both the hose and regulator were on top of the metal. With most of his right arm pinned under the plate, he couldn't reach them.

The heavy plate had his left arm pinned against unyielding rock, so he couldn't use it to reach the spare air canister in his BCD pocket. He'd die very soon unless he could get to his regulator or the spare air.

Without one or the other, at best he had only minutes to live.

He struggled to dislodge the metal plate pinning him to the bottom, but it was so heavy that he couldn't lift it. A few tears leaked from his eyes and pooled in the skirt of his shattered mask. His mouth opened in a scream, releasing the last breath in his body.

FIN

Chapter 2
Bloody Bay Wall

RAFE and I stepped off the platform on the stern of the *Tranquility* at the same time. We met underwater at about five feet of depth and gave each other the okay sign and a big happy grin. This was to be the last dive of our very short honeymoon, and we wanted to make it memorable.

And although I planned to keep my name—Fin Fleming—during our marriage, it still surprised me to remember that now I was also Mrs. Rafe Cummings, wife of Hollywood's hottest action star. I am a lucky woman, in so many ways.

We'd decided to get married on the spur of the moment, and we immediately rushed off on our honeymoon because Rafe had to be on the set of his next movie very soon. In the middle of the night, I'd left my post as VP of marketing and chief underwater photographer at RIO—the Madelyn Anderson Russo Institute of Oceanography—with no notice whatsoever except a gleeful voice mail for Maddy, RIO's CEO, letting her know I'd be away for a few days or maybe even a week. I did not say where I was going.

Maddy is also my mother, so even though what I did was unprofessional, I was pretty sure I'd still have a job when I got back to Grand Cayman. Even so, I didn't like that I'd left her and the rest of the RIO team in the lurch like that. Usually I was hyper-responsible, worrying about every detail and shouldering every task that came my way without comment or complaint.

Things had moved quickly once Rafe and I decided to get married, and we'd eloped in the middle of the night as soon as we'd made the decision. We'd spent our short honeymoon on Little Cayman, diving multiple times per day, taking long walks on the beach with our newly adopted puppy Penny, and eating.

Oh, how we ate.

Even Rafe had relaxed his normally strict eating habits and treated himself to the occasional bite of dessert or a few sips of a cocktail. To my eyes, even after his indulgences he didn't look any different than he had when he subsisted on salad and an occasional bit of meat or carbs.

I smiled at Rafe, and he smiled back. Even with a regulator in his mouth, he looked good. We held hands and drifted slowly toward the reef at Mixing Bowl, one of the most popular sites on Little Cayman. The site was located at the juncture of Bloody Bay Wall and Jackson Bight, so it had a variety of terrain—something for everyone from steep walls to swim throughs to hardpan. The sea life was equally as diverse, and divers often say you can dive the site every day and it will be different every time.

Of course, when it comes to sea life, they follow their own agenda, so that statement could apply to almost every dive site in the world, but it's especially appropriate at this one. Rafe and I had already been to this site several times during our short stay, and we'd loved it each time.

Today we made our way through the big swim-through that dropped us out at around 100 feet. We checked the current and headed into it. We didn't want our accumulated nitrogen load to force us to cut our dive time too short, so almost immediately, we began ascending slowly while we kicked along the wall admiring the coral and abundant sea life.

Right away, two beautiful turtles with bright curious eyes veered our way and swam along beside us until a very large and very friendly grouper decided to join the crowd. The turtles calmly swung away into the blue, and the grouper stayed with us. Fish faces are usually pretty inscrutable, but I'd have sworn this particular grouper wore a happy smile.

An exceptionally large green moray eel stuck his head out of a crevice in the wall and flexed his jaws into the current. He looked menacing, but I knew he was just trying to breathe.

A few feet further on, three dolphins and two eagle rays passed us out in the blue. They were swimming in opposite directions and seemed to take no notice of each other.

A nurse shark slept peacefully under a rocky overhang. She opened one eye and glared at us while we stared at her. Her facial expression clearly told us she would be much happier if we would please go away. We obliged.

We crested the reef top at around twenty feet and checked out the coral groves scattered across the hardpan. One large barrel sponge held a tiny seahorse, and the next was home to a juvenile spotted drum, swimming gracefully back and forth in a tiny circle, almost like he was pacing around a room, impatiently waiting to become an adult.

Next we swung over to the other side of the path we were following and found several Southern stingrays buried in the sand. Stingrays are my favorites, so I was very happy to see them. We swam through a school of horse-eye jacks, and then we stared in awe at a school of chromis so thick the water seemed to have turned into a solid purple wall. A queen triggerfish, three grey angelfish, two black durgon, a couple of Spanish hogfish, and a Caribbean reef shark rounded out the rest of the dive.

The coral was magnificent as well. Huge barrel sponges, elegant elkhorn coral, brain corals, black coral, and more, most in vibrant tones of red, orange, and purple, made the site shine with an unearthly beauty. We were entranced.

Even though we'd been diving on this same site several times already, Mixing Bowl was such a great site we kept coming back for more. We'd vowed to return whenever we could get to Little Cayman, but for now, air supply and bottom time said we had to leave. Reluctantly, we headed back to the mooring where we'd left my boat, the *Tranquility*.

We reached the mooring line, but when I looked up, I realized right away that something was wrong. There was no reassuring shadow of my boat waiting on the surface for our return.

I was sure we were at the right mooring, and I didn't think we'd been careless when we tied the boat off before the dive.

My heart hammered constantly during the three minute safety stop. I loved the *Tranquility*. What could have happened to it? I desperately needed to surface to make sure the boat was okay, but I didn't want to risk our health by skipping the safety stop after several days where we made five dives each day. Our tissues were too saturated with nitrogen to risk skipping the simple safety precaution. And really, how much worse would things be in just three minutes?

We finally surfaced and circled in all directions, looking for any glimpse of my boat. There wasn't a single sign of it anywhere, not even drifting along the horizon. *Tranquility* was simply gone.

I was fraught with worry about the *Tranquility*. My mouth went dry and my heart thudded, making it hard to breathe. The boat meant a lot to me. It had originally belonged to Ray Russo, my late stepfather. I'd spent the happiest days of my childhood on his boat. Ray had left it to me in his will, and I sent a silent thank you to him every time I boarded her.

I couldn't imagine what might have happened to my boat, but there wasn't much we could do to find it in the current circumstances. The lost boat had left us stranded out here in the open sea, far from land.

Rafe took my hand and squeezed it, while removing his regulator from his mouth with his other hand. "We'll get your boat back, wherever it is. Don't you worry. But right now, let's start swimming."

We both blew air into the inflators to conserve the remaining air in our tanks for emergencies rather than use the auto-inflators on our BCDs. Then we put our snorkels in our mouths and started to swim as fast as we could toward the distant shore. After our blissful honeymoon, we were in a hurry to start our new life together—and to begin the hunt for my missing boat.

Chapter 3
Homecoming

RAFE and I are both superb swimmers and in excellent physical condition. We made it safely back to land after the long swim, but other than being extremely thirsty, we were none the worse for wear.

Luckily, we came ashore near the Little Cayman Research Center, and after a long drink of water, we begged a ride to our hotel to pick up Penny and our luggage. They offered to wait at the hotel while we settled our bill.

The team at the research center and I were old friends. They'd known me since I was a small child, and they knew Maddy well. Since our phones were aboard my missing boat, they kindly called the coast guard to report the loss of the *Tranquility* and offered to ferry us back to Grand Cayman aboard one of their cutters rather than take us to the airport as we'd originally requested. We were extremely grateful for the offer because we didn't want to risk flying so soon after multiple days of diving. Our tissues were saturated with nitrogen from diving, and the reduced air pressure during the flight might have set off bouts of decompression sickness.

We had originally planned to use the *Tranquility* to get home, so decompression sickness hadn't entered into our logistics planning. Rafe needed to get back to Grand Cayman for a meeting with the director and the other stars of his upcoming movie. Luckily, they'd all jumped at the chance to hold the meeting in the Caymans, especially after Rafe had offered to foot the bill for their airfare and allow them to stay in private suites in his renovated mansion in Hell.

The trip across the water was uneventful, another blessing because it could be rough. We'd worried about Penny, but she handled the trip like a professional sailor, even wearing her life vest without complaint.

I'd asked the boat's pilot to drop us off at Rum Point. We could walk to my house from there, and after asking for permission, we stored our luggage at the nearby restaurant, promising to pick it up the next day.

During the mile walk home I couldn't stop myself from stressing out about the *Tranquility*. I alternated between berating myself for not double checking that the mooring was secure and speculating that pirates or opportunistic joy riders had taken the boat. Neither scenario felt right to me, but I couldn't imagine any other reason my beloved boat would have disappeared.

I held Penny's leash and Rafe carried the duffle bags containing our gear. I was happy when we finally walked around the bend in the road and I saw my home. Then an unexpected moment of shyness overcame me, and I stumbled a bit.

Rafe and I had gotten married so quickly that we hadn't taken the time to discuss where we'd live after the honeymoon. Soon we'd need to decide where our home would be. I loved my house, and with a sinking heart I realized I didn't want to live anywhere else.

We stopped at the end of my walk. "Good to be home, huh?" Rafe said. "Don't get me wrong—the honeymoon was great. But my life is so crazy that I always crave quiet serenity when I'm home. And that's exactly what I feel when I'm at your place. Will you think I'm too forward if I suggest we make your house our home base instead of my mansion?"

I could feel my face glow with happiness. Every day, with almost every interaction, Rafe proved over and over again that I had made the right choice. I knew I was the luckiest woman alive.

"I'd like that," I said. "I love my home, and I'll love it even more when you're living here with me."

"Whew," he said. "I'm glad you don't want to move into the

mansion. It's beautiful, but it doesn't feel like a real home. Not like your place does."

"Correction. Not like *our* place does," I said.

His smile was as bright as the afternoon sun in the Cayman skies. "How about if you bring Penny in and give her a drink while I clean the gear?"

"It's a deal," I said.

Rafe strolled off toward the garage where I kept the large barrel I used as a rinse tank, while Penny and I walked down the path. I fished my keys out of the canvas tote I use as a purse and unlocked the door. I dropped the keys in the blue bowl on the glass table beside the door and knelt to unhook Penny's leash.

I nearly jumped out of my skin when I heard Liam say, "It's about time you got home. Where have you been?"

He was sitting on my couch, wearing cargo shorts and a blue RIO t-shirt. He'd kicked off his sandals and propped his bare feet up on the coffee table. His computer was on his lap. Several folders and lots of paper littered the couch, the floor, and the tabletop. He looked right at home, which made sense. During our relationship, he'd often worked from my couch.

"What are you doing here?" I stammered.

"Waiting for you, obviously," he said. "I've been here all day for the last three days waiting for you to get home. I was getting nervous because I had no idea where you were."

The front door swung open and Rafe walked in. He looked startled when he saw Liam. "What are you doing here?"

Liam scowled. "Right now, I'm trying to have a conversation with my fiancée," he said. "And I'd appreciate some privacy."

"It looks to me like you're trying to have a conversation with my wife," Rafe said coolly.

Liam blanched and turned to me. "His wife? What's going on? I thought *we* were engaged."

"After our last conversation on the topic, I broke it off, remember? And I left you a note explaining once again why it had to be that way. It was right beside the coffee maker the last time you were home. Didn't you see it?"

He shook his head. "Chico startled me with an unexpected crow, and I spilled the coffee that morning. I remember there was a paper towel on the counter next to your engagement ring. I used the paper towel to mop up the mess." He fished in his pocket. "Here's your ring. You must have forgotten it that day."

I tried to keep my voice steady. "I told you before you went to bed that night that I couldn't live under the conditions you wanted. I thought you knew I meant we were no longer engaged."

I put my hands on my hips. "I knew you weren't listening to what I said. That's why I wrote the note on that paper towel, explaining once again why I couldn't marry a man that would disappear without a word, never let me know where he was while he was gone, and not even bother to call or text while he's away, especially because each time he disappeared I would know that the trip was dangerous. And I didn't forget my ring. I was returning it to you. We're not engaged."

He snorted. "Rafe, Fin and I need a few moments of privacy to straighten this out."

Rafe looked at me with a question on his face.

I squared my shoulders. "There's nothing to straighten out. Anything you want to say to me you can say in front of my husband. And I'll need your key to my house back before you leave."

Liam looked from Rafe to me and back again. "Wow! It didn't take you long to reel him in, now did it?" he said harshly. He gathered up his papers, closed his computer, and put everything into his bag. Then he fished his key out of his pocket and placed it on the coffee table. "See you around." He slammed the glass sliding door on his way out.

Chapter 4
Aftermath

RAFE LOOKED AT ME, uncertainty showing clearly in his glorious blue eyes. He swallowed hard. "Do you want to go to him?" he asked. His voice cracked, and when I heard that forlorn sound, my heart cracked too.

I shook my head. "No. I made it clear weeks ago that our relationship was over for good if he didn't let me know where and when he'd be traveling and connect with me by phone or text at least once a day. I don't think that's too much to ask. He refused to even consider it. When he skipped out on Oliver and Genevra's wedding without a word, he made his own feelings quite clear. Liam and I had been over for a long time. We just couldn't admit it to ourselves. I married you, and I'm very happy I did."

Truthfully, I had a nanosecond's worth of misgiving. I hated that I had hurt Liam. We'd been together for a long time. And obviously, I hadn't made my feelings as clear to him as I'd thought I had. Either that, or he'd deliberately chosen to ignore my needs. Again.

But on balance, I knew I'd done the right thing. Rafe and I had hit it off from the first moment we met. Our interests and abilities were perfectly aligned, and we loved working together and even just being together hanging around and doing nothing. I loved everything about him.

The troubled look cleared from Rafe's face as he listened to me. I was amazed that this man—a man beloved by millions of fans, one who could have married almost any woman in the world—had chosen me. I said a thank you to whatever part of the universe had blessed me with such amazing good luck.

"C'mon," I said. "Let's show Penny around her new yard and introduce her to Chico and Henrietta."

Although Penny had been to my house before, she hadn't spent a lot of time here. And I'd made it a point to keep the free-range rooster and his mate away from my new puppy until I was sure she'd settled in.

But before we could go outside, I heard several loud bangs from the backyard. I rushed out through the slider to see what had caused the racket. One last bang drew my eyes to the fence between Liam's yard and mine. He'd hammered a board over the pass through that Chico and Henrietta used to travel between our yards. The birds were firmly on his side of the fence.

Luckily most of the rest of his yard wasn't fenced in. Before Liam had bought the house next door to mine, the chickens had roamed freely around the neighborhood. They knew how to scratch at my front door if they wanted to see me, but Liam's petty revenge irritated me.

Rafe looked from the makeshift blockade in the fence to the irritation on my face. "I'll handle this." He stalked off toward the gate.

"No, don't aggravate him," I said. "He'll cool down soon enough."

Rafe nodded. "Not planning to annoy him. Just taking care of the livestock." He went into my garage and came out with a hammer, some kind of saw, and a couple of hinges. I hadn't even known I possessed such things.

I watched while he sat cross-legged near the gate that led from my backyard to the street. After he sawed out a rooster-sized piece of the fence. He handled the section he'd removed carefully while he installed hinges on the top of the piece, and on the fence just above where he'd cut the segment out. He fiddled around for a few minutes, then he stood.

"Tada," he said with a flourish. "Behold your new chicken gate."

I smiled with delight. "It's perfect. Thank you so much. Now I just hope Chico and Henrietta can find it."

He laughed. "Gotcha covered." He went inside the house and returned with a handful of seeds. He dropped a few on this side of the chicken gate, and then left through the people gate.

I walked over to watch him as he left a trail of seeds from the edge of my yard that abutted Liam's property directly to the new gate. He went inside the house again and returned with the water bowl I used for the birds. I truly could not believe how caring this man was, and how diligent he was about making me happy.

Yes, I was lucky indeed.

When he'd finished ensuring Chico and Henrietta would know they were welcome, we sat on the edge of the pool and dangled our feet in the water, not speaking, happy just to be together. Penny slept in the shade of the umbrella over the nearby table. I sighed with contentment.

The gate swung open. I was afraid it was Liam, but it was my father, Newton Fleming, with his friend and rival for my mother's affection Dane Scott of the Royal Cayman Islands Police. With them were two men I didn't know. One wore the uniform of the Cayman Coast Guard. The other wore a plain grey business suit and carried a slim leather portfolio. He must have been sweltering in the late-day heat.

I stood up when I saw them. Newton and Dane both kissed my cheek.

"Congratulations. Make her happy," Newton said when he shook Rafe's hand.

"You'll answer to both of us if you don't," Dane said.

Rafe laughed and held up his hands in a warding gesture. "Have no fear. My intention is to make her the happiest woman in the world."

"Good," Dane said. "Now that we have that settled, I have to confess this isn't a social call." He turned to the other men. "This is Captain Peter Roberts of the Coast Guard, and my brother, Marvin Scott of the department of the environment."

"Welcome," I said. "Please have a seat." I gestured to the nearby table, which had enough seating for eight people.

Rafe excused himself and went into the house while the four men and I sat down. Marvin Scott placed his leather folder on the table in front of him. Nobody spoke until Rafe returned a few minutes later, carrying a tray with cheese, fruit, veggies, two kinds of dip, and other snacks along with a pitcher of icy lemonade.

I felt flabbergasted. "Where did all that come from?" I asked. Usually, my house was famously empty of anything edible.

He grinned impishly. "I called Maddy and Theresa while you were in the shower at the research center. They took care of stocking the house for our return."

Newton laughed. "And Maddy called and told me the happy news. Otherwise, I wouldn't have had any idea when you'd be returning home. Luckily, we had a plan in place if we needed it."

His laugh made me feel warm and loved. Not only was I lucky enough to be married to the absolutely incredible Rafe Cummings, I had family and friends that wanted nothing but the best for me.

After a few moments, the smiles at the table faded. "We have a favor to ask of you," Marvin Scott, the department of the environment man said. "It's a big ask, but my brother says you're the best person for the job."

"I have a job," I said. "And I've been away from it far too long already."

He nodded. "I know. Maybe we should start at the beginning so you have the full picture." He turned to my father. "The story starts with you."

Newton poured himself a glass of lemonade and took a sip before he spoke. "Many years ago, my mother hired a young girl to be a maid in her house. Rosalina's primary language was Spanish, and she didn't speak English very well. We became friends, and she taught me a little Spanish and I taught her a little more English."

"Rosalina had grown up on an island very near here. It's a tiny islet, not actually part of the Cayman Islands. Her family owned the island she grew up on and had for centuries. It was just big enough for her family to grow a few vegetables and keep a few goats and chickens. After she'd been with us in Nantucket for a few years, she asked to go back to her home island. She wanted to marry her childhood sweetheart."

"We were sorry to see her go, but we sent her off with a party, a pocket full of money, and our best wishes. Other than a holiday card every year, I never heard from her again. At least, not until I received a letter from her a few weeks ago."

He took another sip of lemonade. "She's an old woman now. Her husband died, and it seems her oldest son, Miguel, sold the island to a construction company without her permission. The company told him they were going to build a resort—one with a few suites of underwater rooms as well as the usual topside accommodation. Miquel took the money they gave him and left the island. She hasn't heard from him for months. Her younger son, Alonzo, got a job working for the construction company, but now he's disappeared too. She hasn't seen him for weeks."

"Meanwhile, she says the construction company is making a mess of her island, digging up random holes and leaving piles of debris everywhere. Worse yet, she says the water surrounding the island is getting more and more polluted. An oily film covers the surface. Dead fish are washing up onto the beach. There's a foul stench. And the fresh water supply, which comes from a spring in the island's center, is now barely drinkable."

"Rosalina knows about my work with environmental causes, so her letter begged me to investigate. I called in the department of the environment and the Coast Guard. Even though the island isn't part of the Cayman Island group, it's close enough that severe pollution is a big concern to them. It's private property, so we can't go onto the island without permission, but we've seen enough from a distance to be really concerned. That's where you come in."

I looked at him, puzzled. "What can I do? I don't have any standing to investigate the company. There must be better ways to find out what's going on."

Dane took over for Newton. "We'd like you to apply for a job with the construction company. They've been advertising for commercial divers to join the team. It would only be for a few days. You can quit and come home as soon as you figure out what they're really doing."

I shook my head. "They'll recognize my name—maybe even my face. It won't work."

Rafe broke in. "I don't like it no matter what. It's much too dangerous for Fin to be out there all alone with no backup."

Marvin Scott, the department of the environment guy, ignored Rafe's protest and spoke for the first time. "We've arranged for you to have a commercial diver's certification under another name. And an extensive resume, which will show your last job. We have a hot line set up that we'll answer like a company, and the phony company's HR department will confirm that they fired you for drinking on duty. You'll be a perfect hire for Kraken because they'll assume you're desperate, and that you won't look too closely at whatever it is they're doing."

Rafe stood up. "That doesn't ensure her safety once she's there all alone on the island. I should be there with her in case she needs a hand."

I shook my head. "You can't go with me. You've got filming starting in a few days, and you're way too recognizable anyway."

Newton bit his lip. "We will have someone else on the scene. Before we knew you and Liam had broken up, we'd hired his company to be in the area, supposedly filming a documentary on environmental remediation methods. He won't actually be on the island, but he'll only be a few miles away. He can get there quickly if you need help. Remember that watch with the beacon you used before? He'll have the receiver with him on the *Enviroman*. He'll know immediately if you summon him."

"That won't be awkward at all, now will it?" I said sarcastically.

Newton and Dane both shrugged. "Sorry, we didn't know about your breakup at the time we brought him into the operation," said Dane.

Dane's brother Marvin spoke up. "There's a lot of environmentally important locations in the area. We know for sure there's at least one octopus nursery and a nearby juvenile lemon shark habitat in the area. We've also picked up at least twenty green turtles sickened by some sort of industrial slime. Liam's team cleaned the turtles up and brought them to the Turtle Centre to nurse them back to health. Once they're well enough, the Centre will return them to the wild."

I glanced between Newton and Dane. They were adept at getting whatever they wanted, and Marvin had mentioned some of my favorite ocean creatures and causes. I wondered if they had rehearsed him. Both men tried to look innocent, but still, I had my suspicions.

"The only one of my favorites you didn't mention is stingrays," I said. "Why the omission?"

Newton bit back a rueful laugh. "I knew you'd catch on that we'd primed Marvin if we led with stingrays, but yes, there are—or were—a lot of them in the area. Take on this project in memory of Harry if for no other reason." Harry was a stingray I'd frequently interacted with a few years ago.

At last Captain Roberts of the Coast Guard spoke up. "We understand the incredible risk you'll be taking if you accept this project. I commit to you that we'll have a cutter nearby the entire time you're working on the island. We can extract you within minutes if you need us."

Rafe gave him a very unhappy look. "When seconds count, the police are only minutes away."

Newton choked back a laugh. "That's a line from one of your movies. My favorite movie, in fact. Wasn't it *Night Dives*?"

Rafe set his chin and hardened his eyes. "Might be a line from a movie, but that doesn't mean it's not true. I can't allow you to risk Fin's life. Get someone else."

I reached over and touched his hand. "I love being your wife, and I thank you for caring about me. But this is a cause I believe in—in fact, protecting the ocean and its inhabitants is the basis of my whole life's work. You know I can take care of myself. And you must also know that Newton would never ask me to do this if he thought there was any real danger."

Rafe stood up and went inside without another word. I heard the sound of the front door slamming.

There was an uncomfortable silence around the table.

Then Newton spoke. "Rafe's right. We shouldn't be asking you to risk your life, especially so soon after your wedding. I'm sorry. We'll find someone else."

He rose to leave.

"Sit down," I said, wondering if I'd regret agreeing to the operation. "I'll do it. What's the plan?"

Chapter 5
A Plan

NEWTON SHRUGGED and sat back down. "We took the liberty of sending your fake resume to the construction company, and you have a video interview set up for ten o'clock tomorrow morning."

Marvin opened the slim leather case he'd placed on the table in front of him and extracted a sheet of paper. He slid it across the table to me. "I suggest you familiarize yourself with the details of your history before then. We have people set up to respond appropriately to any reference calls or emails. But stay on script when you talk to Kraken, because the people on the phone won't have access to any details that aren't in the backgrounder."

His tone rankled. I might not be an undercover pro, but I knew better than to start improvising on the fly. It was hard enough to keep details straight under pressure without embroidering on the cover story.

Rafe had silently returned, and at Marvin's words, he walked over and stood at the head of the table. "If you don't think she's enough of a pro for the job, then don't ask her to do it. And if you think that she's the best person for the job, then don't belittle her with your stupid advice. She knows what she's doing." He folded his arms and glowered in turn at each of the men at the table.

Marvin's cheeks turned pink. "Sorry, Mr. Cummings. I forgot who I was dealing with."

"Apologize to her, not to me," Rafe said.

I stood up. "Rafe, thanks for trying to fight my battles for me, but as you know, I can take care of myself. And Marvin wasn't trying to belittle me. He was just showing his concern for my safety."

Marvin nodded. "That's right. I'm sorry if I offended anyone. My concern is just to get the job done and bring you home safely."

I nodded, but I didn't smile. I wasn't about to undertake such a dangerous job when the people supposedly on my side didn't have faith in my ability to complete it properly. "Good. Now if we're all on the same page, I accept your apology. Tell me the rest of the plan."

We spent the next hour going over the details. When everyone was satisfied that there were no loose ends or unanswered questions—at least, none that we could anticipate up front—we got ready to adjourn the meeting.

When the four men stood to go, I said, "Wait. I have one more question."

The men stopped and turned to me politely.

"Where'd you guys stash the *Tranquility* anyway?"

Newton sighed. "I told you guys she'd figure it out. I'm sorry. We needed you to be here for the interview, and the only way we could be sure you'd be home in time was to force you to cut your honeymoon short. We tied the *Tranquility* safely to the dock at Gus's place."

"What if we hadn't been able to make it back to shore?" I said.

He looked startled, like the thought that I might not have made it to shore safely had never crossed his mind. "I knew you had your beacon watch on. We kept tabs on you the whole time you were away."

I understood what he'd said, but I didn't like it. "I suppose a simple phone call never occurred to any of you?"

They all stared at me blankly, like they'd never heard of a phone. I resolved never to wear or carry anything Newton gave me from now on unless I'd first agreed to allow him to track me. He was very sweet, but there was obviously a lot more to him than the billionaire philanthropist the rest of the world saw. And I was just starting to learn about those hidden depths.

Chapter 6
Interview at the Bar

By ten AM the next morning, Rafe had flown off to his movie set and I was sitting at a table at Nelson's, the bar that belonged to my frenemy Stefan Gibb.

I'd agonized over finding just the right location for the video interview. My house was too upscale looking to fit with my cover story, and anywhere on the RIO grounds or at Fleming Environmental Investments would be too recognizable.

Nelson's was a popular place that wouldn't be associated with the real me in any way. I wanted the bar to be the background they'd see during the video interview because I thought that seeing me sitting in a bar would play into my backstory that my last employer had fired me for drinking on the job.

Stefan had made me a mocktail that looked exactly like a Tequila Sunrise, and I'd placed it prominently next to my left elbow where the interviewer couldn't miss it in the video frame. I took a couple of quick sips so it would look more convincing if the drink wasn't full to the brim. I wore my wireless ear pods to drown out the noise from the other patrons and the television over the bar.

At the last minute. I remembered to remove my new wedding ring. I sighed as I slipped the hammered silver band off my finger. For a moment, I stared at it remembering the words he'd said when he first showed it to me, just a few moments before we got married.

"The gems match the colors I see in your eyes," he'd said. "Each of its gems has a different color, and there's a color for every one of your moods. I bought this ring the first day we met, and I've carried it with me every day since then, hoping that someday this would happen. Thank you for making my dream come true."

I put the ring on the table in front of me, where it wouldn't be visible during the call. Then I took a sip of my drink.

I still had the drink's straw in my mouth when the screen sprang to life, and I was face-to-face with Brock Moran, the head of Kraken Industries and Resorts, and my potential future employer. I hastily put down my drink, making a show of being ultra-careful as I did so.

"Miss Hynes?" he said with a pleasant smile when we'd fully connected.

I nodded. "Nice to meet you, Mr. Kraken. Sorry. I mean, Mr. Moran."

He laughed. "I've often been called a monster, but never so charmingly."

I tried not to puke. "I need this job, so I'm just a little bit nervous," I said, staying in character.

"No need for nerves," he replied. "You're among friends. And you've already got the job if you want it. Your resume is very impressive." He looked down at some papers on the desk in front of him. "Very impressive indeed. The form says you have no family. Is that right?"

"Correct," I said.

"Good. You're exactly what we're looking for."

His tone made me nervous. I wondered whether he was impressed by "my" diving qualifications, or by the fact that I'd listed "none" in the next of kin space on the intake form I'd filled out earlier that morning.

"Your application says you have your own boat, so you won't need us to ferry you out to the island, which is great. That'll save us some time. I'll have my team email you the coordinates of the site as soon as we're done here."

He looked up from the resume and smiled. Maybe it was just a trick of the lighting or the camera angle, but his eyes glittered like ice and his teeth looked vaguely like fangs.

I shook off my fanciful fears. "Great. When can I start?"

"Before you accept the job, I should warn you that you'll be the only female member of the team, and we don't offer separate accommodations. Will that be a problem?"

I smiled like I didn't have a care in the world. "No problem. I'll probably spend my free time on my boat anyway. Most likely I'll sleep on it too if that's okay."

"Certainly," he said. "That's a good solution to the privacy issue if it will make you feel more comfortable. Can you be here by tomorrow morning? Or even better, later today so you can settle in and hit the ground running in the morning."

He looked away. "Oh, yes. And we'll need your banking information so we can deposit your salary. I hope we're offering enough money to tempt you."

"The salary's fine," I said. In fact, if I'd actually been in the market for a diving job, I'd have been overjoyed. "I'll email you my bank info later this morning." I picked up my drink and took a deep sip. "Thanks, Mr. Moran.

"Call me Brock," he said.

I had to glance down at the data sheet in front of me to remember what my cover name was. I'd immediately hated it, so my brain kept blotting it out. When I saw the name again, I almost groaned out loud, but I swallowed the groan and answered brightly. "Okay. And you can call me…Honey."

I cursed whoever on the project team had come up with that for my cover name. Honey Hynes. It sounded like a stage name for an exotic dancer. It was hard for me to even say it with a straight face, and I was pretty sure it would open me up to all kinds of jokes and harassment with the all-male crew. But too late now.

"Excellent. See you tomorrow, Honey." He leered at me, then broke off the call.

I gathered up my things and walked past the bar on my way out. I noticed Stefan had switched from the usual *Sea Hunt* reruns to a RIO documentary, as he often did when I was at his restaurant.

I hated it when he did that, but this time I simply shrugged and kept going. I had a lot on my mind and a very long to-do list if I was going to assume my new persona and start my new job later today.

Chapter 7
Setting Off

MOST DAYS a full-fledged marching band with tubas and bass drums could walk past Fred the chief security guard at RIO, and he might not notice. But today was not one of those days.

"Welcome back, Dr. Fleming," he bellowed when he caught sight of me. "How was the honeymoon?"

Every head in the atrium turned my way, and there were a lot of heads since it was almost time for one of the daily aquarium shows to kick off.

I blushed scarlet and waved as I ducked my head and practically ran for the corridor leading to the executive offices. I reached the conference room and slid into my seat. Dane, Newton, Marvin Scott, and Peter Roberts were sitting at the table, sipping coffee and munching on pastry. Penny was on the floor beside Dane.

I filled a RIO branded mug with coffee and grabbed two cookies from the platter on the sideboard. Despite the many pleasant distractions I'd enjoyed while I was away on my honeymoon, I'd really missed those cookies. I sat down in an empty seat where I could pat my dog and took a sip of coffee. "I'm in."

The men sighed with relief.

"When do you start?" asked Peter.

"Tomorrow morning. But they'd like me to arrive on the island today so I can get acclimated before I start work. I need a boat that's not as recognizable as *Tranquility.*"

Newton nodded. "All set. I've arranged for you to borrow *Sunshine Girl.*" He turned to Marvin and Peter. "It belongs to my friend Gus Simmons. He's a good man. Knows how to keep quiet."

He looked at the men around the table. "And before you ask, we already changed *Sunshine Girl*'s name and her registration numbers, so there's nothing that will lead back to Fin's real identity. Or to RIO or Fleming Environmental."

He pulled a hand drawn map out of his briefcase and placed it on the table between us. "The distances are estimates, but all the important landmarks are on here. It's probably good enough for you to find your way around the island."

He pointed out the dock, a few outbuildings, Rosalina's shack, the freshwater spring, and a spot on the other side of the island from the dock. "As best we can tell, they start all their dives from this spot."

"That makes no sense if they keep all their gear and tanks here." I pointed to the area on the other end of the map where the outbuildings were.

Newton nodded. "We agree. There must be a reason for it, and if you can figure it out, it may help us get what we need to put these bad guys away."

I nodded in agreement. "I'll do my best. Dane, you've got Penny until either Rafe or I return, right?" I asked.

"Right. Maddy and I are already planning to spoil her rotten."

"Her life vest, bedding, food, and clothes are on the *Tranquility*. You can grab them anytime."

He smiled. "Already taken care of."

I ran through a mental checklist of what I'd need for this operation. "I have clothes and everything else I need on *Tranquility*, so I can just pack a few toiletries and books and head out if someone can give me a ride over to Gus's dock."

"Not so fast," Newton said. "Let's talk about communication protocols and extraction procedures first."

He opened his briefcase and pulled out a phone. "Use this one. We'll always know where you are as long as it's with you. And there's nothing on it that links to your real identity."

"It can track me underwater?" I asked, astonished.

He shook his head. "No, but here's a new dive watch. It's not as expensive looking as your old one, so it's more in line with your cover story. But like the old one, it has a built-in locator beacon, plus it has a built-in communicator if you need to talk to me in an emergency. If I'm not able to talk for some reason, Dane will have a duplicate of the other half of the paired communicators. This watch has more range than your old one, so that's good because by necessity we'll be further away. And remember, if anyone other than Dane or me answers when you call, don't talk or give anything away. The code word is muffin. If anyone uses the word in any form of communication, it means you're compromised. Do whatever you have to do to get out of there as fast as you can."

He looked at the other two men. "Sorry, gentlemen. I don't mean to exclude you from communicating with Fin, but we need to keep the circle tight. Her safety is our top priority."

He turned back to me, holding the new watch at an angle so I could see what he showed me. "This button activates the locator beacon. This one is the communicator button. You hold it down when you want to talk, like a walkie-talkie. This is the emergency extraction button. That button will call Liam on the *Environman*."

I frowned. "Let's hope I don't need to use that button."

Newton grinned. "Yes, for multiple reasons. By the way, Liam took Rafe's comments about every second counting in an emergency to heart, so he's been trying to find a way to legitimately get closer to the island so he can be there faster if you need him. He approached Moran about doing some real-time environmental remediation on the island and the surrounding ocean area. He thinks he convinced him that less pollution and a more proactive approach would mean less likelihood of government intervention. He's expecting to hear from Moran with a contract okay later this week."

I nodded but didn't say anything. I was happy to have backup on tap but not looking forward to interacting on the regular with Liam.

Next he handed me a small drawstring bag filled with what looked like a bunch of unrelated objects. "This is a perimeter alarm. Put the items in a circle around the area if you think you might be in danger. The circle can be pretty large, as long as each object has line of sight to at least one other beacon. Two or three of the others is even better."

"Are you joking? That stuff looks like a random assortment of junk," I said.

He laughed. "Yup. It's a Chaun special, and it's supposed to look like that. None of the objects will seem suspicious if you have them lying around. Just a bunch of old knickknacks and tchotchkes."

I nodded. "What else do you have for me?"

Newton smoothly continued as though I hadn't interrupted his presentation. The next thing he pulled out of his bag of tricks was a small pistol. "You know how to use this, right?"

I nodded. Rafe and I had been practicing every week at a nearby shooting range. Rafe needed to be a crack shot for his movie roles, and I'd gone along with him because I liked hanging out with Rafe. It turned out I was a pretty good shot. This was the same model I used at the range, and I was glad to have a weapon that I was comfortable with on this gig.

"Good. There's extra ammunition in the safe compartment on the *Sunshine Girl,* which we temporarily renamed *Thundercloud. Sunshine Girl* was in a few of the early RIO documentaries and we wanted to be sure Moran didn't recognize the boat's name. You know where the compartment is. Same place as the one Ray used. You can pick the boat up whenever you're ready to go. Gus says you already know where the spare key is."

I nodded. I occasionally borrowed *Sunshine Girl,* so I was familiar with her operation.

He pulled out a huge lethal-looking dive knife in a beat up thigh-worn scabbard, "Next…"

"No," I said. "No, no, no. I don't like knives and I don't want a knife. I never bring a knife when I dive. I'll stick with my dive scissors."

He shook his head. "Fin Fleming famously uses dive scissors, but Honey Hynes is not Fin Fleming. She likes having a big knife with her." He put the knife on the table along with the other equipment. "And besides, there may come a time when it'll come in handy. Better to have it and not need it than to need it and not have it."

He pulled a duffle bag out from under the table. "Your wardrobe," he said.

"I'm all set. I have plenty of clothes," I said.

He nodded. "You do, except that virtually every item you own has the RIO brand on it. It'll be sure to break your cover. We can't let them connect you with RIO in any way. You'll find another bag on the *Tranquility*. Be sure to bring it all with you."

Then he pulled a wrist worn dive computer from the bag. It looked like the latest model from one of the most popular manufacturers. "This will track you underwater to a depth of about two hundred feet, so we'll be able to find you if you're in trouble. And as soon as your air supply falls below 2700 PSI, it will continually register your available air supply as though you had 500 PSI less than you actually do. You'll have an unexpected margin of safety if anyone tries to mess with you."

"Cool," I said. "They'll just think I'm an air hog."

"Better an air hog than a dead diver," he chided me. "We want to keep you safe and give you every possible advantage. You'll probably never need some of this stuff, but if you do, you'll be very glad to have it."

I nodded. "I'm sorry. You're right."

"I understand. That's all I've got. Any questions?"

"Yeah," I said. "Just one. Who the heck came up with that alias? It sounds like a Bond girl, or something even worse, and it's embarrassing. Next time—if there ever is a next time—I choose my own cover name. Agreed?"

They nodded, and the meeting broke up.

I was supposed to use a loaner car in case anyone from Kraken Industries and Resorts was following me. I didn't understand how they would have been able to track down my real identity so quickly, but some members of the team had insisted.

"Always begin a case as you mean to continue," Newton had said. "Stay in character every minute. That way, mistakes are less likely to happen."

They'd parked the loaner car at the long term parking area at Owen Roberts International Airport. Bari Blackthorne, my new assistant, was waiting for me outside RIO's main entrance to drive me over to pick it up.

"Why all the subterfuge?" she asked when I got in her car.

"Just something Newton cooked up. He's concerned that people will try to follow me now that Rafe and I are married," I said.

"Unlikely. Nobody even knows you guys eloped. Even I just found out this morning." She sounded hurt that I hadn't confided in her.

"Sorry, Bari. It was a spur of the moment thing. Plus we didn't want to take any of the spotlight off Genevra and Oliver's wedding." I smiled at her to show her I hadn't meant to hurt her feelings.

She grinned. "You're now Mrs. Rafe Cummings. That's something people are going to want to talk about."

"They might want to, but I don't," I said. "It's private. Now tell me what's been going on at RIO while I've been away."

Bari filled the short drive to the airport with chatter about the latest happenings. A large portion of her conversation focused on Austin Gibb. She'd developed an immediate crush on him when they met, and he'd returned the feeling. I'd always been a fan of Austin, and it was easy to like Bari. Her bubbly happiness always gave me a lift and made me happy too.

"Benjamin has another mermaid class running this week," she said. "He asked me to see if you could drop by sometime before it's over. And Joely wants to review the quarterly financials with you..."

I interrupted her. "I'm only here for now. I'll be gone for a few days, maybe even a week or more. Please try to keep my schedule open until I give you the okay."

I could see she thought Rafe and I were planning to hole up somewhere and continue our abbreviated honeymoon. I didn't say anything to dispel the idea. It would make a good cover story for my continued absence. I only wished it were true.

Bari pulled up in front of the airport's passenger entrance. I walked through the heavy doors and then walked over to one side, watching until Bari had driven away. Then I went back out through the doors and hiked over to the airport's long-term parking area.

When they'd told me they were giving me the anonymous loaner car, I'd shrugged. Cars meant nothing to me as long as they carried me from place to place efficiently and with minimal pollution. The loaner was pushing its luck as far as efficiency went, and it left a trail of smog behind me wherever I went. I hated that, but luckily, I wouldn't be driving it much.

Chapter 8
Check Out Dive

I DROVE the clunker over to Gus and Theresa's place to pick up the *Sunshine Girl,* recently renamed the *Thundercloud*. The paint job had been masterful. You would never guess it had been repainted or renamed recently. Although Gus always kept *Sunshine Girl* perfectly pristine, whoever did the makeover had even managed to make *Thundercloud* look a little bit battered, which fit in well with the rest of my cover story.

Before boarding *Thundercloud,* I stopped on the *Tranquility* to pick up some toiletries and other necessities. I was so happy to see my boat safe and intact that I nearly cried with relief when I stepped aboard.

An unfamiliar duffle bag sat on the daybed. I unzipped it, and found the contents consisted of a handful of belly-skimming t-shirts, several pairs of very short shorts, and a bunch of tiny bikini bathing suits.

I groaned at the sight of the impractical swimwear. I usually only wore athletically cut tank-style suits so I didn't have to worry about straps slipping or strings coming untied while I worked. Apparently Honey never had that type of problem, because there wasn't a single suit in the bunch I'd have chosen for myself.

Nothing I could do about that now. I tied the sleeves of a generic grey sweatshirt around the bag's straps and tossed it across to *Thundercloud*.

When I did that, I noticed a well-worn gear bag on *Thundercloud*'s deck. I stepped over the gunwales and zipped open the bag. The committee had stuffed it with all the gear and equipment I could possibly need, even including a full-face mask equipped with an underwater communication setup. All of the gear looked like someone had used it for hundreds of dives. Most of it was top of the line equipment and the same models from the same brands I used in my real life, which made total sense. To be convincing, I'd need to look as comfortable with my gear as though I'd been using it for a long time.

Honey Hynes is a dive pro. Of course she'd have the best gear she could afford, and she'd use it hard. The gear looked legitimately used, even to my critical eyes. I pulled out the dive skins and suits. They were plain, scuffed, faded and frayed. Generic. You could buy them in any dive shop in the world. Good choices.

Satisfied there was nothing on the boat that would give my real identity away, I unpacked my clothing and gear and stored it all in exactly the same places I would have if *Thundercloud* had actually been my boat.

Next I checked the refrigerator and the cabinets and found them well stocked with snacks and junk food. Apparently Honey and I had the same bad eating habits. Several bottles of liquor and a couple of cases of beer were in the hold, which made sense given Honey's supposed alcoholic tendencies. In the storage locker below deck, I found a large plastic bin for rinsing gear, a container of the environmentally safe cleaning solutions Liam's company used, and a whole rack full of large jugs of fresh water.

I went back to the *Tranquility* and locked my personal phone and my ID's in the hidden compartment inside *Tranquility's* head. Then I checked my new phone for any messages. As promised, Brock Moran had texted the coordinates of the island, so I climbed up to *Thundercloud*'s flying bridge. Once I'd entered the coordinates into the GPS, I headed out.

Before leaving the peaceful waters around Grand Cayman, I stopped for a quick dive to shakedown the unfamiliar gear and make sure everything worked as it should. I wanted to really put the gear through its paces, so I chose a deep site with lots of current.

I cruised over to Ghost Mountain, one of the more difficult dive sites on Grand Cayman. It's an advanced site for several reasons. First off, it's deep—the ghostly pinnacle that gives the site its name starts at about seventy-five feet. The current can often be strong, another reason that usually only more advanced divers visit the site. Because of those characteristics, the reef is pristine, and there's a vibrant array of healthy sea life.

I tied up at the mooring and took a few minutes checking over my gear before I assembled my tank/regulator/BCD. I needed to make absolutely sure I seemed totally familiar with the gear when I dove with the Kraken team.

Even though Newton's group had provided all the same models I used in my real life, sometimes there could be minor differences due to maintenance or manufacturer's changes because of safety concerns, component costs, or to improve reliability. These types of changes were usually minor, but they could possibly cause a fumble during set up or use that would give me away. I couldn't allow that to happen.

After I set up my rig, I took a few breaths from the regulator. Satisfied that everything worked exactly as I expected, I donned the gear and stepped off the *Thundercloud*'s rear dive platform. As always in the Caymans, the water was warm and crystal clear, although I felt a strong current as I descended. The current wasn't unexpected, but it made me work a little harder than I normally would have. I was actually glad about that because it was an additional test of my gear.

I kept descending but made special note of some landmarks near the mooring line so I'd have no trouble returning to my boat. Then I relaxed and let myself enjoy the dive.

As I neared seventy-five feet, I saw the ghostly pinnacle rising from the depths up ahead. I stopped to admire its majesty for a moment, and wished I'd brought my camera along on the dive. I'd been here before, of course, but the site's majesty was always breathtaking.

No matter. I could always come back again when I'd finished this job for Newton.

The reef and the pinnacle were both thickly covered with gorgonians in a variety of brilliant colors. The reds, oranges, purples, and greens made the reef look very festive, and the variety of delicate patterns and shapes made for a visual delight as the sea fans danced in the current.

As I popped over the top of the reef, heading for the pinnacle, a huge school of jacks swam by me, and for a brief moment, I was part of the school. They had no interest in hanging out with me, and I had no interest in trying to keep up with their rapid pace, so they soon left me behind.

I stopped swimming for a moment, and the current grabbed me and started pushing back in the direction I had come from. I had two reasons to stop swimming mid-dive like that. I wanted to estimate the speed and strength of the current so I would know how far and how fast it would take me when it was time to turn around.

The second reason is that it's fun to fly through the water like superman. I only indulged for a moment before I went back to swimming against the current.

I was keeping a close eye on my tank pressure, making sure that the doctored gauge worked as Newton had said it did. I knew the tank had held 3,000 PSIs of air at the start of the dive, and I was close to the 2700 PSI mark where Newton had said it would adjust itself to show 500 PSI less than the tank's actual contents. I swam into a small overhang in the reef that shielded me from the current a little bit, and breathing normally, stared at my pressure readout.

One breath. Two.

Immediately, the pressure readout went from 2700 PSI to 2200 PSI. As long as nobody but me was looking at the gauge at exactly that moment, the subterfuge would work, but it made me uneasy. The only reason I might want my tank to read less than the actual air I had left would be if somebody was looking at it and hoping I'd run out of air soon. The thought made me shudder because if that were the case, it meant I was in some super dangerous situation I didn't want to think about right now.

Or ever.

I looked out into the blue and watched a scalloped hammerhead cruising by, swinging his ungainly head from side to side. He knew I was there, but he wasn't interested in making my acquaintance. Most sharks don't interfere with divers unless the divers interfere with them first.

A long silvery barracuda swam by, but he too ignored me.

I finned back out to the pinnacle and circumnavigated it at about ninety feet. I saw several stands of fire coral, and I was careful to stay far away from it.

Both the pinnacle and the main body of the reef were home to thousands of fish and interesting sea life. I saw a couple of black durgon, two French angelfish, a gigantic princess parrotfish, a couple of rock beauties, a trumpet fish, and a pair of banded butterfly fish. There was so much life here I resolved that Rafe and I would have to come back as soon as we were both free again.

I looked at my gauge, and it read 1000 PSI, which I knew really meant 1500. But it would be in my best interest never to count on that hidden extra 500 PSI of air, so I began my ascent, swimming along the reef and allowing the current to push me, increasing the speed of my return.

As I ascended over the reef top, I crossed paths with a spotted eagle ray, heading out toward the blue. I smiled at him, happy that this symbol of good luck had graced me with his presence at the start of what could be a dangerous undertaking.

After a three minute safety stop, I climbed aboard the *Thundercloud* and took off my gear. I rinsed it in fresh water and spread it out on the bow to dry. Within a few minutes, the hot Cayman sun had completed its job, and I packed all the gear back in my gear bag. At the last minute, after checking that the safety was on, I stowed the gun Newton had given me at the bottom of the bag. Then I spent a few minutes soaking up some sun before I started the engines and headed to the Kraken island.

It took a couple of hours to reach the destination, but the trip was uneventful. I arrived salty, un-showered, and disheveled, which I thought was a perfect look for Honey.

Chapter 9
Brock Moran

THERE WERE a couple of Kraken employees lounging on the dock when I pulled into a slip, and they helped me tie up. One of them held out a hand to help me step down from the *Thundercloud*'s gunwales to the dock.

"I'm Garth. You must be Honey," he said.

"Nice to meet you, Garth. I'm Honey Hynes." Once again I cringed inside at my alias.

Garth gave me an oily leer. "I can see that you are quite a Honey," he said. "Can't wait to get to know you better."

The three men standing behind him laughed and whooped as they moved closer, forming a semicircle around me.

I narrowed my eyes and glared. "I'm just here to work."

I could see that Garth was about to add another unwelcome innuendo, but Brock Moran came striding along the dock. As soon as they saw him coming, the crew backed down and each man took a few steps away from me.

Moran didn't appear to notice. He reached out for my hand and gave me an enthusiastic handshake. "So glad you've agreed to join us, and very happy you could make it so soon. Welcome."

He was wearing a wrinkled denim shirt with the sleeves rolled up and baggy linen pants. The creases across his hips bore testament to the fact that he'd been sitting for quite a while in the humid heat. A bright blue image of a kraken adorned the chest pocket of his shirt. The kraken's tentacles held tools, including a lab beaker, a test tube, a Bunsen burner, and a calculator. Some others held icons that looked like money or coins.

The items seemed like odd choices for the logo of a hospitality company. I would have expected plates of food, cocktail glasses, beds, or spa tables. But if that was the company's logo, no one could accuse the company of false advertising when it turned out they were only interested in money.

What a difference between Brock Moran, who was clearly interested in money and profits, and my father. Of course Newton was interested in profits for his investors, but he'd built his company on the iron principle of only investing in enterprises that made a positive environmental impact. And his company gave away huge sums of money every year to humanitarian and health care causes while still delivering a strong return to his investors.

I knew it was petty, but in addition to the differences in their investment strategies, I couldn't help comparing Brock Moran's appearance unfavorably to my father's. Newton always looked neat, stylish, and perfectly tailored. His clothes were always appropriate, and they fitted him so well that they looked as though someone had created them just for him—probably because almost everything he wore really was bespoke.

But I put those catty thoughts aside and smiled brightly at my temporary boss. "I'm pleased to be here, Brock. When do I start?"

He laughed. "That's what I like to hear. An eager employee. I'll show you around the office, and then Garth here will show you the crew quarters and where we keep all the equipment. He'll also fill you in on your work schedule." He looked at Garth. "You'll be keeping her busy, right?"

Garth smiled. "Sure will," he said.

The crew behind him snickered, and my skin crawled. I already didn't trust the crew one bit. From the way they were leering at me, some of these men seemed practically feral. I was glad I had my own boat to sleep on.

Brock and I walked away, and I had to work hard not to speak up about the appalling destruction the project had wrought on the island. No wonder Newton's friend Rosalina was upset.

Heaps of dirt and sand were everywhere, with mounds of rocks and dead coral next to them near the shore. I could see there had once been a rudimentary dirt track running from the dock to the island's interior, but now it was nothing but ruts and piles of debris. They'd uprooted every tree or shrub in sight, and their desiccated remains lay randomly on the ground. Except for one tree, I couldn't see any living vegetation anywhere.

Brock and I picked our way carefully along the rutted track. He talked continually while we walked, waving his arm at various locations. "That's where the main swimming pool will be. And the bar will be right behind it." He pointed across the island to a slight rise in the center. "The main hotel will be right about there, and every room will have a view of the ocean."

I nodded politely as he spoke, but I didn't say anything. I was no builder, but I couldn't see how this mess would ever turn into the luxury resort Brock was describing.

We had walked about halfway around the island when the most horrible odor I'd ever smelled assailed us.

I couldn't help it. I gagged.

Brock smiled sympathetically but kept on walking. "It's pretty bad, I know, but you'll get used to it. I don't even smell it anymore."

We rounded a pile of construction debris, and I saw the source of the stench—a huge pile of dead fish heaped beside a small stagnant pool of water that stunk. The water might once have been fresh, but now it was turbid and brackish looking. Whatever had done that to the water must have been what killed all those poor fish.

"What happened to the fish? Something really bad must have occurred to kill them all."

He paused to try to look sad for a moment. "We do some underwater blasting. Lot of them can't survive the concussion. They wash up on shore and we pile them here to keep the odor confined to one area."

I thought back to the hand-drawn map of the island that Newton had shown me. "Isn't this the island's fresh water source? I thought there was only one source of fresh water on the island. Won't putting the rotting fish so close to it contaminate the water?"

He frowned. "I see someone's been doing her homework. But don't worry. It's not a problem because we brought our own fresh water. You can never be too safe when it comes to your drinking water in these backwater places. I'll have someone look into cleaning it up even though I don't think that pool is fresh water anyway."

"Is there anybody else on the island who depends on the spring as their fresh water source besides you? I mean besides you and your crew."

"Nope. Nobody," he lied.

I was fuming. He and his team were deliberately contaminating Rosalina's fresh water supply, obviously hoping to drive her off the island. What a monster.

By this time we were nearly back to the dock area. Brock stopped next to a small prefab building.

Garth came out, carrying two cans of beer. "Here you go, Boss," he said.

Brock took a deep swig from the icy can. "Now it's your turn to show Honey the operation and explain her job." He walked away without another word.

Garth watched him go until Brock was out of sight. Then he turned to me and gestured toward the dilapidated metal building behind us. "This here's the bunkhouse. We hung a sheet over a clothesline to set up a partition for you so you have some privacy while you sleep. Or whenever."

I smiled stiffly. "Thank you. That was very kind, but I'll probably be sleeping on *Thundercloud*. That way my presence won't bother your crew."

"Smart," he said. "You'll have a lot more privacy for whatever you want to get into than that sheet ever could provide. Let's go this way." He held out an arm for me to follow his direction.

There wasn't much else to see. A thatch-roofed shack housed the air compressor they used to fill the scuba tanks, and there were several large tanks of pure oxygen and helium for when they needed to mix Nitrox or Trimix.

We walked another few feet to an open air thatched building. A metal cabinet full of tools and spare parts took up an entire wall, and there was a long worktable in front of the cabinet. I peeked inside. It looked like an equipment repair shop.

I was adept at repairing my own scuba gear. If I ever had a problem while I was here, I didn't want to rely on anyone else to do it right. "Can I use this area to tune up my personal gear?"

"Sure. If you don't tune it up, no one else will," he said.

Although I knew it was probably an unsafe operational practice, his statement still made me feel better. I didn't want to get into a turf war with someone who thought keeping everyone else's equipment repaired was their personal responsibility, especially because they might not have the depth of experience I have.

Plus I didn't want to take the chance that they might uncover the modifications to my pressure gauge. "Great. What else should I see?"

We walked to the third building, which housed a variety of tools and industrial equipment, such as torches, drills, and welders. "You'll get your assignments from me every morning, then you report here and Ken will issue your tools and equipment for your part of the job each day. At the end of the shift, you bring it all back here and he'll check it in. You pick up and drop off your tanks at the filling station back there." He jerked his thumb over his shoulder toward the first building in the row. "We use steel tanks with a DIN valve. You okay with that? You know what that is?"

Since I was certain he was testing me, I did an exaggerated double take. "Of course. I'm a pro."

"Good. There's coffee all day in the bunkhouse, and there's usually chili or something simmering on the stove in case you get hungry between meals. Breakfast is at seven after the first dive, lunch is whenever you surface from your next dive, and dinner is at six. The bar opens whenever you're done diving for the day."

I knew my character was supposed to have a problem with alcohol, so I said, "The bar? There's a bar in the bunkhouse? Maybe I need to rethink my sleeping arrangements."

He snickered. "As much as we'd all enjoy your company, the bar is really just a few cans of beer and a bottle or two. Nothing elaborate. No way we can make something like that fancy drink you were swilling during your interview."

I stopped short, realizing that although he hadn't been visible on the screen, Garth had been privy to my interview. I peered at his face. I didn't recognize him from anywhere, but I wondered if it was possible he'd been at Nelson's during my interview.

That thought sent a chill down my spine. If he'd been there, it meant that Brock Moran had more than likely known my real identity even before the interview. Which meant he knew about Newton and the team's investigation.

Which also meant I might be in even more danger than I'd realized. I'd have to be more alert while I was here than I'd thought. Obviously, I needed to figure out what game Moran was playing before he launched his plan.

Chapter 10
Island Diving

GARTH FINISHED HIS TOUR. "Ready for a beer?" he asked.

I shook my head. "Sorry. I was up late last night and it's been a busy day. I want to be in good shape for my first dive tomorrow. I think I'll just head out to the *Thundercloud* and turn in early." I smiled vacantly at him, trying to seem like the "dim bulb" I was supposed to be.

He looked at his watch. It was only late afternoon—nowhere near late enough to be thinking about turning in. "You've gotta eat. And the guys won't like it if you get hungry later and come crashing in during the night looking for food and waking them all up. Stick around for a while. Grab some grub. Chat with the boys. To be honest, we're all pretty sick of each other's company by now. A fresh face would do us good. Especially a face as pretty as yours."

UGH.

I smiled as vacantly as I could and turned it into a big yawn. I patted my mouth with my hand. "Maybe tomorrow. I don't have the energy to be social tonight."

Before he could ask again, I walked away toward my boat. I had just stepped aboard when he yelled out, "You're on the early shift tomorrow. You hit the water at five AM."

I didn't turn around. "Got it. See you then."

I hopped aboard the boat, loosed the lines, and then climbed up to the flying bridge. I took the boat out far enough that I didn't think anyone would venture to swim that far to bother me during the night. I climbed down, dropped the anchor over a sandy spot, set up the perimeter alarm, and then poured myself a glass of lemonade.

The late day sunshine was inviting, but I stayed below. I didn't want anyone watching me. The boat had come equipped with a bunch of magazines—all fashion and celebrity focused. There was also an iPad, preloaded with emails and texts from my supposed friends. I assumed the new messages from "Nadine" and "Diana" were actually Newton and Dane's cover names. "Leeann" must be Liam. There was no cover name for anyone who wasn't part of the operation, so no contact for Maddy, Theresa, Joely, Bari, or Genevra.

My friends. I desperately needed them.

Definitely no contact info for Rafe. I obviously knew his details, but I was aware I shouldn't contact him. Knowing I couldn't talk to him made me want to even more.

I shivered, feeling alone despite the heat. I missed him, and I missed Penny.

The iPad had a bunch of books loaded into the reading app. Wayne Stinnett, David Berens, Nick Sullivan, and a few more authors who wrote novels set in the tropics. I'd already read most of the books, including one or two that were pretty new releases. But I was too restless to read, so I decided to save them for later

I got up, rummaged through the cupboards, and found the makings of a peanut butter sandwich. Whoever had stocked the boat's provisions knew me well, because in my opinion, a peanut butter sandwich makes a perfect dinner. I pulled the PB&J together and put some chips on a plate with it. I sat at the table and read my "email" while I ate.

Newton's messages—or rather, Nadine's messages—talked about hoping I'd be home soon. Diana's were similar, along with several admonishments to be careful.

Leeann's were more of the same, but each one insisted that she missed me so much she needed to hear from me at least a couple of times a day—and 'she' begged me to be careful and come home soon. If the bad guys read these messages, it would be very easy for them to assume that the writer and I were lovers.

I finished my sandwich and put the iPad aside. I grabbed a couple of magazines from the pile, but I had no interest in the topics they covered. I don't care about fashion, and I didn't know who any of the celebs in the other magazines were. I tossed them all aside.

What now? It was too early to go to bed and there was nothing to do except dive.

Why not? Sunset dives are my favorite, so I geared up. At the last second I remembered I was supposed to be wearing that giant dive knife on my thigh. I pulled it out of the bottom of my bag and fastened the Velcro strap around my leg. As soon as it was securely in place, I stepped off the rear transom into the warm water.

Almost immediately after I submerged, my mask became coated with an oily, slimy film, making it hard to see. At first I thought that nobody had prepped the mask properly so the manufacturing process oils still coated the lens. But then I remembered I'd already used this mask and it had been fine at Ghost Mountain.

Then I noticed the density and grey color of the coating, and I knew it was something else. I grimaced and used my fingers to rub at the mask's lens, hoping that the friction would clear some of whatever that thick gunk was off the lenses.

The edges of the lens accumulated a small pile of sludge, but the center of the glass was now clear enough to see, so I descended along my anchor line. It wasn't very deep here. The reef started at about forty feet.

There was enough light from the surface to see that this reef was in trouble. The corals were extensively bleached, gleaming a pure white in the rapidly dimming sunlight. Many of the sea fans and elkhorns had broken off, the branches lying forlornly in piles atop the dead coral.

Worst of all was seeing the ailing fish. There weren't as many of the usual reef denizens as I expected, and those that were here were very clearly sick.

They swam in circles. They swam upside down. They wobbled as they swam. Or worse yet, they just lay on the reef, their gills heaving in death throes.

There were no large specimens. No sharks or rays. It looked like any sea creature that had the ability to survive away from a reef had already fled the area.

I had no idea what was causing such distress, but I didn't want to expose myself to whatever it was any more than necessary. I pulled a pair of diving gloves out of my BCD and put them on before picking up a couple of the dead fish and dropping them into my catch bag. I planned to put them in the freezer for Maddy and her team of scientists to analyze as soon as I returned to RIO.

A few minutes later, I ascended according to protocol and climbed the ladder to the boat. I didn't want to touch the specimens I'd collected with my bare hands, so I kept the gloves in place while I put the dead fish in a small glass container of sea water and then put the container in the tiny freezer compartment in the galley refrigerator.

I kept my gloves on and used one finger to push some of the sludge that had accumulated on my mask into another specimen bag. Then I stripped off the gloves and filled a large bucket with fresh water from the hose on the dock and threw in a handful of the environmental cleaner I'd found below. I dumped everything I'd worn or used during the dive into the cleaning solution. No telling what that gunk was, but I was pretty sure it couldn't be healthy.

By now the sun had set, so I used my iPad to surf the web, searching for info on Brock Moran and Kraken Industries. Most of what I found was either a puff piece about one of their properties or just a press release issued by the company itself. I looked up a few of the resorts the travel sites had featured and discovered none of the resorts had online booking capabilities or even a website. That seemed very odd in this day and age.

I sent a few of the links to my "friend" Nadine and then erased my browsing history, just to be on the safe side. After that, I went to bed.

My alarm went off at 3:30 AM. I put on a bathing suit, some shorts, and a t-shirt and piloted my boat back to the island. I wanted to take a shower, but I didn't want to do it while the crew was around. I didn't expect anybody to be up, so I was surprised when I saw all the lights in the bunkhouse were on.

After walking along the rutted track to the ramshackle building, I stopped outside one of the windows and peered in. Even though it wasn't yet four o'clock in the morning, the entire crew was up, sitting at the table drinking coffee and eating scrambled eggs, bacon, and pancakes. My stomach gurgled at the sight of the food.

Apparently, that gurgle was one of the loudest sounds ever heard by man, because the entire team looked up and saw me in the window. Drat. I smiled and waved before I went inside. Since they were all up, I would have to delay my shower, but that didn't mean I couldn't have some breakfast.

I poured a cup of coffee and joined the crew at the large table in the center of the common area. "You guys are early risers," I said as I sat down.

"I told you first dive is usually at five," Garth said. "You'd better hurry if you want breakfast."

"Right. You did tell me that last night." I smiled, put down my coffee and rose to fill a plate with pancakes from the buffet table. I made a point of not hurrying. I decided Honey Hynes was someone who would not be easy to intimidate.

Once I sat down again, nobody spoke. The silence was uncomfortable, so I ate as quickly as I could. When my plate was empty, I loaded it into the dishwasher near the stove. Nobody else had cleaned up after themselves.

"You sure eat a lot for a girl," said one of the crew. I remembered Garth had said his name was Bert.

I smiled. "I do. But diving is hard work. Uses a lot of calories."

Bert eyed me up and down. "Doesn't look like you're overeating though. You look pretty good. Nice figure."

Before I could tell him that his words and demeanor were objectionable, Garth spoke up. "Watch it, Bert. That kind of talk is unacceptable and will get you canned. Honey is a member of the team, not your girlfriend. She's here to work. Same as you. Now apologize."

Bert scowled. "Sorry."

I could tell he didn't mean it, so I didn't say anything, just gave a curt nod.

The other members of the team were watching avidly, which made me extremely uncomfortable. I don't like being the center of attention under any circumstances, but this could easily become intolerable if Garth couldn't keep Bert and the others in line.

Garth seemed to have a handle on it. He looked at his watch. "Time to go. Let's move."

Everybody stood and walked out of the bunkhouse, heading across the road to the tool shed. When he arrived, Garth sat on a stool behind the bench and picked up a clipboard. He looked at the top sheet for a minute, picked up a pen, and made a few changes.

"Honey, you'll be with me today. Bert, you work with Ken on second dive. Arthur, you sit this one out. I'll set up new teams for tomorrow."

"Aw, man. I hate second dive," said Bert. "Can't I be first dive with you as usual?"

Garth glowered. "Quit your whining or you won't be diving at all. You'll be on kitchen duty instead. Got it?"

Bert nodded sullenly but didn't say anything else while Ken broke off from the group and trotted to the equipment shack. By the time the rest of us had strolled over, he stood behind the counter.

"Garth, you have the lights. Honey, you've got the torch." He smirked as he pointed to an underwater welding setup in the corner.

I nodded and went to check it out. It was old, but it seemed to be in good repair. Garth took our job ticket from Ken and stuffed in in the pocket of his bathing suit before he picked up a large array of underwater lights and a small toolbox from a pile of equipment sitting on the end of the counter.

Garth took off carrying his gear bag, and I quickly gathered my welding equipment and ran after him. The equipment was heavy and awkward. I wondered why we didn't have a cart to move it back and forth between the site and the tool crib, but I didn't say anything.

Behind me, I could hear Bert still whining about his assignment for the day, and I was happy to know that he whined about everything, not just things that had to do with me.

Garth walked about halfway around the islet before he stopped. "We'll be working this part of the site today." He looked around. "Where's your gear?"

"Sorry. I thought we'd be diving from the dock or on a boat. I left it at the end of the pier when I went to breakfast. I wasn't expecting a shore dive." His disappointed look made me feel like a naughty child.

"Go get your stuff. And hurry up. You'll throw the whole schedule off." He looked pointedly at his watch.

I took off jogging, glancing at my watch as I ran. It was still only 4:45. I'd be back in plenty of time to make the five AM dive time.

I ran down the dock, grabbed my bag, and turned back to where I'd left Garth. He was already in his dive suit by the time I returned, but still he seemed surprised that I'd made the roundtrip so quickly. Thanks to my daily runs with Rafe, I wasn't even breathing fast, and I noticed him noticing.

I dropped the gear bag on the sand and slid into my dive suit. Garth's regulator was already set up on a double tank rig lying on the sand near the entry point. I quickly set up my own regulator on the identical rig beside it. The last thing I did was strap that annoying dive knife on my thigh. Garth leered at me with obvious lust as I twisted my leg to reach the sheath's clasp. He didn't even bother trying to hide his ogling.

It only took me a minute to get ready, and I could see that despite himself, Garth was impressed with my competence and speed. He grudgingly handed me a full face mask with built in underwater communication.

Without hesitation, I pulled the mouthpiece off my regulator's second stage and attached it to the intake port on the mask. "Tomorrow, I'll bring my own."

He shrugged. "Suit yourself, but it'll be a hassle to set up the comms. Nobody here will help you, so you'll have to do that on your own. And on your own time."

"Okaaay. Maybe not then. I'll keep using the mask you issued. I'm ready when you are. You lead. I'll follow you," I replied before sliding the mask on.

His half smile was cold, but he waded into the water and I followed behind.

The water at this spot got deeper really fast, and we started to surface swim almost right away. We were in water about forty feet deep before we'd gone ten yards from the beach. Garth made a rapid descent. I had no problem keeping up and keeping my ears clear. I was grateful for the full-face mask because the water here was slime filled, and the lenses on my mask were quickly covered with gunk.

I held my welding machine's strap with one hand while I pulled my gloves out of my BCD pocket with the other. I put them on and wiped the glop off my mask without pausing in the descent or losing my hold on the welder.

When my mask's lenses were clear again, I noticed Garth hovering nearby watching me. He gave a slight nod. We both knew that the number of people who could have pulled that underwater maneuver off without dropping anything were few and far between.

Garth swam off around a dying coral pinnacle, and I followed a few feet behind him. We were just above the bottom when I saw the source of the sludge in the water. There was an open barrel of a grey ashy substance. A screened cover fit over the top of the barrel, so the mess inside drifted out in small quantities as the gentle current stirred it up.

Garth seemed unconcerned by the presence of the substance because he swam straight through the cloud. Since I still didn't know exactly what it was, I swam out a little way so I could bypass the worst of the mess. When I looked ahead to see where Garth was so I could catch up with him, I noticed a second barrel a few feet in front of him, and another beyond that. Seeing the many sludgy dark clouds misting the water ahead, I could only assume that the Kraken team had surrounded the island with similar barrels leaking whatever noxious substance they contained into the water.

I stayed further away from the reef, outside the perimeter where the leaking barrels were, because I wanted to avoid the worst of the pollution. Whatever the substance was, if it was responsible for the neurological problems the fish were having, I wanted to stay as far away as I could.

At last Garth stopped under a coral overhang, in an area equidistant between two barrels. He turned to see where I was, and I quickly finned over to join him. Once we were side-by-side, he opened a waterproof case attached to the coral with a polypropylene rope and pulled out several sheets of white plastic. Even before he held them up close enough for me to see the details, I realized each sheet bore an engineering drawing for some type of machinery.

Garth rifled through the sheets until he found the one he wanted, then he gestured for me to come nearer. He held the sheet in front of me and used the hand signal for look, pointing to the sheet. When I'd studied the diagram for a minute, I nodded. He smiled and then gestured beyond him to where a partially assembled and rather strange looking electronic device rested on the ledge.

"That's the job," he said into the mic in his mask. "You got it?"

I'd forgotten our full face masks included underwater communication technology, so I jumped when I heard his voice. "Got it," I replied. "What is it?"

"We only give out that information on a need to know basis, and you don't need to know. Your job is just to follow the instructions. Got it?"

I swallowed my irritation and gave him the ok sign before I studied the diagram again. "Where are the rest of the parts?" I asked through the comms link.

He opened a large plastic tote bin that someone had attached to the reef with another sturdy rope. "Take what you need for today's task and get to work. I'll keep watch," he said using the comms system.

I didn't like his attitude, but this was not the place to discuss it. I took the diagram from his hand and studied it. Along one side was a list of manufacturing steps. Someone had already checked off several operations as completed, so I read the detailed instructions for the next step in the process. Then I rummaged through the bin until I found the parts I'd be welding today.

As part of prepping for the welding, I selected the designated electrodes and picked up a grungy welding mask that someone had stowed in the bin. I signaled to Garth that I was ready.

"Follow me," he said through the comms link. He swam over the edge of the nearby wall and descended to about eighty feet where there was a natural shelf. On the rocky ledge stood a tall metal tower with what looked like a satellite dish near its top. Used welding rods, parts wrappers, and other assorted debris littered the coral around it. I worked hard not to show my anger and disgust.

"Get to work," said Garth. "I'll keep watch."

I wasn't sure what he was watching for until I started welding. Almost immediately, Garth said. "Two sharks. Twelve o'clock. I got them."

A minute later, I felt something large bump me. I assumed it was one of the sharks. I was supposed to rely on Garth to keep watch and prevent anything dangerous from coming too close, but it left me feeling uncomfortable. I didn't trust him to live up to his responsibility.

I didn't like not being able to see through the dark welding mask, but not wearing it wasn't an option unless I wanted to risk blindness. I gritted my teeth and finished the assigned process step as fast as I could and shut off the welder. I tore off the welding mask and looked around for the sharks.

I didn't see any.

I didn't see any sign of Garth either.

I checked my pressure gauge and it showed that it was time for me to surface. I knew I had that extra 500 PSI of air, but I didn't want to use it. If I ever needed the extra air in a tussle with the Kraken team, I didn't want them to realize I might have more air than my gauge showed.

Staying close to the wall, I swam back around the pinnacle to the point where Garth and I had started our descent. The water here was about forty feet deep, and the bottom sloped up so sharply that it grew shallow abruptly. I made my ascent while swimming slowly along the gritty looking bottom. It took me about ten minutes to reach a depth of fifteen feet. I hung out there for about three minutes, although the thought of lingering in that nasty water revolted me. After the safety stop, I resumed swimming slowly for shore. The depth changed quickly, and after just a few kicks the water was shallow enough to stand up in.

When I waded onto the beach, carrying my gear, the sight of Garth, Arthur, and Ken sitting in lounge chairs, smoking cigars and sipping beers, was shocking.

I looked Garth over. He seemed fully intact. Not a scratch on him. "You're okay?"

Garth nodded. "Yup. You finish the weld?"

"I did," I said. "What happened to the sharks?"

The men started laughing.

He smirked. "There weren't any sharks. I was just pulling your leg."

"Very amusing," I said. "I'll be doing my surface interval on *Thundercloud.*" I turned and walked away toward camp and the dock. I could feel their eyes boring into my back as I stopped to drop off my empty tanks at the filling station.

Chapter 11
The Kraken Team

AN HOUR LATER, I was back on the beach at the end of the dock, ready to dive. I'd set up my gear on my newly filled tanks. I had the dive knife on my thigh and my full face mask ready. Garth and Bert moseyed slowly along the road toward me, pulling a small cart behind them. The cart held their dive gear, and I realized that Garth had made me hand carry my gear as we walked around the island to the entry point just to deliberately hassle me.

The two men stopped in front of me. Bert was gnawing on a toothpick. Garth smiled, but the smile held no warmth. "The three of us will be diving together this time. After that, you and Bert will be buddies on every dive."

"Right," I said. "Sounds good. Where'd you get the cart?"

"It was in the shop this morning. Bad tire. But it's all fixed now," Garth replied.

Bert gave me a big, sloppy looking smile. "It's okay if you want to put your stuff in the cart with ours," he said.

I lifted the heavy double tank rig with one hand and put it in the cart next to their gear. "Gee, thanks," I said.

The two men didn't seem to catch the sarcasm in my reply.

"New guy pulls the cart," Bert said. Unencumbered, he and Garth walked off in the direction of the entry point, leaving me alone to deal with the cart full of tools and heavy scuba gear.

While I was on the track, the cart was heavy and awkward to handle, but as soon as I left the track to cross the beach toward the entry point, it became nearly impossible to move. The wheels sank deeply into the loose sand, and there was no traction at all. I pulled with all my might, but the cart didn't move.

My dive buddies turned around to watch me, but neither one offered to lend a hand. I could hear their gleeful snickers. They obviously thought the task would prove too hard for me and I would give up. Rather than let them get the better of me, I looked around for something to give the wheels enough traction that they could glide across the sand.

A nearby pile of debris looked promising. I rummaged around for a few minutes and came up with a broken wooden pallet. I picked it up and whacked it against the ground until I had several loose boards. After placing a board in front of each wheel, I tugged the cart forward. When it had traveled the length of the boards, I repositioned them so I could move the cart another few feet.

It was an arduous process and it took quite a while and a ton of effort to push and pull the cart across the loose sand. Sweaty and red-faced, I finally reached the entry point for the dives. Garth was standing ankle deep in the water, staring out to sea. Bert was sitting on the sand, letting the waves wash up against his gnarly toes while blatantly laughing at me.

For a moment I considered using one of the boards I'd been using to smack him with, but even though it would have been extremely satisfying, I thought better of it at the last minute.

While we were gearing up, I considered leaving the dive knife in my bag. Even against Newton's advice I had my trusty scuba scissors in my BCD pocket, so I knew I'd be safe from entanglements.

But then I sighed. The knife was an important part of Honey's disguise. I wrapped the sheath's neoprene and Velcro strap around my thigh and fastened it tightly.

We finished gearing up, and as before, we descended quickly. We swam around the pinnacles until we reached the spot where Garth and I'd been working this morning. Once again, he opened the waterproof crate and shuffled through the plastic sheets while I waited nearby, hovering in the water and wasting both air and bottom time. When he finally selected the right process sheet for the task, he handed it to me.

I reviewed the assigned job and then swam over to the nearby crate that held the parts. This time Garth had assigned me to a step that didn't require welding, just some mechanical assembly.

That was beyond annoying. He'd watched me load up the cart with the welding gear, and he could have told me then that the plan for this dive didn't require it. It would have saved time and energy if I hadn't added all the heavy welding equipment to the cart and then laboriously pushed and pulled it across the sand.

I had trouble believing that anyone would be more interested in hazing a new employee than in being productive for their employer, but it seemed like Garth had no qualms at all about his behavior. After giving him a disgusted look, I grabbed a wrench and some pliers along with the components from the open crate. Neither Bert nor Garth moved a muscle. They simply hovered nearby for a few minutes, watching me set up the work area.

As soon as I was ready to begin, the two of them swam away, drifting slowly around the site. They were having a nice leisurely pleasure dive while I completed the work. They weren't even keeping a lookout for dangerous sea creatures as they should have been.

But it didn't seem to matter if they didn't bother to keep watch. Because of the fish kill and the death of the nearby coral, no healthy or dangerous creatures were in the area.

Since my dive companions had been diving on this site many times, there was little of interest to keep them occupied. They soon tired of hanging out looking at the empty blue water and the reef destruction. They swam back and hovered over my shoulder to watch me work.

I had just finished the job when I looked up out into the blue and saw two juvenile lemon sharks headed our way. I remembered Newton telling me that this area had a large population of young sharks. They spent time near here in a "shark nursery" while attaining their full growth and learning how to navigate while they were still safely in a protected area with plenty of reefs for food, safety, and cover.

I could understand why the sharks had chosen this spot. It had probably been beautiful and teeming with life at one point. Sadly, that was no longer the case.

With plenty of reefs to provide an abundant food supply, very little current, and an absence of larger predators, it made a great location for sharks to hang out until they'd reached their full size. But now with the fish and coral dying, they no longer had access to an ample food supply. As a result, these guys might be feeling a mite peckish.

Lemon sharks don't usually bite humans, and if they do, often it's because someone provoked them or because the sharks just made a mistake.

Garth and Bert hadn't seen the sharks because they were busy watching me instead of keeping watch. The sharks caught sight of us and immediately veered toward our location. I was safely between the reef wall and the equipment we were building, but the men were more exposed with their backs to the open sea.

The larger of the two sharks bumped Bert, who threw his hands in the air and screamed.

The scream echoed through the water and nearly destroyed my hearing when it came through the comms link in my mask. Bert turned and started frantically swimming away, his breathing and movements jerky and hurried.

The rapid random motions excited the sharks, who charged after Bert. Garth didn't move, although his bubble pattern indicated extreme agitation. If one of us was going to save Bert, it would obviously have to be me.

The sharks had easily caught up to Bert, and now they were taking turns bumping him. He'd stopped any attempts at swimming away, although he continued to flail. He must not have known that the flailing only increased his danger.

Still carrying the heavy wrench I'd been using, I launched myself from the area behind the construction, and my momentum carried me most of the way toward the unfolding drama. A few gentle kicks, and I'd joined the group.

I swam up to the larger of the two sharks and brought the wrench down hard on his delicate snout. He turned to me with a snarl, and I let him have it again. Meanwhile, his friend joined the attack, so I whacked his snout too with the recoil from the earlier blow.

Rather than helping to save himself, Bert had shut his eyes and was gibbering incoherently, but it was okay. The sharks had now turned their attention to me. They bumped me on each side, one after the other, but every time as they passed me I wielded the wrench to deliver hard knocks to them on whatever body part I could reach.

It felt like a lifetime, but in reality it was only a few seconds until the sharks wisely decided Bert and I weren't worth the pain and trouble. They turned away and headed off into the blue. Garth finally left his safe hidey-hole and swam over to join us. He took Bert's arm and pulled him along toward the exit point. I followed slowly behind, keeping a sharp eye out for the possible return of the sharks.

We reached the point where we normally left the water, and the three of us quickly waded to shore once we were in the shallows.

On the beach, Bert fell to his knees and kissed the sandy earth. Garth dropped his tanks into the waiting cart and helped Bert to stand. He removed his friend's rig and placed it into the cart, then they walked away, leaning on each other. Neither said anything to me, not even a simple thank you.

I picked up the handles of the cart and using the boards as I had before, I trudged back to the air filling station to drop off our tanks. Garth had me scheduled for another dive at three PM, and for the first time in my life, I wasn't looking forward to diving.

I wasn't sure if Bert and Garth would be up for it either after their scare with the sharks, but we wouldn't be canceling the dive because of anything I did or didn't do.

Arthur was manning the tank filling station. I smiled when I saw him, but the compressor was too loud for conversation so I merely waved and unloaded the tanks. Then I walked over to the tool crib, where Ken was still behind the counter. He was rebuilding a couple of well-used regulators.

"Mind if I borrow a couple of your tools? I'll bring them back as soon as I'm done," I said.

"Sure. Whaddaya need?" He quickly looked back down at the bench in front of him.

"A hammer, a wood chisel, some nails. Maybe a small saw. Some sandpaper. Wood glue. A couple of really strong tie wraps if you have them."

"No problem." He hopped down off his stool and assembled the items I'd asked for, placing them all in a small plastic basket. "Here you go," he said when he'd finished.

I went outside to where I'd left the gear cart. I used the saw to create a rough point on the ends of the boards I'd been using as runners and planed and sanded them until the ends were smooth. I went back to the trash heap and found another long board. I sawed two pieces off and glued and nailed them onto the original boards, a few inches from the pointed edges.

While the glue dried, I walked down the dock to *Thundercloud* and rummaged through the gear bag Newton had provided until I found what I was looking for—an old pair of dive booties. Back where I'd been working, I slipped the booties over the pointed ends of the boards and nailed them in place. Then I used the tie wraps to fasten the boards to the wheels of the cart, so instead of rolling on four wheels, it now slid on two blades, almost like skis.

I picked up the tanks we'd be using for the afternoon dive and loaded them in the cart. Then I pushed it down the road and across the sand to the entry point. As I'd hoped, the new blades more or less glided over the sand rather than digging into it.

Pushing the cart was still no picnic, but it was infinitely easier than trying to force the wheels through the deep and unyielding sand. Satisfied with my modifications, I left the cart at the entry point and went in search of lunch.

Chapter 12
The Bunkhouse

By now I was starving and I didn't have much time left before my next scheduled dive, so I decided to grab a hot lunch in the bunkhouse with the team rather than scarf down a cold peanut butter sandwich alone on my boat.

The roar of laughter reached me while I was still about twenty feet away. Garth was telling the guys how he'd saved his crew from this morning's vicious shark attack by smacking the sharks with the wrench. I waited outside for a moment listening, but he never mentioned my part in the event. I rolled my eyes and went inside.

Instantly, the room went silent.

I ignored their stares and headed over to the sideboard where lunch was set out. Today's fare was a hearty veggie soup, a tray of assorted cold cuts, crusty fresh rolls, salad, fruit, cookies, and coffee. I ladled out some soup, then added a roll and a couple of cookies to my plate before looking around for a seat. Nobody waved me over to join them.

Ordinarily, since it was obvious the team didn't like me, I'd have been fine with the exclusion and just gone my own way. But I was here on a mission.

I'd grown up without any friends of my own age, but in my job at RIO, I'd learned how to fit in with strangers. I needed to make friends with my teammates and hear what the crew talked about among themselves in case they slipped up and said something that might help the investigation.

So I ignored their glares and walked over to the table, squeezing onto the end of the bench next to Arthur. Grudgingly, Arthur moved over a few scant inches to give me room. I hid my irritation and smiled a thank you.

I wasn't expecting much from the food, but then again, I usually didn't require much beyond a full stomach. My tastebuds and I were both pleasantly surprised when I took my first spoonful of the spicy soup. I savored the complex flavor for a moment before I spoke. "This soup is delicious," I said. "Who made it?"

Arthur blushed. "I did. I do most of the cooking around here."

"If this soup is typical of your creations, I can see why they ask you to cook. It's amazing."

He looked down at his lap, his eyes glowing with pleasure at my words. Maybe I'd just made an ally.

None of the guys said anything for a minute. Finally, Garth brought up a soccer rivalry currently playing out in Europe. I don't pay much attention to sports unless they take place underwater, so I just sat back to listen while enjoying the rest of my lunch.

A few minutes after I'd finished eating, Brock Moran walked in. "Who did that to the tank cart?" he asked.

Everyone at the table sat up straight and looked at someone else. I knew they had no idea what he was talking about.

"I did," I said, putting my hand in the air.

"Does it work?" he asked.

I nodded. "It's still not ideal, but it's much, much better. Cuts down the time to move the tanks to the entry point by more than half."

His face broke into a grin. "Brilliant," he said. "Expect a bonus in your check. I'll make it one-half of the estimated savings. Come talk to me directly if you have any more ideas for improvements. It'll be faster that way." He glared at Garth for a second without saying anything, but everybody in the room could see he was annoyed with his second in command. Without another word, he went to the sideboard to pour himself a cup of coffee and left the bunkhouse.

After Brock was gone, everyone in the room lapsed into an angry silence. The guys all scowled at me. I was the new team member, and they were clearly infuriated that I'd had a good idea and just gone ahead and implemented it. They'd had months to do so before my arrival, and on my first full day, I'd made them look bad for not having already thought of the same idea. And of course, they were jealous of the extra money.

I don't know which of my transgressions angered them more, but it was obvious that now they'd frozen me out completely. There was no hope they'd ever confide anything in me or even accidentally speak out of turn while I was in the room. I gave a mental shrug. I didn't mind being on my own. In fact, I preferred it.

There was no sense in my staying there making everyone uncomfortable, so I picked up my tray. After putting the dirty utensils and dishes in the dishwasher I said, "I'll see you guys at three."

Nobody replied or even looked up when I walked out.

Chapter 13
Lawton Environmental Remediation

I HEADED FOR *THUNDERCLOUD*, where I planned to spend the rest of the time between dives sending update messages to Newton and Dane, but as I rounded the corner of the bunkhouse, I saw Liam's *Enviroman* pulling up to the dock.

Since he was still angry about my marriage to Rafe, his presence here worried me. I was afraid he'd say or do something to blow my cover, but then I calmed myself down by remembering that Liam was an experienced undercover agent and he knew what to do. And even more important, he knew what not to do.

Plus I knew he still loved me. I was sure he'd never deliberately do anything to hurt me, no matter how mad he was.

Even so, given the current state of our relationship, I considered turning around and heading to the interior of the tiny island to hide out while Liam was here. Before I could take a step off the path, Brock Moran came out of nowhere and started walking beside me.

"I'm glad I ran into you," he said. "There's someone here I'd like you to meet. I'm interested in your opinion of what he's trying to sell me."

"I'm sure I'd have no idea about that, Mr. Moran."

"Brock. The name is Brock. And I think you're a lot smarter than you let on. Those lunkheads back there have been knocking themselves out dragging that foolish cart through the sand for months and it never occurred to them to do anything to make it less demanding."

"I'm sure they'd have thought of it eventually," I said. "And it's easier to come into an existing operation and see problems than it is to see them while you're in the middle of following established procedures."

He rubbed his jaw. "Hmmm, maybe so. But I'm still impressed with you and your motivation to make the change. Have you seen anything else you'd like to address?"

I nodded. "I have several ideas. Maybe we can talk after you meet with this guy, whoever he is? Would that work?"

"Perfect," he said as we stepped onto the dock's wooden boards. He put a hand on the small of my back, subtly forcing me to walk with him as he strode rapidly down the pier. Liam finished tying off *Enviroman* and straightened up as we approached.

Brock held out his hand. "You must be Liam Lawton. I'm Brock Moran, CEO of Kraken Industries and Resorts. And this is one of my employees, Honey Hynes."

Liam shook Brock's hand. "Pleased to meet you both." He didn't look at me.

Brock looked around, sighing after he sniffed the soft salty air. "We can go back to my stuffy office, or we can meet out here where we can see the sky and the sea. It's up to you two."

I didn't want Brock on my boat just in case there was something I hadn't noticed that might give me away. I jumped right in to make sure that didn't happen. "I've heard a lot about you, Mr. Lawton, and about the *Enviroman*. I'd love to see it up close."

"Of course you're both welcome to come aboard. But *Enviroman* is nothing special. I'm sure you've been on boats just like her hundreds of times, Honey." Liam tightened his lips in a very fake-looking smile. Or maybe I only recognized it as fake because I knew him so well.

Brock's gaze swiveled between Liam and me. He'd obviously sensed the undercurrent of tension. "Do you two know each other?" he asked.

"No," I said.

"Yes," Liam said at the same time.

Brock laughed, but it didn't sound merry. "Which is it?"

"We've met. I've seen Mr. Lawton around at industry events and on other jobs. But I wouldn't say we're friends," I said, glaring at Liam.

"Oh, I agree. We're definitely not friends," Liam said, staring at me with hard eyes. "C'mon aboard and we can get this meeting started."

Brock and I followed Liam onto *Enviroman*. The first thing he did was show us around, pointing out many of the boat's features—especially the ones I'd helped him design. I didn't say a word, although Brock asked intelligent questions about every detail.

Liam said, "*Enviroman* is mostly my floating office and living quarters when my team and I are on a job. Why don't we head into my office now and I'll talk to you about what I'm proposing."

He led the way to his small on-board office. Before sitting down, he flipped his desktop monitor around so we could see his presentation. I had seen this spiel hundreds of times, and I'd even helped him develop it. I knew the presentation cold, so I stayed silent and let my mind wander while Liam delivered his spiel.

Brock asked several questions, and Liam answered with polished ease. When the session was winding down, Brock said, "Do you have any questions, Honey?"

Liam flinched when Brock called me Honey, although he knew perfectly well it was my undercover name. He'd already used it himself, but I knew he'd done that to make me uncomfortable.

I shook my head. "Mr. Lawton explained everything very clearly."

Brock nodded. "Good, because I would like you to be the liaison with the Lawton Environmental Remediation team. You'll be my eyes and ears on the cleanup work, and you'll keep me up to date on the progress or any problems that crop up. Can you handle that? It's a big promotion."

"I think Garth would be a better choice," I said. "He knows your company's project and the island much better than I do."

Brock snorted. "But you're ten times smarter than he is. I know you'll be perfect for the job. When can your team start, Liam?"

"Right now, if you like," said Liam. "It'll take me a few minutes to print out the contracts, and then we're good to go."

"Give me an hour," said Brock. "I want to talk to Honey about some ideas she mentioned."

"I can tell. already that Honey would be full of ideas," Liam responded. "So I'll see you two in an hour to finalize the contract?"

"Oh, you won't need me for that at all. Email me the documents whenever you're ready. I'll e-sign them right away, and I'll send Honey out to join you as soon as she and I finish our meeting. No time to waste when the environment is at stake." Brock smiled and headed for the dock.

I looked at Liam's angry face and shrugged, then I followed Brock down the dock back to the island.

Chapter 14
An Assignment

BROCK LIVED in a small but luxurious building smack in the center of the island. In the states, people might call his place a tiny house, but it was practically palatial here on this rustic island. As a comparison, the small diver dormitory building had cooking, sleeping, and laundry facilities for six divers crammed into an area smaller than the conference room at RIO.

The space inside Brock's home was set up in an open floorplan. One end contained a full gourmet kitchen, with stone countertops, tile floors, and sleek appliances. I assumed the closed door at the far end led to a bedroom or bath.

A plush leather couch in one of the corners faced the floor-to-ceiling windows that made up the opposite wall. In another corner, two leather recliners angled toward a gigantic television set mounted high above a gas fireplace. Thick rugs covered most of the floor, which was a rich, dark hardwood.

He'd devoted at least one quarter of the square footage to his office. A sleek teak desk sat against the wall next to two matching file cabinets. The desk chair was one of those pricey ergonomic status symbol models. A satellite phone lay across the desktop next to an expensive looking monitor and computer setup.

He'd arranged several small gold figurines of exquisite workmanship near the sat phone. At first glance they all seemed to be images of mythical sea monsters, armed and ready for war. I noticed a helmeted kraken held pride of place, front and center of the group, as though leading them into battle. There were also a few seahorses, a small castle, and a mermaid wearing a crown. With a start, I realized they were pieces of an elaborate chess set, although it wasn't complete.

"Have a seat," Brock said when we'd walked inside. "Would you like something to drink?"

"No thanks," I said. "I'd like to get back to work. I think my surface interval is just about up. Garth will be looking for me, and he'll be angry if I'm late."

"No problem," he said. "You're off the dive rotation effective immediately. You can dive at will anytime you like, and I want you to use your eyes and ears to gather intel, but you don't have to dive with Garth's crew. Keep me informed about anything you see going on with the worker bees."

I frowned slightly. "I'm not sure I'm comfortable with that. Garth won't like having me spying on him and his team."

He shrugged. "What Garth likes is of no concern to me, but regardless, I'm not really asking you to spy on him. Certainly let me know if you see things that you think we could improve, or just fix them yourself if you can. But right now, what I actually want is for you to watch the team from Lawton Environmental Remediation. Keep them away from certain things that are none of their business, if you know what I mean."

My heart was pounding. Was Brock about to spill the bad stuff Kraken had been doing? I hoped that was the case because it meant I could go home sooner. I tried to put a puzzled but innocent expression on my face. "I'm sorry, but I don't actually understand what you mean."

"No? I think you do, but I'll explain anyway. I definitely want you to keep the Lawton crew away from the side of the island where the team is working. And by all means, keep them away from the kill zone."

I gulped. "The kill zone?"

"You know what I mean by the term. It's where we saw the dead fish the other day. And the barrels underwater near the work site?

Keep them away from that area too. It's important that we get a clean bill of health from Lawton Environmental Remediation so that neither international nor the Cayman Islands environmental police come poking around anymore than they already have. If you need Garth to move anything out of sight for some reason, just give him an hour or two notice. Got it?"

I nodded, wishing I'd been quick witted enough to record this conversation. "Got it."

He smiled. The expression made him look like a predator, sending shivers down my spine. "Now, you mentioned some ideas you had..."

"Uh, yeah," I said, trying to put myself back in that mind space. "The first thing is to move the cases with the work instructions and the component parts up to dry land. The divers can study their assignment and gather the right parts during their surface intervals. They can just bring the single process sheet on the dive with them in case they need to refresh their memories, but not having to plan out the whole process underwater will give them a lot more productive time on the dive."

He looked thoughtful. "That seems reasonable. Any idea why Garth is storing the parts and the process sheets underwater? It seems like your way would be much more practical."

I shook my head. "No idea. Maybe it's just the way they did it in whatever training program he took."

Brock gazed out the window, his mind obviously elsewhere at this point. "You're probably right. You can go now. If you get a chance, tell Garth about the idea you've suggested and that I approved the changes. But your most important priority is to stick close to Lawton, especially if he wants to dive, and then report everything you've seen or heard to me every evening."

"Got it. Will do," I said.

Chapter 15
Kayak and Diving

I LEFT Brock's office and walked back along the pier to where Liam had tied up his boat. "Permission to come aboard, Captain Lawton," I said from the dock.

"Welcome aboard, Miss Hynes," he said. "Need a hand?" There was no warmth in his voice and he didn't smile.

Great. This should be fun.

"I can handle it," I said.

He grimaced. "I'm sure you can. I bet you can handle just about anything."

I glared at him. "Would you like to see the island's whole coastline? Since the area is pretty small, it won't take long, and I thought it would be a good way for you to kick off the project."

I was trying to stay in character just in case Brock had managed to plant a bug on the *Enviroman* while he'd been aboard. "Maybe we can take one of your kayaks and circumnavigate the whole island so you can get an idea of how you want to proceed."

I scratched my ear, trying to signal that I was concerned about anyone hearing us talk.

Liam nodded. "Good idea." He walked to the gunwale and lifted the two-seater kayak hanging from the rail. When we'd been a couple we'd always preferred to be in separate kayaks, but this time, I agreed with Liam's quick assessment that the two-seater would be a better choice. To minimize the risk of anyone overhearing us while we were both undercover, it would obviously be better for us to stay close together and as far away as possible from any locations that Brock could easily bug.

Liam and I launched the kayak and took off paddling. After our years together, I was so comfortable kayaking with Liam that I automatically synched my strokes to his.

"Stop it," he hissed. "Try not to make it look so smooth. Anyone watching us would be able to tell we've done this together before. Screw up every now and then, willya?"

I immediately altered my stroke so I was off Liam's rhythm by a beat or two, and every few feet, I skipped a stroke entirely. I knew the lack of synchronization would irritate him, but he'd asked for it. And he was right that we needed to look and act like strangers if we were going to credibly maintain our cover.

We moved slowly along the area near the dock, passing close by the shore so Liam could get a good look at the layout of the island. The project team buildings clustered near each other and all of them were close to the shoreline, so it was easy for us to check them out as we slowly passed by. As we paddled by each of the buildings, I explained to Liam its purpose and who was likely to be in it at various times of the day, given the rhythm of the work on the island. Liam kept the kayak on a course that hovered in the shallows near the beach so we had a good view.

As we rounded a curve in the island's shape, I pointed out the spot where the divers made their entries. Soon after that, we passed the area where I knew the divers were working a short distance from shore but far below us underwater. Only now did I realize that the work zone and the entry point were quite a distance from each other. It hadn't felt like it had been a long way on the dives, but I chalked that up to nerves.

As we hovered above the work area, I asked Liam to swing out further from shore. "Brock especially wanted me to keep you away from this area. But maybe we can do a secret night dive together and you can see what's down there for yourself."

"Good idea," he said. "Moran needs to see you following his

instructions to the letter. We wouldn't want him to get suspicious of you."

We'd gone a little more than halfway around the island now, and we were coming up on the spot where the pile of dead fish rotted in the freshwater spring. This was the place Brock had called the kill zone.

I held my paddle upright in the water to slow our forward progress. "We should turn around now. Brock specifically told me to keep you away from this area. There's something really bad going on here."

I described what I had seen, and my concerns that Kraken was deliberately killing the sea life and polluting the island's only source of fresh water. "I think this spot and the worksite are the areas you'll be most interested in. That's where these monsters are despoiling the undersea environment. But I'm not sure I can help you investigate up close since I'm supposed to keep you away from those spots, although maybe we can sneak in a couple of dives late at night."

"Hmmm," he said when I'd finished. "Then we should definitely go back now. Moran is probably watching you, and if he's as ruthless as we think he is, he needs to see that you're following his orders or it could become very dangerous for you."

He thought for a minute. "And you're right that it's probably too dangerous for us to dive together near here. I'll come back later on my own, and if they catch me you can claim you told me to stay away from here. I'll confirm your story if he asks." He swung the kayak around and we began heading back toward the *Enviroman*.

As we'd agreed earlier, I pretended to be unable to match his cadence. I was doing what he asked, but his shoulders tensed up anyway. He obviously found the lack of rhythm annoying. There was nothing I could do about that except stick to the plan

A few strokes later, he spoke. "I'd really like to see what's going on underwater though. Do you think we can go for a dive when we get back to the dock?" he asked, still smoothly paddling.

"Sure. Brock specifically told me we can dive, but it's a long swim to where the really interesting stuff is. And you'll want to wear a full face mask. They're spewing something really nasty into the water…"

Liam abruptly stopped paddling. "Then you can't dive here again until we know what that substance in the water is. It's too dangerous. Go home where it's safe. Let Newton know you're done with undercover work. We all know you hate it anyway. Then you can quit the job with Kraken. Tell Moran you just don't want to dive with his crew anymore."

I desperately wanted to do exactly what Liam was advocating, but I couldn't. Newton and Dane were depending on me. "I'm not leaving until we figure out what's going on. And avoiding diving here isn't a problem. Brock already told me I'm permanently off the project's dive rotation. He wants me to work with him and Garth's team to improve their productivity. I think he's frustrated by their lack of progress."

"But that's only my job's secondary priority. The first priority is you. He wants me to spend most of my time with you and your team. It's obvious he's hoping you'll give this project a clean bill of health to keep the environmental police at bay."

Liam harumphed, clearly more annoyed than ever. I'd managed to achieve exactly what he wanted me to, but without needing him to intervene or advise me. That would aggravate him.

And I was infuriated at Liam for thinking he could tell me what to do, especially when it came to diving, my primary profession. He had no right to tell me what I could or couldn't do, and he certainly should know better than to use that commanding tone of voice and expect me to react well.

I gritted my teeth. Liam's edicts were especially irritating now because we weren't even together anymore. What I chose to do or not do was no longer any of his business.

With a sinking heart I realized that working together was never going to be a viable option. We'd only spent an hour and a half in each other's company and we were already angry and annoyed with each other. Not to mention that we'd come dangerously close to blowing our cover stories in front of Brock.

While Liam and I paddled the rest of the way back to the dock without speaking, I contemplated how to let Newton know he needed to revise his plan. Liam could not be my backup, and he most certainly could not be my boss.

I'd spent the return trip lost in thought, so it seemed shorter than the journey out had been. When the kayak bumped against the sand near the start of the dock, the jolt startled me out of my reverie. I hopped out of the kayak and offered Liam a hand. Unlike in the past, he didn't take it, just smoothly lifted himself out of the kayak and stepped out onto the beach.

It was nearing sundown by now, and as usual, I was starving. "What are you doing for dinner?" I asked him. "Do you want me to take you in to eat with the Kraken team?"

"Not tonight," he said. "I'd like to get that dive in before it gets too late. Maybe we can dive while they're all at dinner."

I looked up at the sky, gauging the time by the angle of the sun. "Let's have a sandwich and something to drink before we dive. By the time we finish eating it'll be perfect timing for a sunset dive. And better yet, it'll coincide with the Kraken crew's dinner time so they'll be less likely to notice us."

His smile was wistful. "That makes sense. Sandwiches for dinner sounds like a good plan. I have sliced turkey I'm willing to share. What have you got?"

"Just PB and J. But I have chips and a bag of cookies."

That made him laugh. "Of course you do."

We pooled our food and sat on *Enviroman*'s deck munching our sandwiches and watching the sun go down. Other than "Please pass the mustard," or "Would you like another cookie?" we didn't speak. It was beyond awkward.

By the time we finished eating, the evening was dark enough that I thought we could probably dive without the Kraken crew noticing us, but not yet so dark that we'd need lights to do our entries. But just in case they were watching, we geared up inside *Enviroman*'s cabin to avoid prying eyes.

As we were finishing our preparations, I told Liam, "If you have a full face mask with you, you'll definitely want to wear it and some gloves to minimize skin exposure."

Gloves sometimes make divers careless, and a single heedless touch can kill years' worth of coral growth. Not wearing gloves while diving is a point of honor with divers who care about the environment.

Liam never wore gloves while diving, so he scowled at my suggestion. "No thanks."

"At least take a pair with you. You'll see what I mean pretty quickly. It's nasty down there, and all the fish are dying. You don't know what the substance in the water is, so you can't know if it's absorbed through your skin. Just wear the gloves until we know what that stuff down there is. Better safe than sorry." I said.

I could see he wasn't happy with my suggestions, but for once, he decided not to argue. He rummaged through his gear bag for a few minutes and at last he found what he'd been looking for. He stood up holding a pair of brand new gloves still in their packaging. He tore the package open and grudgingly stuffed the gloves in his BCD pocket.

He walked to the *Enviroman*'s stern and slipped quietly into the water. Less than a minute later, after gearing up and strapping the much-despised dive knife to my thigh, I followed. We met up on the bottom, directly beneath the boat.

I pointed in the direction I wanted us to swim, and Liam signed okay. As we moved into deeper water, we left the sandy area near the dock and approached the nearby reefs. I could tell that Liam was upset by the extent of the bleached and dead coral he saw.

A few minutes of swimming later, we came to an area where a few fish still lived. As I'd seen on my own dives, the fish were alive but obviously sick. They swam in circles, or upside down, or with an odd wobbly motion. Not a single creature was moving normally.

It was heartbreaking to see, especially because we could contrast this ailing area with our memories of the vibrant reefs teeming with life where we usually dove.

Liam was swimming slightly behind me, but after taking in the extent of the unhealthy sea life, he surged forward, looking at me with a question in his eyes. It was obvious he wanted to know what was causing the problem. I shrugged my shoulders in the "I don't know sign," and he scowled at me.

I wasn't sure why he was annoyed at me. After all, trying to figure out the problem was the whole reason we were here.

By this time, both our masks had become covered with the gritty grey substance I'd noticed on previous dives. I hovered in place and slipped on my own gloves to wipe the grit and slime off my mask.

Liam watched me for a second, peering through the now nearly opaque lens of his mask. The pattern of his bubbles told me he'd sighed with frustration, but then he pulled out his own gloves and put them on so he could wipe the disgusting debris from his mask.

Once we were both able to see clearly again, we swam on. Soon one of the barrels I'd noted on my dives loomed out of the murky water, emitting a thick spray of grey grit into the sea. We paused, and watched the unknown substance it was discharging drift slowly out of the fine mesh cover topping the barrel.

Liam pulled a specimen jar out of his BCD pocket and swam close to the misty grey cloud. He held his arm in the thickest part of the foul stream and took the cover off the jar to capture some of the toxin, then quickly sealed it again. He replaced the jar in his pocket and then signaled that he was ready to move on and that I should continue to lead.

After all the years we'd spent diving together, we automatically matched each other's pace, and we both knew exactly where the other diver was at all times. We inevitably fell into our usual rhythm and habits.

Diving with Liam was easy. It was comfortable.

Living with him had been neither.

We swam fast toward where the Kraken team was working, but because we'd started so far away we were almost at the turn-around point for air consumption when the first of the small oddly shaped towers came into view. The murky water and fading sunlight made it hard to pick out details, so I took a small flashlight out of my BCD pocket and played the beam closely over the tower's details.

Liam tapped my shoulder and looked quizzically at me.

I shrugged again. I'd been up close and even worked on the towers, but I still had no idea what they were for.

We put on a short burst of speed and ended up near enough to the first tower that we could make out some of the details. I had a small point-and-shoot underwater camera in my BCD pocket. I pulled it out and took a few quick shots, hoping nobody on the surface would see the flash.

Liam pointed at his pressure readout. I gave him the okay sign, and we turned around and swam back to *Enviroman*.

Back aboard *Thundercloud,* I emailed the photos I had taken to Liam and Newton. Then I stepped across the dock to *Enviroman* and gave

Liam the dead fish I'd collected on the first day. He could bring the sample to RIO for an analysis of the cause of death to help us identify what was creating the neurological issues all the fish were manifesting.

He put everything away, and then I said goodnight. I'd just stepped off his boat to return to *Thundercloud* when he spoke.

"Thanks for being so cool about working with me. I'm sure it's as awkward for you as it is…"

I held up a hand to stop his words. "It's fine. Go home and get some sleep."

He turned away to start *Enviroman's* engines as soon as I stepped onto *Thundercloud*'s deck. The boat roared away in a mist of spray, and I knew working together must have been a lot harder for Liam than for me.

Chapter 16
Photo Shoot

I WAS up before dawn the next morning and went out on *Thundercloud*'s deck while waiting for the coffee to brew. It was so early that Liam and the *Enviroman* hadn't returned yet, so I sat on the bench and watched the stars wink out, one by one.

As soon as the coffee was ready, I took a few gulps and then geared up for an early morning dive. The sea was as smooth as glass and its ethereal beauty gave no hint to the destruction occurring below. For this dive, I decided to swim in the opposite direction from all my previous dives, to see if there was any noticeable difference in the underwater conditions that might explain the poor health of the reef and the sea life I'd observed on the construction side.

I slipped into my gear, grimacing as I strapped the dive knife onto my thigh. I still hated wearing it, and much preferred my dive scissors. But the knife was part of the Honey Hynes persona, so I needed to wear it on every dive no matter how much it rankled me.

When I was ready, I took a large professional-level camera and strobe setup as well as my little pocket camera on the dive with me. The large camera was just for show. If Brock Moran or the Kraken crew caught me nosing around and wanted to confiscate my photo equipment, I hoped they'd take the obvious route by commandeering the very visible pro gear and leaving the small unobtrusive pocket camera behind.

The pictures I planned to take today were to document any damage to the area, not for art or publication like my usual photography. Since that was the case, the lower pixel quality and feebler flash of the small camera wouldn't make much difference in the usefulness of the photos.

The underwater landscape on this side of the island was very different than on the side where the Kraken crew was working. The reef walls were steeper, and although the coral was starting to bleach in spots, the devastation was nowhere near as advanced as it was on the other side. Using my professional camera setup, I took a bunch of innocuous pictures of fish and closeups of coral. I had to work hard to take photos that looked amateurish, but not nearly as hard as I had to work to find healthy looking specimens. If Brock Moran looked at these images, I didn't want him to know I'd seen anything that might make me question his project. The more incriminating pictures I took with the small camera, and I stowed it back in my BCD pocket for safe keeping as soon as I'd taken each shot.

After I'd taken enough decoy pictures to make my dive seem legit, I swam around a large coral pinnacle that jutted out from the wall and explored the sides.

It was an interesting formation. Approached from the direction I'd come from, it appeared to be a solid wall of coral, but once you were up close, it was easy to see that in multiple locations, the coral curved and coiled in behind itself, leaving several narrow passageways between the wall and the pinnacle. I swam into a small gap a little way, and instead of a quick dead end, the passageway led into an open area.

I'd been swimming at about sixty feet of depth, but when I looked down along the coral, I noticed a dark spot in the main wall at about eighty feet. It looked like the entrance to another cavern. Unless you passed through the narrow opening between the wall and the pinnacle, you would never see it at all. Curious, I descended and peered inside.

Naturally, it was as dark as the darkest night in there, so I switched on my camera's powerful strobe lights. Even they didn't do much to illuminate the cavern's interior. It was almost as though a light-eating monster lived in the cavern because the visibility didn't extend more than a few feet.

I know better than to enter a cave or cavern without the proper equipment—especially a guide rope to help me find my way out in an emergency. And the air in my tank was already getting low—even considering the extra 500 PSI that it didn't register. I realized that for my own safety, I'd have to come back another time to explore the cavern's interior.

I swam back out the way I'd come and headed to the dock area where I'd tied *Thundercloud*. I made my ascent behind it, hoping the boat's bulk would keep the Kraken team from seeing me, but this wasn't my lucky day. Brock Moran was on the dock talking with Liam, who must have returned on *Enviroman* while I was underwater.

I reached up to put my camera and attached strobe lights on the dock so I could climb the ladder, but the faint clunk when I put the camera down alerted Moran of my presence.

"There you are," he said with a smile. "I might have known you'd be up early. I was on my way to invite you to breakfast when Liam arrived for his day's work. Maybe the three of us can have breakfast together and talk about the project."

"I've already had breakfast," I said, hoping my stomach didn't growl, since as usual, I was actually starving. I just didn't want to have my breakfast with him and Liam.

Brock nodded. "Okay. Another day then. Probably just as well. This way Liam and the team from Lawton Environmental Remediation can get right to work. The sooner we resolve the perceived issues, the better. These unfounded allegations have been holding up our work."

"Allegations?" I asked. "About what? Who complained?"

Moran scowled. "A young busybody who used to live on the island complained to the Cayman Islands department of the environment. I own this island outright, and it isn't part of the Cayman Islands, so they have no jurisdiction here. But they're saying our operation is polluting their waters and harming their marine park and therefore hurting their economy. I guess their entire economy is dependent on diving tourism."

Liam and I both knew that the Cayman Islands had a vibrant and healthy economy supported by multiple industries, not just tourism.

As a businessperson, Brock must also be aware of that fact. It was obvious that he was lying to us for some reason.

Liam and I exchanged subtle nods indicating that we'd decided to ignore the lie and focus on getting more information about the whistle-blower that had Brock so riled up. He must be referring to Rosalina's youngest son, the missing Alonzo.

Liam took the lead. "Where is this guy now? It would be helpful to talk to him and see what his main concerns were. You know— to provide a better idea of what to look for. It might save you some money if I knew what set him off."

Moran's nostrils flared. "I like the idea of saving money, but I have no idea where that young busybody is. He left the island right after he filed his complaint."

"Does he have any relatives on the island? Maybe one of them knows where he went," I said. I was hoping he'd mention Rosalina, which would give me the opening I needed to meet her and make sure she was alright.

"I told you nobody lives on this island. I own it." Moran sounded exasperated.

I slapped my forehead and tried to sound like a ditz while I looked at him with what I hoped was a clueless expression. "That's right. You did say that. It's just that I thought I saw some chickens and a goat the other day. Do they belong to you?"

"You were seeing things," he said rudely. "Probably spending too much time underwater breathing compressed gases. Why don't you stay on the surface today? You can work in the office with me, or in the toolshed with Ken."

I bit my tongue to avoid saying something that would blow my cover. "Okay," I said. "That sounds great."

He started to walk away, but then thought better of it. He turned back and held out his hand. "By the way, there's no photography allowed anywhere on the island or underwater. I'll need your memory card."

"What?" I squawked. I'd been expecting this, but still, I had to put on a show. "Those things are expensive!"

Brock Moran had a faint half smile when he said, "I'll buy you a new one when it's time for you to leave for good. You shouldn't be taking pictures here anyway. It violates the terms of your contract. Didn't you even read it?" He extended his hand further, waiting to receive the memory card from me.

Pretending reluctance, I picked up my camera and opened the casing. I popped out the memory card and slapped it into his hand. "Here," I said rudely.

He put it in his pocket and walked away without saying anything more.

Chapter 17
A Discovery

LIAM WATCHED HIM WALK AWAY. Once he was out of earshot, he whispered "Was there anything good on that memory card?"

"You know me better than that," I said. "The real photos are on my little point-and-shoot camera in my pocket. That big camera setup was just a decoy."

He laughed. "You're right. I should have known you'd be one step ahead of him." His eyes glowed for a second, then he bit his lip and looked away. "What's our plan for the day?"

"I can show your crew around, and that will give us an excuse to be in places where we maybe shouldn't be. And then they can wander around on their own and we can plead ignorance if Moran catches them. What time are they arriving?"

"Sorry. I'm not sure when they'll get here, but right now, I have some important news. I already got the analysis back on that water sample I took yesterday." He looked grim.

"And?" I didn't like the angry look in his eyes. He had to get a handle on that or it would be hard for him to interact with Brock.

He ran his hands through his blonde hair. "It's Tephrosia. Not sure which specific plant in the family it came from yet, but it's one of them. It's highly lethal to fish, but fortunately, it's not harmful to humans. So we're safe, although I'd stick with the gloves and the full face mask when you're diving, just in case."

I thought about this finding for a few seconds. "Why would Kraken Industries want to poison the fish in the area? They're supposed to be building underwater suites as part of their new hotel. I should think they'd want a healthy marine ecosystem."

"That's what I thought, but then I did some research. When they're dissolved in sea water, some forms of Tephrosia inhibit the corrosion of steel. The Kraken engineers may have been looking at using it to help reduce the deterioration of their underwater structures, without factoring in the harmful effects on the local sea life."

"Things look pretty far gone to me. Can you still reverse the effects?" I asked.

"Maybe, at least partially. If enough of the coral survives, the fish may eventually return. Once Kraken stops dumping Tephrosia in the water, the ocean will disperse the toxin widely enough that it won't harm most sea life, except maybe some fry who were unlucky enough to catch a dose of the last of it."

I shuddered. All I could think of was Rosie, my beloved Atlantic Pygmy octopus. She was so cute, so smart, so small—and so utterly defenseless. And there could be thousands just like her in the nearby octopus nursery.

"The octopus nursery... I haven't had a chance to visit it yet, but the Tephrosia could destroy it. It might wipe out a whole generation in this area. Maybe forever. We have to stop it."

"Let's see what we can do to save them on our dives today. You can tell Moran you're showing me the healthy reefs and keeping me away from the construction zone."

It was a brilliant excuse. I could have kissed him. Except I couldn't kiss him. I was married to Rafe Cummings, and I knew I loved Rafe with all my heart. But it was confusing working so closely with Liam after having been together for so long. Old habits die hard, as they say. I inhaled deeply and took a step back. "What's your team's plan?"

"The first thing is to get my team to replace the Tephrosia in the barrels with an inert substance that looks pretty similar. From what you say the Kraken divers aren't very diligent or observant, so they probably won't notice the change. The water will still be murky for a while—at least until we figure out what's going on. Once we do, we'll pull all the dispensing barrels out of the water and then it will clear up quickly. Meanwhile, you and I can dive on the nursery site and relocate as many of the octopus fry as we can to another spot…"

I interrupted. "We'll lose a lot of them. And the change will confuse the regional population. They've probably been coming here for generations to lay their eggs and nurture their young…"

Liam sighed. "I know that. But if we act, we can just lose some of them, and if we don't, we may lose them all. I vote to save as many as we possible while we still can, but this is your operation. It's your choice."

I nodded. "I get it, and I vote to save what we can, as long as it doesn't blow the bigger operation. What's the plan you worked out with Moran? Your team will need to look like they're following that plan while they actively work on the cleanup. How will your team be able operate around that?"

"They'll be arriving later today. Although Brock Moran will think they're working on remediation, their first step will be to replace the Tephrosia in those barrels. Then they'll be working on cleaning and reseeding the coral, trying to help it recover. Eventually, we may relocate some typical reef denizens to the area—kind of giving the neighborhood a kick start." He started pacing along the deck.

"So far, so good. I need to make sure Moran still thinks I'm on his side. What can I do to help you?" I said.

He held up his fingers in a vee. "Two things in particular I want you to do. I brought some dive scooters, so we can cover more ground when we're diving. I'll want you to dive with me most of the time so the Kraken team doesn't get nervous thinking I'm blundering around down there on my own."

I nodded. "And…"

He bit his lip nervously. "You may not like it. I want to bring Rafe and T-8 over to the island. Pretend we're scouting for our next documentary. We'll tell Brock we plan to focus it on him and his brilliant vision for the eco-resort…"

"I'm gonna barf," I said.

He looked startled. "Are you okay? You didn't drink the water, did you?"

"Figure of speech," I said, laughing. "It's just that the idea of creating a documentary around that monster Moran makes me sick."

Chapter 18
The Octopus Nursery

Even though I'd anticipated it, I was still brooding over Brock's confiscation of my memory card. "Let's take this opportunity to check out the octopus nursery. Brock will probably spend all day gloating about catching me in breach of contract, and the crew won't be around for another hour or so."

"I'm game, but I thought you didn't have the coordinates?" he said.

"I don't, and I can't contact Newton to ask for them. But you can. You're not undercover. You're exactly who you say you are. Sort of."

We both laughed at that, because Liam spent more time undercover in various personas than he did as his real self. With a shock, I realized I didn't actually know for sure that the Liam I'd been engaged to actually was his real identity and not just another undercover persona. The thought made me want to cry.

Not catching the sadness engendered by my last statement, Liam nodded. "I'll call him now while you set up the scooters in case we need them."

"On it," I said. "And I'll grab some Trimix from the tank house. We may need it."

He was already on the phone trying to track down Newton, so he just wiggled his fingers to send me on my way.

Nobody was in the tank hut when I arrived, so I simply helped myself to four tanks of Trimix and two of Nitrox, along with a couple of spare air canisters. I bundled it all into the cart and wheeled it over to the end of the dock. The runners I'd created for it wouldn't work well on the wooden planks, so I hand carried the tanks down to *Enviroman*. Liam hung up on his call with Newton just as I arrived, so we retrieved the remaining tanks together. When we'd stowed everything, I returned the cart and left a note that I'd borrowed the tanks.

Liam put the nursery's coordinates in the GPS system and then started *Enviroman*'s engines. We moved quietly and smoothly away from the dock. When we were far enough away, Liam opened the throttle so we could reach our destination quickly. Luckily, the nursery wasn't near either of the areas Brock had said to stay away from, so even if he questioned me about where we'd been, I wouldn't have to lie.

The location wasn't far from the island. Liam found a sandy patch on the reef top to drop the anchor in. We looked at the bottom topography on *Enviroman*'s sonar, and it looked like the reef top was about 150 feet down, although a massive pinnacle rose from the central area up to about thirty feet from the surface. And as usual, there was a steep vertical wall at the edge of the reef that plunged to unknowable depths.

We decided to use the Nitrox tanks to dive the first ninety feet, and then switch over to Trimix. Liam attached our backplates with the Trimix tanks to a weighted line he dropped off *Enviroman*'s bow so we could swap out our Nitrox tanks at depth and pick them up on our way back up.

We planned the dive this way because we wanted to preserve our options in case we needed to intervene by relocating some of the nursery's residents to save them. It wouldn't be the weight of all those tanks that gave us a hassle down there—just their sheer bulk. By leaving them at the "way station" for later pickup, we could have plenty of breathing gas for the dive without having to deal with the cumbersome extra tanks at depth.

We geared up and then dropped the scooters over the platform. After we entered the water, we each grabbed one and used it to increase our speed while reducing the necessary effort as we swam toward the pinnacle. I noticed that the current was fairly strong in the shallows down to about sixty-five feet, and it came from the direction of the island. The corals that made up the upper portions of the pinnacle were dead or dying—probably from the effects of the poison the Kraken crew had unleashed in the water. It was disheartening to realize that those monsters were destroying the environment even this far from the island. Once again, I wondered about their motivation for such wanton destruction.

As we descended, the coral seemed to become increasingly healthy, and the sea life grew more abundant. That was good news for the octopus nursery if it was as close to the pinnacle as Newton had said.

At about eighty-five feet we switched over to the Trimix tanks and continued our descent. Near the bottom of the pinnacle, the current switched course once again. It was now coming from the direction of the island, and the coral here was beginning to wither and die.

As we continued our descent. I looked down at the reef spreading below us and saw the nursery. It was about fifteen feet wide and filled with hundreds of baby octopus in all stages of development. The mother octopuses huddled near their eggs, with their tentacles surrounding them for protection.

Even from a distance I could see that many of the eggs had withered and died. Fry filled the water, but many of them were dead too, floating inertly in the current. But the babies on the bottom were even more heartrending. They ranged in development from near adult to just out of the fry stage, and most of them lay curled into balls with their tentacles protecting their bodies.

Many of them looked sick. Some of the larger ones peered at us with their enigmatic eyes. I imagined my beautiful Rosie, my Atlantic Pygmy octopus, suffering out here, and my heart felt as though I shard of ice had pierced my heart.

I looked at Liam. He too looked horrified. We had to do something.

With fingers crossed that my hunch was right, I quickly steered my scooter around to the other side of the pinnacle. The current pushed me along at a rapid pace right up until I rounded the curve of the coral. There was a moment of turbulence as currents coming from opposite directions slammed into one another, and the force sent me tumbling. I switched the scooter to full power and swam as hard as I could to break through the turbulence, and within a few seconds, I had popped around the bend.

The water on this side was clearer, and the reef looked healthy. That meant the Tephrosia hadn't reached this area.

At least, not yet.

I knew what we had to do. I swam back to where Liam hovered over the nursery and pulled a catch bag from my BCD pocket. I loaded it up with as many of the egg sacs and mother and baby octopuses as I could.

It only took Liam a second to figure out what I had in mind. Then he too started loading up a catch bag of his own. As soon as my bag was full, I pointed my scooter back to the clean side of the coral mountain. Once there, I opened the catch bag and began placing the babies in coral crevices that would help provide shelter. A moment later, Liam joined me and began unloading his own catch bag. He'd also taken the time to swish a sample bag through the open water on the other side, and now he opened it to release a small swarm of fry. There was no guarantee our plan would work, but it was a sure thing that doing nothing would wipe out generations of octopus from the area.

Octopuses give birth only once in a lifetime. The mother stands guard over the eggs full time, not even leaving to forage for food. After the eggs hatch, the mother dies. Disrupting a generation of octopuses in the area could completely wipe them out for years into the future and maybe even lead to extinction.

We were able to make three trips around the pinnacle before we ran low on breathing gas. We'd managed to relocate nearly a hundred of the babies and an uncountable number of eggs and fry. We were both elated as we began our ascents.

Once back aboard the *Enviroman,* I noticed Liam's shining eyes and happy smile. "Relocating the nursery was a great idea," he said. "That pinnacle is diverting the flow of poison from the island, so the side where we relocated the babies seems totally clean. I'll get my team to relocate another batch as soon as they can. And if they can take care of the poison in the next day or two, the rest should be fine."

I nodded. "We may lose a few, and the fry have definitely taken a hit, but I think you're right. Thanks for the help. I'm glad you were with me today,"

Liam beamed. I could have kicked myself as soon as I said it.

I bit my lip and didn't speak again until we returned to the island.

Chapter 19
Cave Discovery

As I STEPPED off the boat onto the island's dock, two Lawton Environmental Remediation boats came over the horizon and into view. This was my cue to find an out of the way place to spend the next few hours. And I knew exactly what I wanted to do.

"I'd better make myself scarce. I know most of your team, and although they wouldn't purposely do anything that might give me away, they aren't undercover professionals and something could easily slip. We'll catch up later."

I waved goodbye and hopped onto *Thundercloud* where I quickly geared up for a dive. Before I made my entry off the stern, I slipped a couple of extra flashlights in my BCD pocket and grabbed a rope reel. I wanted to spend some time exploring that cavern I'd found.

This time I headed straight for the cavern instead of meandering around. That was partly because I didn't want to risk anyone seeing me while I was diving in the area, and partly because it broke my heart to see all the ocean creatures suffering. But mostly I went straight to the cavern because it was down deep and I wanted to maximize my bottom time once I reached the cave. I'd already made a couple of dives this morning, and my tissues were probably nearing maximum gas saturation. After this one last dive today, I knew I'd have to spend at least the rest of the day and all night off-gassing on land.

When I arrived at the mouth of the cavern, I spent a few minutes securing my reel to a conveniently located rock. Satisfied that it wouldn't come loose while I was inside the cavern, I flicked on a flashlight and swam into the darkness, letting the rope unspool as I went along.

Healthy looking coral coated the first few feet of the cavern, and I saw no evidence of any bleaching or distress. As I moved away from the meager sunlight that made its way inside the entrance, the coral on the cavern walls grew sparser, eventually becoming bare limestone. A few sergeant majors and a parrot fish glided serenely by me on their way out, although I swear they gave me dirty looks as they passed. Possibly they annoyed at me because I had invaded their sanctuary.

I was surprised at how large what I'd thought was a smallish cavern actually turned out to be. This was no cavern—it was a full-fledged limestone cave of an exceptionally large size.

The ceiling wasn't visible even when I shone my light straight up, and when I flicked the beam around in all directions, I couldn't see any walls except the one I was swimming next to. The floor was at least twenty or thirty feet below the cave's entry point, which I'd noted was at eighty-three feet of depth. The cave must extend well into the reef in all directions, and the interior of the cavern was immense.

I kept my pace slow and easy so I could look around and get a feel for the space, and I stayed next to the wall even though I had the reel unspooling along with me as I swam. About fifteen feet inside the cave, a spotted moray eel popped out of his crevice in the coral. His motion was so sudden that it startled me and I jumped back. My abrupt motion obviously startled him in turn because he rapidly exited his home and swam for the mouth of the cave.

The eel was at least ten or twelve feet long, and as thick around his body as one of my thighs. He was a prime example of how healthy and vibrant this reef must once have been. I mourned all the other residents who'd been deliberately poisoned.

When my heart rate returned to normal after the eel sighting, I moved deeper into the cave, flashing the beam of my light around me as I progressed. I'd gone quite a way inside when my light's rays landed on a large protuberance rising from the floor of the cavern twenty feet below me.

In the dim glow of the beam, I noticed a metallic gleam coming from the base of the mound. I stared at it for a moment, thinking it must be a fish's sparkling scales, but even after what felt like a long time, whatever it was, it never moved. So not a fish.

I was torn. I wanted to see what could be creating that shimmer, but I also wanted to continue my methodical exploration of the cave. I knew the systematic approach I was taking would pay off if and when I returned to the cave, but my curious thoughts about that strange glint had my mind churning.

A soft beep from my computer told me my bottom time was at an end. No matter what I wanted to do, that beep meant I should head for the surface. Right now.

I'd already spent a long time underwater today, and I hadn't respected the required surface intervals to let my body off-gas the extra nitrogen I'd absorbed during those dives. I knew pushing my bottom time further was taking a risk that could kill me.

I wasted a moment weighing my choices, then I swam as fast as I could toward the tiny glint. I grabbed whatever it was I saw in one gloved hand. It felt spiky and hard, with no give at all, so I knew it wasn't a living creature. I stuffed it in my BCD pocket to examine later, and spooling my rope back onto the reel as I went, I quickly left the cave to return to my boat.

I took the ascent slowly, letting my body use the extra time to off-gas, and I extended my safety stop to ten minutes at fifteen feet. It would have to be enough because I was now completely out of air.

Chapter 20
A Change in Plans

When I climbed quietly up the ladder on *Thundercloud*'s stern, I could hear Brock and Liam talking. Moran's voice was loud and he sounded upset. Liam was using his infuriatingly reasonable voice—the one I hated. I had no idea what they were discussing, but it didn't bode well for the rest of my day.

In the distance I saw several people walking around the island in groups of two. They were wearing the bright green Lawton Remediation t-shirts that Liam's crews usually wore. I guessed that while I was on my dive, they must have started the reconnaissance that was a standard first step in the company's projects.

Brock wouldn't like that. He seemed intent on keeping outside people penned up in the area near the dock, and well away from the work areas.

Luckily Moran was facing in toward the center of the island when I came aboard the *Thundercloud,* so he didn't see me as I tiptoed across the deck in my scuba gear. I carefully placed my BCD and tank on the floor under the tank racks and quietly secured them in place with a wad of wet towels and dirty t-shirts so my gear wouldn't roll around or make any tell-tale clanking noises that might draw Brock's attention to me.

Once I'd safely stowed my gear out of the way, I tiptoed below to change into dry clothes. I slicked my wet hair back and slid my feet into a pair of plastic flip-flops, then I went back on deck.

I yawned ostentatiously, as though I'd just gotten up. I hoped Moran would think I'd taken a nap after he left us earlier this morning —not unreasonable considering it wasn't even eight AM yet.

Sticking my hands in the pockets of my shorts, I scuffed along the dock to join Liam and Brock. "Hey, guys, what's up?" I called out as I drew closer.

Brock turned to me, looking highly annoyed. "Where have you been? I thought I told you to stick close to Lawton. First he sent his crew on a dive without clearing it with you first. Who knows what kind of trouble they could have gotten into?"

He glowered at me while shaking a large blue loose leaf binder. "And now his team is wandering all over the island unattended. They're not construction experts and they're not prepared to understand a complex construction site. They could have injured themselves or damaged the construction equipment with their meddling. I expected better of you."

I looked him straight in the eye and spoke evenly. "I don't appreciate you scolding me in public. I trust it won't happen again."

His ears turned red as he tightened his lips. "I gave you a direct order, which you disregarded. I trust THAT won't happen again."

"Well, excuse me for taking a shower," I said. "And I was close to Lawton. Our boats are docked side by side, no more than four feet apart. How much closer do you want me?"

I took a big gamble with my next words. "But it doesn't matter, because apparently you didn't hear me when I told you that a public scolding had better not happen again. But whether you heard me or not, it doesn't matter because you've already done it again. I won't allow you to treat me like that. I quit."

I turned around and headed back to the *Thundercloud*. Honestly, I'd have been thrilled if he'd just let me leave, but I wasn't that lucky.

"Honey, wait," he called after me. "I'm sorry I was rude. I was frustrated, and I admit I have a terrible temper. I'll try not to let it happen again if you'll agree to stay through the term of your contract."

I stopped walking but kept my back turned to him. "If I stay, I'm either a commercial diver and I dive the regular rotation with the crew according to the same rules the whole crew follows, or I'm this guy's babysitter and I do that undefined job in a way that works for Lawton and me. Choose one or the other, but either way, I will not put up with your bullying."

Liam gasped, but there was total silence from Moran for at least a full minute. I started walking away again, but I hadn't yet taken three steps when he caved.

"You're right. I apologize again. It is an undefined job, and it requires you to use your own good judgment. You can't read my mind about what I expect or what I would recommend in a particular situation, and I can't expect you to be on duty every minute of every day. I don't consider you a babysitter. You're a liaison, and I think you'll make a darn good one. Maybe the three of us should have a meeting later this morning and discuss how this will all work."

I was surprised and extremely suspicious that he was so conciliatory. I turned around and looked at Liam. I could see he was skeptical too about the change in Brock's attitude and about his real motives for throwing Liam and me together. But I felt like I owed it to Newton and Dane to play this out if I could.

"Sure. Let's have a meeting. Where and when?" I stared hard at him with an angry expression on my face, exactly as I imagined Honey Hynes would have done if she were real.

"How about over lunch?" he said, turning to Liam. "Are you free?"

Liam shrugged. "Sure. But what about my team? Should they join us too? Our contract says you supply their meals while they're on site."

"Not necessary. They can eat in the bunkhouse with my crew." His disdainful expression said he had no desire to eat with any members of anyone's crew, even his own.

Liam shrugged. "Fine. What would you like Honey and me to do until then?"

"Why don't you sit on the beach or on one of your boats and study the project specs. See if you can identify any areas that might be contributing to the alleged environmental damage. But stay where I can see you. There are enough unaccompanied people who don't understand what we're trying to accomplish roaming around getting into who knows what."

He thrust the huge blue binder at Liam. "Check this out, write down any questions, and we can discuss it at lunch. Meanwhile, gather your crew and send them away until you and I have a clearer plan in place.

Liam's mouth dropped open. "We have a contract. I spelled out the plan in great detail in the terms."

"I'm changing the plan. I'll pay you for your expenses and the time you've already put in, but that's it." Brock turned and walked away.

Liam and I stared at his back.

"Looks like we have a free morning," Liam said.

I nodded. "And better yet, so does your crew. Do you think they can sneak in a dive and replace the Tephrosia?"

"Already done," he said smugly. "I think that's what actually set Moran off. They probably got too close to something he wanted to keep hidden."

"Great work anyway. Now you and I can dive here safely. But before you send them home, why don't you send your crew back to finish what we started at the octopus nursery? It's outside Moran's domain, and at least that will do some good."

Chapter 21
Sea Monsters

Liam went off to gather his crew and give them the location of the octopus nursery while I scouted around for a place where we could review the material Brock had given us. I finally decided on a small picnic table near Brock's trailer. Four chairs surrounded the table, and a large palm tree—the last healthy one on the island—provided some shade. I grabbed a couple of cans of lemonade from the stack Newton had included in my provisions and a plate of cookies. Then I sat down to wait for Liam to join me.

I'd originally put five cookies on the plate. There were two left when Liam arrived. He smiled. "One for you and one for me, right?"

"Right," I said. With a straight face, I picked up what would now be my fourth cookie.

Liam grinned. He was quite familiar with my cookie obsession, and he knew full well I'd have eaten several cookies before his arrival. The only question in his mind would be how many cookies I'd put on the plate to begin with. I didn't plan to tell him.

When he'd finished his lone cookie, he scooched his chair around so we were sitting side by side with the binder open on the table between us. By the time I opened the book to the first page, he was ready to take notes on his tablet.

The first section was a marketing document describing the project in lavish terms. It was to be a luxury resort with all the expected indulgent amenities. The most interesting part was the description of the underwater suites, which included everything you'd want in a luxury hotel suite, including incredible ocean views. Of course, from these special rooms the views were underwater, not the usual sand and surf.

By the time Liam and I finished paging through the contracts, the architectural drawings, and the material specs, my eyes were glazing over. I bit back a yawn. "I don't see anything that feels out of place, do you?"

Liam shook his head. "No, it all looks pretty standard to me."

I tapped my fingers thoughtfully on the table. "So then, why poison the water? And what exactly are those satellite dish things I've been working on underwater?" I paused to think things through. "Something doesn't make sense."

I jumped at the sound of Brock's voice. "Ask me your questions. I'll answer whatever you need to know." He'd approached silently from his tiny house behind us.

Liam and I looked at each other, eyes wide. I was under strict orders from Brock to keep Liam in the dark about whatever I saw. Had Brock heard me mention the underwater towers and the poison water to Liam? What would his response be if he had? We could be in incredible danger because of my carelessness.

I shrugged. "It's a lot to take in, and it's not my area of expertise. I'm just a diver."

"Oh, come now," he said. "We all know you're a lot more than just a diver."

My blood ran cold. Could he possibly know my real identity? I looked at Liam for a way out, and as usual, he came through.

"For sure," he said. "She's the best looking diver I've seen in years. She should be a model." He waggled his eyebrows suggestively at me.

Had he done this in real life I would have been beyond irate, but it was exactly the right thing to say because Brock forgot about me and turned on Liam.

"I'm shocked that a man with your business expertise would say such a thing. It's beyond inappropriate, and I won't have you creating an unhealthy atmosphere for my employees. If Honey has any complaints, just know that she'll be the one who stays, and you'll be the one to go. Got it?"

There were red blotches on Liam's cheeks when he looked down at his feet. "Got it. It won't happen again."

I had to admit Liam was a pretty great actor, because he managed to look and sound defiant and yet properly chastened.

Brock pursed his lips and stared at him for a minute. "Good. Now, any questions about the project?"

Neither Liam nor I had a question that we thought Brock would answer, so we stayed quiet.

Brock sighed. "I heard you ask about the underwater towers before you knew I was here. Those are to enhance communication for the underwater suites. When we're ready, we'll attach them to the outer steel beams."

Liam and I both nodded, but I was the one who asked the big question.

"Wouldn't it make more sense to build the suites and then attach the communication devices to the building's beams later? It would make it a whole lot easier to do it that way than to try to get the suites to conform to the placement of the devices."

"There are a few technical reasons. But even if there weren't, that's how I've decided to do it, and I'm the boss. Next?"

I gulped. So much for Brock's promise to answer our questions. "The grey stuff floating in the water seems to be killing the fish and causing coral bleaching. What is it?" I didn't want him to know we'd already analyzed the substance.

"The reefs and the fish were dying well before we got here. But for your information, the "grey stuff" is a homemade shark repellent. Garth mixes it up. It won't hurt you. It's good for business to have beautiful reefs surrounding the underwater suites. That's why we originally brought in Lawton Remediation. We need to be sure the reefs stay viable. Once we've finished construction, we'll do whatever it takes to mitigate any damage and restore the reefs to full health."

We both nodded thoughtfully, acting as hard as we could since we both knew he was lying.

"That's all my questions. Liam?" I said brightly.

"I'm good," he said. "For now, Honey and I just need to put our heads together to come up with a plan."

Brock shook his head. "I appreciate that, but I've changed my mind about needing you and your team here before we finish building. I'll call you in a few months when we're actually ready for you."

Liam paused for a moment. I could tell he was debating what to do, but there wasn't much that he could do. He looked at me and I gave a slight nod letting him know I was okay with him leaving me here alone on the island.

"Okay," he said finally. "I'll await your call."

"I think I might have left my sweatshirt on *Enviroman*," I said. "I'll walk with you to get it." I hadn't left my sweatshirt anywhere, but I wanted to give him the gold sea monster figurine I'd found this morning. He could pass it on to Dane and Newton for evaluation. I had a feeling it might be one of the keys to what was going on.

"I'll be back in a minute," I said to Brock.

"Take your time," he said. "You know where to find me." He turned and headed to his office.

Liam and I walked toward the dock. As soon as we reached the *Enviroman*, Liam boarded. I walked to the next slip where I moored *Thundercloud*. My BCD was still sitting on the stern, with the figurine in its pocket.

I pulled the statuette out of the BCD pocket and gasped at its beauty. It was an intricately carved seahorse wearing armor. The horse's eyes were brilliant green gems, and a variety of colored jewels studded the armor as well. There was an upright lance protruding from a jeweled holder on its white enameled saddle, and an equally bejeweled spear hung from its right flank. The seahorse looked like it might be a missing piece from the same set I'd seen displayed on Brock's desk.

I really missed my usual baggy cargo shorts with their voluminous pockets. In the tight pocketless shorts that Honey wore, I had no place to hide the statuette from view if Brock was watching. Without pockets, I needed another way to discreetly transport the seahorse to Liam. Then I remembered I'd told Brock I needed to get a sweatshirt, so I grabbed a generic grey hoodie and draped it over my hands before hurrying back to Liam's boat.

"I found it," I said loudly as I approached him. "It was on *Thunder-cloud* all along." I stepped aboard *Enviroman*. I was deliberately loud in case anyone was listening.

"No," Liam said equally loudly. He was holding an identical grey sweatshirt in his hand. "I think that one's mine. This one is yours." We swapped garments, and I passed Liam the little sea monster along with the sweatshirt I'd been holding.

"Well, it's been nice meeting you, Mr. Lawton," I said. "I hope I see you again soon."

He smiled sadly. "You'll always know where to find me."

I hopped over *Enviroman*'s gunwale back to the dock. Liam climbed up to the flying bridge and started the boat's engines. He waved his hat in the air and left. I was on my own again.

Chapter 22
Brock's Move

I WATCHED Liam's boat until it disappeared over the horizon before I walked back to the island and Brock's office. I knocked on his door but there was no answer, so I strolled over to the crew quarters to see if he was there or if anyone knew where he was.

As soon as I walked in, Garth stood up with a gloating smile on his face. "I knew you'd blow it. Your new job didn't last long, now did it? I guess this means you're back on the dive rotation. You'll do the 3 o'clock dive this afternoon and the 6 o'clock and 8 o'clock dives tonight, and then the 5 AM dive tomorrow morning to make up for your slacking off. Got it?"

"I've got it," I said. That was barely enough time to off-gas completely between multiple deep dives, so I knew I'd have to be careful. I also knew I had never been slacking off from my assignments, but I didn't want to argue with Garth, especially because he was telling me to do pretty much exactly what I wanted to do anyway.

Then I heard Brock's voice from behind me. "I told you Honey is off the dive rotation. I'll be the one who decides when and if she goes back on it. Understand?"

Garth glared at me like it was my fault he was in trouble with his boss. "Got it," he said sullenly.

"Honey, meet me in my office in five minutes." Brock turned and walked away.

I raced back to *Thundercloud* to grab a notebook and pen, as well as Honey's iPad. Then I scurried to Brock's trailer and knocked on the door.

"It's open," hollered Brock.

I lifted the latch and climbed the two metal steps to enter the tiny house where Brock both lived and worked. He was sitting on the couch with a glass of white wine in his hand. A second glass stood on a tray on the small coffee table in front of the couch. I ignored it and sat in the leather chair across from him.

"Don't you like wine?" he asked. "I've got beer, gin, and tequila if one of them would suit you better."

I shook my head. "I'm working. And I don't drink much alcohol anyway" I said demurely.

He looked momentarily confused. "I thought you were a hard drinker. It's one of the reasons I wanted to hire you. It can get pretty boring on this island. I was hoping we could party a bit."

Immediately I realized my blunder. I'd answered the way Fin Fleming would, but here I was Honey Hynes, a serious drinker indeed. I'd broken my cover, and Brock—no dummy—had caught me. I had to find a way to recover.

I giggled. "In my past I have been a heavy drinker, but I'm trying to turn over a new leaf. That's one of the reasons I wanted this job. I figured some time away from alcohol would do me good. Sorry if you were hoping otherwise." I looked down at my lap as though I were ashamed of myself for refusing to have a drink with him.

Brock picked up the glass of wine and poured it down the sink. He handed me a bottle of water from his mini fridge. "No problem. Let's get to work then."

We spent the rest of the afternoon talking about the project. I took a lot of notes and jotted down some quick ideas. He seemed honestly confused and unhappy about the lack of progress. Just as the clock on the wall clicked over to five PM, he gathered up his own notes. "That's enough for today. You're off the clock. I don't suppose I could interest you in a cocktail now, could I?"

I shook my head. "No thank you. I'm seriously trying to cut back."

He nodded. "I get it. When can you get back to me with your ideas about how to get the project back on track?"

"I'd like a full day to pull it all together into a nice, coherent presentation. Would that work for you?"

He looked startled at my professionalism, then he smiled. "It would. So let's say 8 AM day after tomorrow unless you hear otherwise from me. And in the meantime, you're on this full time. Don't let anyone tell you differently."

I really wanted to go back to the cave and do some more exploring, so I said. "I'd like to do a few dives tomorrow to document some of my ideas. Is that okay?"

He smiled a thin cold smile. "No. Come up with your presentation, and just mark the ones that are tentative pending a confirmation dive. Does that work?"

It would have to. "Sure thing," I said. "See you at 8 AM day after tomorrow." I gathered my things and headed back to *Thundercloud.*

Chapter 23
Penny

I DIDN'T WANT to interact with Garth and his team, so I spent the next day sequestered on my boat, trying to come up with suggestions for getting the stalled resort project back on track. It was easy work because from what I'd seen, someone had taken pains to design every single process in the most cumbersome, time-consuming, least-productive way possible.

At first I didn't see how someone could accidentally set up EVERY process so badly, but then it hit me. Whoever had done this had done it deliberately to drag out the construction for as long as possible. And I could think of several reasons why someone would want to extend the construction process.

The dive crew might have wanted to ensure that this easy job lasted as long as possible. That was a best case scenario with an easy fix.

Kraken Industries and Resorts—and therefore its owner Brock Moran—might be scamming the project's other investors if there were any. I'd have to get Newton to look into that aspect.

Either Brock or someone on the crew might have heard about the cave from Miguel or Alonzo, and now they could be looking for the location of the cave where the gold sea monsters lay hidden.

Or possibly all of or any combination of these possible scenarios.

The idea made my head spin. So I started trying to solve the mystery. The first thing I thought of was that if Brock were looking to delay the project, why would he ask me to find ways to speed up the process? Unless he was trying to convince his investors that he was doing everything in his power to complete the project on time, and he was using my involvement as a proof point—albeit one not likely to have a major impact on production.

As far as he knew, I had no expertise in business or construction, so I wasn't a good choice for the role he'd given me. Yet he seemed adamant that I continue, and he tried to keep me isolated from the crew and refused to let them distract me.

What I found the most frustrating was trying to figure out who had an incentive to destroy the ecology of the island and its underwater habitat. In the long run that would hurt the resort's ability to attract customers, so in my mind it was unlikely that Brock Moran was behind it. I was beginning to wonder if he was even aware of the devastation below the surface.

That is, unless he was trying to drag things out to find the sea monsters or scam his investors. In which case, it was in his best interest to be able to say the project was no longer viable, but thanks for the money.

In the short term, the dive crew had to do their diving in polluted waters several times a day. Granted, the dead fish and unpalatable gunk permeating the water also kept people who didn't have to work underwater out of the ocean, which allowed the crew to work at their current leisurely pace without interference. If they did know about the sea monster statuettes, that freedom also gave them time to search for them.

All in all, it was quite a puzzle, and I was no closer to solving it than I had been on the day I arrived.

By now it was almost time for my meeting with Brock, so I slipped on a hoodie and gathered all my notes and my iPad so I could show him the presentation I'd created. Looking ahead as I walked, I noticed him sitting at the table under the tree, sipping a coffee and probably waiting for me. I wasn't late, so I refused to hurry. I waved a greeting but continued my leisurely amble.

I'd just stepped off the wooden dock onto the sandy beach when I heard the sound of a boat not too far behind me. The engine quieted quickly, and a familiar voice called out. "Ahoy. Are you Honey Hynes?"

I knew that voice quite well. It had sung lullabies to me when I was a baby and the speaker had kissed my scrapes and scratches when I was a toddler. More recently, its owner had worked with me at RIO, and even saved my life once. Could it be?

I turned around.

Yup, there he was. Stewie Belcher. Since he'd successfully gained control over his alcoholism, he'd become one of the most important members of my team at RIO. His arrival here could only mean there was a problem somewhere.

I waved my arm over my head. "Yes, I'm Honey. You can moor in that slip next to *Thundercloud*."

Brock had risen and now stood beside me. "Who is that?" he asked.

"Dunno. I'll go find out." I bit my lip.

"I'll join you as backup," he said. "Just in case it's some weirdo. And if he is a friend of yours, I'd love to meet him."

I cringed. There was no escaping Brock's all seeing presence.

He and I strolled down the dock, arriving at Stewie's boat just in time for me to catch his mooring line and tie it off on one of the cleats at the end of the slip. I coiled the rope neatly and stood up.

Then I noticed the tiny, quivering, red-gold dog at Stewie's feet. It was Penny, the wire-haired miniature dachshund I'd adopted with Rafe Cummings. She was whining and clawing at the gunwales trying to reach me. I couldn't imagine why on earth Stewie would have brought her here. It was way too dangerous for her, and her presence might even blow my cover.

Stewie lifted Penny off the deck and put her in my arms. Her joy at our reunion was so great that she wiggled almost uncontrollably. She whimpered and licked my face, frantic to show how much she'd missed me. Her reaction to me was so joyous there was no sense in trying to pretend I didn't know this dog. I cooed in her ear and scratched her belly while her little legs kicked in ecstasy.

While Penny and I were expressing our mutual joy, Brock stood by watching. When there was a break in our little lovefest, he asked "Who is this?"

"This is my dog, Penny. Isn't she beautiful?" I couldn't keep my joy at our reunion with her out of my voice.

He rolled his eyes. "Yes, she's an attractive dog. The bigger question is what she's doing here on my island."

I met Stewie's eyes and hoped he had an explanation that wouldn't blow my cover. He gave a slight nod. "I don't know. You'd have to ask this gentleman," I said.

Stewie hopped over the gunwales onto the deck. "Annie asked me to bring your dog to you."

If I hadn't been so curious about why Doc and Stewie were dog sitting Penny instead of Dane and Maddy as I'd arranged, I would have laughed when he referred to my dogsitter as Annie. That was Doc Warren's first name, and it was a deep, dark secret. Everyone called her Doc, and you could count on the fingers of one hand the number of people who actually knew her traditional name.

But right now, I needed to know why Stewie and Penny were here, and I had to speak in code to keep Brock from catching on that I knew Stewie. I had so many questions, I didn't know where to start. I decided to fall back on my 'Honey is a ditz' persona.

"Annie? Who is Annie again?"

"Your dogsitter, remember?"

"Oh, right. So what happened? She knows I'm paying her, right? I told her I'd give her cash as soon as I get back. Or I can Venmo… Why'd she change her mind about keeping Penny anyway?"

Stewie hopped over the gunwale to the dock. "Her mother came to visit and she's allergic to dogs, so Annie has to bow out of your agreement. She knew you wouldn't want the dog to go back in a shelter, so here I am. Penny's all yours now." Stewie turned to get back on his boat.

"Wait. Don't go. I can't have Penny with me. I'm working and it isn't safe for her here. Isn't there another solution?"

Stewie was unloading a crate of Penny's dog food onto the dock, but he looked up with a frown. "Not unless you know another dogsitter who can take her on a moment's notice." He wiped his hands on his cargo shorts. "That's everything. I'll be going now." He held out his hand as though expecting a tip.

Since there was no place to spend money on this island and my clothes had no pockets anyway, I didn't have any cash on me. I put up a hand in the wait signal. "Hang on a sec. Let me get you something for your trouble."

I raced over to *Thundercloud* and rifled through Honey's gigantic faux leather purse. Luckily she had a few pieces of folding money in her wallet. I grabbed one at random and rushed back.

"Here you go," I said with a smile. "And thank you." I held out my hand with the wrinkled currency in it.

Stewie reached out and took it, and when we made the exchange, he slipped a tightly folded note into my hand. He put the cash in his pocket and pulled out a crumpled business card. "Thank you, Miss Hynes. If you ever need anything, you can call on me. My contact info's on there if you ever decide to call."

I looked at the card while keeping the note hidden in my cupped palm. The card read 'Thomas Jones. Odd jobs.' There was no phone number, but there was an email address. I tucked both pieces of paper under the cuff of my sleeve.

"Thank you, Thomas. I'll be sure to do that." I tried to smile but I was still upset about having Penny on the island with me. With bad water and poison around, not to mention a slightly sadistic crew, it wasn't safe for her here, especially because I would have to leave her alone for long periods while I was diving.

Stewie jumped back on his boat, which I recognized as a rental from one of the marinas on Grand Cayman. He quickly uncoiled the mooring line, started the engine, and backed out. He waved before he engaged the throttle fully.

I was bereft. I hated being on this island. I hated being Honey Hynes. And I hated being away from my friends and family. Most of all, I hated being afraid.

And I was very afraid. Something sinister was going down here, and now I had Penny as well as myself to worry about.

"Let me just drop this card on *Thundercloud,* and then we can get to work," I said, wondering how it was possible that there wasn't a single pocket in Honey's entire wardrobe.

I signaled to Penny to stay, then I ran along the dock to *Thundercloud,* went down to the galley, and put the business card in a junk drawer. With Brock waiting, I knew I didn't have time to read the note now.

Gus kept the boat's spare key taped to the underside of the drawer, so I peeled back a corner of the tape and slipped the folded note under the tape, where I hoped it would be safe. Then I rejoined Brock on the dock, where Penny had remained, sitting quietly beside him.

"What do you plan to do with Penny now?" asked Brock.

I shrugged. "I'm not sure. I guess I'll have to keep her on my boat while I'm working so she'll be out of the way. I know you don't want any more delays in the project."

Brock looked at Penny's wagging tail and bright button eyes. I saw on his face the exact moment when he melted.

"She can stay with you while you're on the island, as long as she doesn't cause any trouble. And as long as you clean up after her."

Thank you," I said, beaming with joy while trying to tamp down my fears. I was thrilled to have my dog with me, but terrified of what might happen to her while she was here.

Chapter 24
Disappearance

BROCK and I walked back to his home office building to start work for the day. Penny obediently followed along behind us, sniffing the air and looking around, but never straying far from my heels. As we approached the office structure, Brock abruptly stopped moving.

"Let's work outside today," he said. "Despite the mess the guys have made of the island, it's still a nicer view than the four walls of my trailer and not nearly as claustrophobic. Plus there's the added bonus that Penny can roam around freely rather than having to stay cooped up inside with us."

I wasn't sure whether his concern for Penny was real or if he just didn't want her in his home, but either way, being outside suited me much better than being alone inside with him. "Great idea," I said, trying hard to suppress the relief I felt from my voice. His constant mood swings and inappropriate innuendos made me nervous.

We brought our work materials and electronic devices to the picnic table where Liam and I had worked yesterday. I tied Penny's harness to a table leg and we all sat down. Roaming freely was all well and good, but there were a lot of unaccustomed dangers on this island. I'd need to train her on her boundaries before I'd be comfortable letting her loose.

Brock dropped his blue looseleaf binder on the table. "Before we start, I'll bring us something to drink and maybe some munchies. Let me see what I've got." He turned and strode across the dirt track back to his combination home and office.

Lost in thought, I scratched Penny's ears. I was having trouble getting a handle on Brock Moran. I couldn't decide if he was the shrewd businessperson his reputation said he was, or a clueless figurehead whose team was taking him for a ride while they did nothing except collect their paychecks. Was he the nice guy who brought me snacks or the cold ruthless boss who berated his employees in public. Each facet of his personality also had its opposite on display.

Which was the real Brock Moran—the man ruthlessly destroying the island's environment or the soft hearted person who'd invited a puppy to join him while he worked? Was he the man who made me uneasy to be alone with him in his office or the nice guy about to serve me coffee and cookies? I couldn't tell, and that made me tense around him.

He was smiling when he came out of his office, carrying a tray laden with snacks and drinks.

He placed the tray on the table. "Help yourself," he said. He picked up one of the water bottles on the tray, and I heard the seal break as he twisted the cap. He poured the cool water into a small metal bowl and put it on the ground where Penny could reach it.

'This has to be an act' I thought.

"I know you've been worried about the quality of the water supply on the island. I'll have Arthur send some extra water to *Thundercloud* so you don't have to worry about Penny." He smiled at me.

His kindness did nothing to dispel my questions about his true nature. I couldn't tell if he was truly concerned about Penny's health or if he was just trying to alleviate my suspicions but setting me up with extra water for Penny inadvertently told me he was well aware that the work his team was doing had tainted the island's water supply. That alone was more than enough to condemn him in my eyes.

Brock had brought another large looseleaf book with him, and he flipped it open to the first page. "This is the procedures manual the team is supposed to use. I'd like to get your opinion on the procedures themselves as well as how well the team is actually following them."

I stared at him, utterly amazed. "What makes you think I'm qualified to evaluate these procedures? I'm sure the people who put them together in the first place had a lot more expertise and experience than I do."

He beamed. "Exactly the point. I'm looking for fresh eyes. You picked out the problems with the underwater welding procedures after just one dive. I want you to look at the entire operation."

He took a sip from his water bottle. "Between us, I think there's something strange going on with this project. But I need help. I just can't figure it out on my own."

The hair on my arms stood up at his words. He sounded sincere, but the words didn't make any sense. This man had a reputation for being a shrewd businessperson, and he had access to some of the world's foremost experts to help put his mind at ease if he had concerns. Yet he was asking me for help. As far as I knew, he still thought I was a relatively inexperienced commercial diver with no college degree—and a pretty big problem with alcohol.

It didn't add up. Either he was on to me, or he was coming on to me.

Either way, I didn't like it.

I thought about the situation for a minute. "Just off the top of my head after a quick glance at a few pages, I don't think what you're asking me to do will be easy. It will take some analysis and study. I'd like to propose a different methodology to accomplish your goals."

"Okaay," he said, drawing out the word. "What 'methodology' do you have in mind?" He made air quotes with his fingers when he said the word, and I knew using it instead of the simpler form of the word might have been out of character for Honey.

Ignoring my potential mistake, I took a deep breath to calm down before I spoke. "Let me take the manual and read the whole thing so I have a good grasp of the entire project. Then I'll review a few items and take detailed notes on what I think. After that we can meet every few days to review the next batch of processes. Agreed?"

His smile was creepy and more like a leer than an expression of good humor. "Excellent. I knew there was a reason I wanted you to run this project."

"Great," I said gathering up the books and papers. "I'll take this stuff and work on *Thundercloud* until I'm ready to start discussing my findings." I bent to unhook Penny's leash, but his next words brought me upright in a hurry.

"Don't take too long. I can't wait for you forever," he said in a low, throaty voice.

I stood up quickly and held Penny's leash tightly in one hand. I shifted the massive binders toward my body's center, almost like I expected them to be a shield. That made me feel even more self-conscious, so I relaxed my grip and tried to hold them more naturally.

Brock chuckled. The sound made my skin crawl. I could feel his eyes on my back, following my every step as I walked away toward the boat.

It was all I could do not to run.

The first thing I did when I got to *Thundercloud* was to make sure Penny was comfortable and that I'd taken care of all her needs.

Next I read the note Stewie had given me. It was no help. It merely said, "Hold on," with a smiley face. I growled with frustration.

Next I sat on the daybed to write emails to Newton and Dane using the personas they had set up on the iPad they'd left with me. I had to be careful what I wrote, since they'd seemed convinced that Brock would be monitoring my communications with the outside world, so it took me a while to finish sending the messages. If I hadn't worried about Brock finding out he was under surveillance from me, I would have been more open with what I wrote. Even better, I would have left and gone home right away.

Here's what I sent:

I miss you both and I want to come home right NOW. The big boss is taking a great interest in me and my work, but I'm not prepared to meet his expectations. The rest of the crew are not very welcoming. Maybe they just don't like me because I'm the new hire. Or maybe because I'm not doing anything like what they hired me for. I mostly just look at project specs with the boss.

BORING.

Some guy dropped Penny off the other day because he said someone developed an allergy, but there's so much going on around here I don't think it's safe for Penny to be with me. I wish one of you could take her in while I'm away. I also wish I knew a sharp lawyer who could get me out of my contract with Kraken Industries. Any suggestions?

Anyway, see you both soon. I hope.

I sat on the bow, sipping lemonade and reading the documents in the massive project binder Brock had given me. Penny sat at my feet. I had to admit it was a comfort having her there. Even though I worried about her safety, I didn't feel so alone and isolated with her by my side.

After I'd been reading for several hours, we both needed a break. I clipped Penny's leash to her harness and took her for a run along the beach. When she'd tired herself out, we returned to the boat, but I wasn't ready to get back to work. I needed to dive. It's the best way I know to calm down and quiet the thoughts swirling through my mind.

I put Penny inside the cabin with some water, her favorite blankets, and a few toys, and then I carefully shut and locked the door to make sure she couldn't get out while I was gone. I geared up for my dive. I wanted to check out that cave again, and maybe bring up another of those sea monster statuettes.

I held tight to my reel and a large underwater flashlight when I stepped off the *Thundercloud*'s stern and descended quickly, swimming at an angle toward my objective as I went deeper. I was happy to see that the sea life was already springing back to health since Liam's team had replaced the Tephrosia with a non-toxic substance. The water was still a murky grey, but I wasn't as concerned about a mask leak as I had been, and I hoped the fish and coral would soon adjust and the reef ecosystem would return to health. I also hoped that Garth didn't catch on that Liam had changed the substance and rat him out to Brock.

But as always, as soon as I was underwater, all my problems slipped away to the back of my mind and I focused on the wonders around me. I was delighted when I looked down and saw a healthy looking stingray swooping across the sand. It was the first stingray I'd seen since I'd been here, and I hoped it was a sign that the sea life was returning.

Nearby, two nearly full grown—but still juvenile—hammerhead sharks mock-sparred for supremacy. I assumed they had ventured away from the nearby spawning grounds and were getting ready to leave for the open seas soon. I wished them luck and continued on my path.

Two gorgeous French angelfish swam past, and a barely visible lobster watched me warily as I neared his home. Hundreds of small reef dwellers—yellowtail damselfish, creole wrasse, brown chromis, and two glassy sweepers—swarmed the coral along the reef top. It was more healthy sea life than I'd seen since I'd been here, and I made a mental note to let Liam know that his work was already having an impact.

The pinnacle was straight ahead, and I swam as fast as I could toward the slender, nearly invisible fold in the coral wall that hid the entrance to the cave. When I was safely behind its concealing bend, I pulled my smaller flashlight from my BCD pocket and switched it on.

The mouth of the cave was as dark and forbidding as ever, but I was determined to explore it more fully. Once again I secured the reel to the rock just outside the cave's entrance and swam inside.

My plan had been to go directly to the cache of golden figurines, but once inside the cave, I thought better of it. I wanted to understand the dimensions of the cave, and to know if there was another entrance.

Carefully unspooling my reel of rope behind me, I swam straight ahead, keeping the cavern wall on my left. I came to a narrow opening that looked like it might be another entrance to the cavern, but it was so slender that I didn't want to enter—especially as I was already nearing the turnaround point for my air. I wanted to make it all the way around the cavern on this dive, but the space seemed immense.

It wasn't a good idea keep smuggling a reel with me on each dive, because sooner or later I was bound to bump into Garth or one of the other Kraken divers, and they'd wonder why I had a reel with me. Reluctantly, I tied my rope off to another conveniently located rock and turned around to go back the way I'd come.

My small flashlight began to flicker, so I put it back in my BCD pocket and flipped on the larger flashlight I'd brought clipped to a D-ring on the side of my BCD. Its stronger beam managed to light up most of the cavern, and I was surprised to realize that I was already nearly back at the entrance.

I mentally berated myself for not switching to the larger flashlight as soon as I'd gone inside the mouth of the cave, but I'd been worried that someone from Kraken might see the beam of moving light and follow it to the cave entrance. But if I'd used it right away, I'd have easily seen the cave's contours and had plenty of time to check out the stash of gold figurines.

I gauged the distance to the entrance if I continued in my original path along the wall versus cutting back across the cave and stopping at the huge central rock to pick up another of the small statues. I decided the difference in time would be negligible, so I left my reel where it was and took off across the cavern floor.

The pile of figurines appeared undisturbed since I'd been here last. I picked one up and examined it in the bright ray of my large flashlight. It was a kraken, wearing battle armor and flailing its long tentacles. Their span was about twice the Kraken's height, and its helmet had a spike in the center, just below its eyes. The battle armor covered much of its mantle, and there were two larger spikes, one on each side of the helmet. The spikes made the kraken—already a fearsome beast —a very dangerous adversary indeed.

The entire statue was about six or eight inches tall, with a similar wingspan. No way was it going to fit in a BCD pocket, so I wedged it under the vest and secured it with the Velcro cummerbund. The helmet's top spike stuck out slightly from the BCD's shoulder openings and the ones on its side poked my abdomen.

I swam out of the cavern and headed back toward *Thundercloud,* angling my path upward to facilitate off-gassing while I swam. I didn't want to spend much time in open water in case someone from the Kraken dive team saw me and noticed the poorly concealed statue I carried. I climbed the ladder as soon as I reached my boat.

I tossed my fins onto the deck to get them out of the way, then tore open my BCD's cummerbund and quickly removed the kraken figurine and zipped it into my bag even before I removed the rest of my gear. I wanted it out of sight in case anyone decided to drop by.

I had set up a shallow trough of fresh water on the deck to use as a rinse tank because I didn't want to share the dirty rinse water the Kraken team members used. I dropped my mask, regulator, and BCD into the tank and hurried to the cabin door to greet Penny.

I opened the door, expecting the small golden bundle to leap into my arms, wiggling joyfully at our reunion, but she didn't come running. Thinking maybe she was asleep in the stateroom, so I went inside to look, calling her name as I went. There was no answering bark, and the stateroom was empty.

I scurried back out onto the deck and called her again.

Nothing.

My heart froze with terror. What if she'd gotten out of the cabin somehow and jumped overboard looking for me?

I rushed back to the *Thundercloud*'s stern and put on my mask and fins, then I jumped in the water to look for her. Using my snorkel, I covered the area under the boats, the entire length of the dock, and the nearby open water areas.

There was no sign of her. The thought of what might have befallen her if she'd jumped in the water was too scary to even contemplate.

As bad as the idea was, it was better to think maybe she'd gone ashore.

I climbed back on the boat, tossed my mask and fins away, and ran barefoot along the dock to the island, screaming her name as I ran. Again there was no response of any kind.

I raced to the tool shed and the tank shack to see if she was there. I ran to the bunkhouse and looked inside. I even banged on Brock's door. When he didn't answer, I opened the door and peeked inside. She wasn't there.

I rushed back to the beach and started running along the shore, calling her name with every step, but I got no response. Soon I'd run around the entire circumference of the island without seeing or hearing any sign of her, so I cut across into the island's interior to see if she was exploring something in there, still calling her name as I ran.

About halfway across the island's diameter, I saw an old and small woman dressed in a vivid red dress and a paisley shawl. A brightly colored scarf wrapped her head, but a few tendrils of dark hair mixed with silver peeked out around its edges. She held a small goat by a rope tied to its collar, and several chickens pecked the dirt by her bare feet.

This must be Rosalina.

"Have you seen my dog?" Panting, I bent over with my hands on my thighs, trying to catch my breath. Although I hadn't run more than a few miles, I'd been shouting for Penny the whole time so I was much more winded than I'd have been after a normal run of that distance.

I stood up straight and took a deep breath so I could speak more normally. "Her name is Penny. She's a dachshund—a wiener dog. She has curly blonde hair—"

Rosalina interrupted. "The bad men have her. They took her off your boat. She didn't want to go with them but they forced her. They picked her up and carried her. She tried to get loose…"

Penny is tiny, weighing in at about twelve pounds. And she's so sweet and trusting that she's defenseless against evil.

My heart stopped. "Where did they take her?"

Rosalina bit her lip. "I don't know. I was afraid of what they would do if they saw me watching. I ran away." She looked down at the sand. "I was a coward. I am sorry."

I wanted to shout at Rosalina. Wanted to berate her for putting her own fear over the life of my dog.

But that was wrong.

This was my fault. I was the one who'd left Penny alone at the mercy of people I knew had none. It was up to me to get her back safely.

Chapter 25
Making Enemies

I TOOK off at a run toward Brock's tiny combination home and office building, yelling, "Moran, I need to talk to you right now" all the way.

When I reached the structure, I drew in a deep breath and banged my fist as hard as I could on the door. "Brock! Open up right now. We need to talk." Another flurry of pounding and banging. "Brock, get..."

He opened the door, looking sleepy and disheveled. His hair stuck up in clumps, and a red crease marred his cheek. Obviously, he'd been taking a nap.

"What is it?" he asked. "Has something happened?"

"What have you done with Penny? If you've harmed so much as one strand of her fur..."

He rubbed his forehead. "Please stop yelling at me. I was lying down because I have a migraine and loud noise makes it worse."

He did look awful, but he would have to take care of himself. My mission was to rescue my dog. He obviously hadn't been involved in taking Penny if he'd been sleeping, and I wasn't going to get any help from him if I kept yelling. Then again, maybe he'd given orders to his crew and then callously gone off to take a nap.

I decided to give him the benefit of the doubt. I needed him on my side to get Penny back from wherever the crew had stashed her.

"I'm sorry you're not feeling well, and I'm sorry I yelled. Penny is missing. I left her locked in the cabin of my boat and went for a dive. When I came back, the door was open and she was gone..."

He looked at me condescendingly. "Maybe you forgot to lock the door. Maybe she got out and ran away."

I bit my tongue to keep from yelling again. "I didn't forget to lock it, and she can't open it anyway. She stays there all the time when I dive, and this has never happened before. And besides, Rosalina saw them take her off my boat."

He frowned. "What was Rosalina doing up here? She's supposed to stay in her own space."

"Focus, Brock, focus. You and Rosalina can hash out whatever your problem is later, but right now my dog is missing. She's only a baby, and you promised she'd be safe here. Are you going to help me or not?"

He pulled his cell out of the pocket of his cut-off jeans and hit a speed dial button. "Garth, have you seen Honey's dog? No? Can you get the guys together for a search party? Thanks." He put the phone back in his pocket. "Garth is going to go out looking for her..."

I held up my hand to stop him from talking. "He shouldn't have to search very hard since he took her and stashed her someplace. I've covered most of the island myself already. Wherever he put her, it's a doozy of a hiding place."

Garth, Bert, Ken, and Arthur swaggered across the rutted dirt from the direction of the bunkhouse, with identical nasty grins on their faces. They walked as slowly as human beings could move and still claim to be making progress.

When they finally arrived within easy conversational range, Garth asked "What's the problem, Boss?"

"Honey's dog is missing. Have any of you seen her?" Although he stayed in the open doorway, he took a step back inside his quarters, making it clear the fight was going to be just between me and the men.

Garth turned to me. "Well, that's a shame. Such a sweet little dog, and who knows what kind of trouble she could get into out here on her own. You sure she didn't fall in the water?"

Brock spoke into the air. "Help her look for her dog, guys. I've got one of those migraines or I'd join you." He turned away and shut the door.

Garth smiled at his crew. "Looks like we're on our own here. But that's okay. We're happy to help you find your sweet little doggo."

I was so scared for Penny I wanted to vomit. "Cut the crap, Garth. I know you guys went on my boat and took her. I have a witness."

An evil gleam sparkled in his eye. "Dunno what you're talking about, Honey. There's no one on the island except us, and we would never do something so mean, would we guys?" He turned to look at them.

Obediently, they shook their heads and tried to look angelic. They failed.

"I said cut the crap, Garth. I have a witness." I tried to keep my voice even, but my stress was rising with each minute Penny remained missing.

"A witness?" he said. "There's nobody else on the island besides us." The guys all nodded in agreement, even though they knew it was a lie.

"Give it up. I know you're lying. Rosalina saw you take her. Now where is Penny?"

He smiled. "That old witch. She lies and…"

"No, I don't lie, Garth Henson, and you know it." Rosalina had quietly approached from behind Brock's tiny house, leaning heavily on a walking stick with a yellow metal handle and tip. "I saw you. You better not have hurt that sweet puppy." She stood up and shook the stick at Garth.

His eyes widened when he noticed the stick, so I turned to see what had drawn his attention. The handle, which I'd assumed was brass, caught a gleam of sunshine and I realized it was gold. The gold figurine was a tiny replica of a winged horse wearing battle armor like the kraken I'd brought up only a short time ago. The only difference was that the armor this horse wore wasn't spiked, and Rosalina's hand rested comfortably on the intricately carved saddle that graced his back.

I wasn't sure if her having the cane meant that Rosalina knew about the figurines in the cave. It didn't seem as if she could be aware of the potential value of her cane since she waved it so casually under the avaricious gazes of the Kraken crew.

But they were very interested in the cane. To a man, their eyes lit up with greed.

Even though I hadn't seen her before today, I'd been uneasy about her safety. Now she'd be in real danger because she'd dared to help me. I'd have to find a way to get her off the island, at least until I figured out what was really going on. But first, I needed to get Penny back.

Garth's eyes glittered as he stared at the cane in Rosalina's hand. He reached out to take it from her.

Without conscious thought, I grabbed his arm to stop him from touching her or the cane. He was obviously surprised by my speed and the strength of my grip.

"Let go," he said. "I only want to see that walking stick."

"Sure thing," I said, not relaxing my grip in the slightest. "As soon as you tell the guys to bring Penny back safely."

He tried to pull his arm away, but I was ready for him. I twisted it around to his back and pulled him close to me so I could whisper in his ear. "Don't make me hurt you in front of the guys. Tell them to bring Penny back here, right now. Otherwise, I'll put you on your knees."

That was probably an idle boast. I'm very strong, but I was already just about at my limit, and if Garth chose to test me any harder, he could probably break my grip.

But knowing him, I was pretty sure he wouldn't want to chance having a "girl" best him in front of his men.

He inhaled slowly. "Okay. I guess we've had enough fun. There's no reason to get so upset about it. We'll take you to the blasted dog."

"Good." I held onto his arm. "Rosalina, you and I need to talk. Please go to my boat and lock yourself in the cabin until I return."

"Si, Missus Hynes," she said. "I will wait there for your return.

She started walking along the rutted dirt road toward the dock. She'd only taken a few steps when she stopped and turned around. "I know how to use the radio to call for help if you are not back soon."

"Excellent." I gave Garth's arm another little twist. "Hear that? So don't try anything stupid. Now let's go."

Garth gestured with his head to the men, and as a group, we all walked into the island's interior. Garth was staggering, off balance in my grip, but he didn't make a sound. The cowardly crew ignored his predicament, although if they'd come at me as a group I'd have been no match for them.

We trudged up to one of the giant piles of sand that they'd created as part of the project work. A small pile of desiccated palm fronds leaned against the bottom of the pile.

Arthur walked over and pushed the fronds aside, revealing a small wooden door with a padlock. He pulled a key from his pocket and opened the door. A blast of heat rolled out when the door opened.

Penny cowered in the back of the tiny crate, which was too small even for her. I didn't see any water bowl or food inside. She was trembling with fright, panting hard from too much heat and not enough water.

I called to her. Her head moved slowly in my direction, but she stayed in the buried crate. She was obviously too afraid of the men to come out.

"See," Garth said. "She's fine. She likes it in there."

I was still holding Garth's arm twisted behind his back, and his head was still close to mine. I whispered in his ear. "Take your men and go back to the bunkhouse. If any of you come out again before first dive tomorrow, I really will break your arm. And if you ever so much as look at my dog again, I'll kill you. Got it?"

He took a deep, ragged breath then gave a nod. "Let's go guys. We've had enough fun for today. First round of drinks is on me."

The crew looked at each other, unsure if Garth really meant for them to just walk away leaving me and Penny alone.

Garth jutted his chin in the direction of the bunkhouse. "Let's go. Get a move on."

The men started walking. When they'd gone about twenty paces, I released Garth's arm.

"You don't ever want to mess with me again. Now get going before I decide to stuff you in that crate. Then we'll see how much you like it in there."

He took a few steps and then turned back to stare at me. I held his gaze without flinching, and he broke off the stare first. He took off after his crew without another word.

I rushed to the crate where Penny still cowered. The heat rolling out of the tiny, enclosed space was almost unbearable. I reached inside to help her out. As soon as she was sure it was me, she hopped weakly toward me.

I stood up with her in my arms and strode as rapidly as I could back to my boat.

Chapter 26
The Movie Crew

As soon as we reached *Thundercloud,* I brought Penny into the cabin where it was cool. I poured her a bowl of water, and she drank the entire contents. Twice. Even after that, she was still shaky, so I filled the galley sink with water and put her in to give her a quick cool down.

Within a few minutes, she had stopped panting and trembling. She stood up in the sink to lick my face and gave herself a mighty shake to throw off the water from her heavy, lush fur.

Her shake soaked me, the cabinet doors under the sink, and the floor, but I didn't care. She was telling me she'd be okay, and I was grateful I'd gotten to her in time.

Rosalina brought me a towel and I rubbed Penny dry and then brushed her thick wiry coat. She took a few more sips of water, then went to her bed, circled twice, and went to sleep.

I couldn't really blame her. After all, she was only a baby, and she'd had a terrible day.

Once I knew for sure Penny was in a deep easy sleep, I turned to Rosalina. "You're welcome to stay here with me tonight, and for that matter, as long as you want to. The crew is likely to be out for blood."

She nodded. "Thank you. I will stay here. But won't they just wait until we're asleep to come aboard?"

"Probably. I have an alarm that I'll set up to give us an early warning and then I'll move the boat away from the dock and anchor at a distance where it's deep. They've made such a mess of the water with all their pollutants, they probably won't want to swim very far, especially at night. We should be safe. And I'm going to contact some friends of mine. They'll take you to safety as soon as they get here."

"Oh, don't worry. I will sleep on your boat tonight, but I'm sure the evil ones will have calmed down by tomorrow. I have to stay on the island to take care of my chickens and my goat."

She bit her lip. "I think they'll be okay for one night. May I cook your dinner as a thank you for letting me stay with you?"

I laughed. "I should be the one cooking for you. I never would have found Penny if it weren't for your help. But sorry to say, I'm a terrible cook. I usually just have a sandwich for dinner."

She sniffed. "I will cook. It is no trouble"

"Thank you. I have some work to do, so I'll go on deck to do it. I'll be out of your way and I can keep watch at the same time."

I grabbed my iPad to send messages to Newton, Dane, and Liam. Despite what she said, Rosalina could not safely stay on the island after she'd helped me, but Newton would have to be the one to convince her to leave her island and her pets.

Once again writing the emails took a long time. I'm usually very direct, so it was hard for me to write something I felt sure the recipients would understand that wouldn't be equally obvious to Brock or his crew if they intercepted the messages.

I finally managed to convey the idea that they needed to find someone to watch Penny because she was not safe here on the island. Since Dane had committed to keeping her while I was undercover, in my opinion the burden of keeping her safe was on them. I mentioned that if someone didn't come up with a safe place for her to stay by tomorrow morning, I would leave the island myself.

Newton must have had other professional operatives he could have sent instead of me, so I felt justified in insisting he keep to the terms of our agreement. Working undercover for his organization wasn't my job, and I'd made a commitment to Penny when I adopted her. She had to be my first responsibility.

I knew that if I left the island prematurely it would put an end to my undercover work forever, and probably kill their current investigation, but there was no way I was going to stay here if staying put my beloved Penny in jeopardy.

Once I'd made it clear that ensuring Penny's safety was key to my continued involvement, I mentioned that Rosalina was staying on *Thundercloud* with me for a few days because of a disagreement with the Kraken crew. She could not stay safely on the island, and she needed a new place to stay as much as Penny did. I said nothing in the message about Rosalina's unwillingness to leave her livestock behind. We'd have to cross that bridge when we came to it.

By the time I'd finished writing the messages, the aromas of Rosalina's cooking had wafted out onto the deck. Whatever it was, it smelled heavenly. I would have sworn there was nothing worth cooking on the boat, but with Rosalina in the kitchen, I would have been wrong.

"Five minutes to dinner," she said when I looked up.

"Just enough time to take Penny for a quick walk," I said, noticing that my pet's head had popped up from her bed when she heard my voice. "I'll be back in five minutes, but if I'm not, go ahead and start eating without me."

She frowned. "Never."

I smiled while I hooked Penny up to a leash and we ran down the dock to the ruined beach. Penny was as happy, frisky, and excited as she usually was when we went for a walk, so I concluded that she probably hadn't suffered any permanent damage from her ordeal. She quickly took care of business. I cleaned up after her, and then we raced back up the dock. The less time we were on that cursed island, the happier I'd be.

Rosalina and I ate the dinner she'd prepared sitting at the small galley table. I was amazed that she put together such a tasty meal from the random ingredients on *Thundercloud*. After we finished eating, we sat on the deck, and I idly rolled a ball for Penny to fetch while Rosalina and I chatted and got to know each other.

It was after dark when I heard a ping from my iPad. Email from Newton—or Nadine, his cover name.

"Solution in process. Hang tight."

Leave it to my father to be so cryptic. But I trusted him, so I assumed he would honor my request to find a way to keep Penny safe.

A little while later, I grabbed a heavy flashlight and took Penny for her last walk of the day. When we returned, I started the engines and took the boat out about a half mile from the dock. That was far enough away from the island that the crew would have to think twice about disturbing us, but close enough that we could return quickly in the morning. Since I planned to sleep on the daybed in the main cabin so I could keep watch, I showed Rosalina to the master cabin where she'd be sleeping and demonstrated how to use the fixtures in the head. Then I checked the perimeter alarm one last time before we all went to bed.

The next morning dawned bright and sunny. Penny snuggled up next to me on the daybed, still snoring softly. I didn't remember boosting her up to join me, so I guess she took matters into her own hands and jumped. Clearly, she was feeling a lot better.

I hopped out of bed and started the coffee. Then I gathered all the pieces of the perimeter alarm and put them away before I piloted the boat back to the dock and tied off in my usual slip. By the time Penny and I returned from her walk, Rosalina was up, sipping coffee and flipping pancakes in the galley. If she kept feeding me like this, I'd have to consider asking her to become my long term boatmate. I already knew I'd miss her company even more than her cooking when she left.

I'd just put Penny's breakfast bowl on the galley floor when Brock shouted from the dock. "Honey, are you awake? Can I come aboard?"

Rosalina gasped and started to shake. It was obvious Brock frightened her. I put my hand on her arm. "Relax. I won't let him hurt you," I whispered.

I shouted back to Brock. "No, stay where you are. I'll come to you."

I strolled out onto the deck, a mug of coffee in my hand. I shut the door to the main cabin behind me to keep Penny and Rosalina safe before addressing him. "You're up early. What's going on?"

"I wanted to apologize that I couldn't help you look for your dog yesterday. I get these migraines and they literally knock me onto my back. I'm completely non-functional when I get them. But Garth told me he helped you find your Penny. I'm glad she's alright."

I took a sip of my coffee to buy time while I gained control of my anger. When I thought I could speak without attacking him, I said, "Penny is fine, but it's no thanks to Garth or your team of thugs. They locked her in a tiny crate, buried the crate in one of those dirt piles, and hid the evidence of their digging under a pile of palm fronds. I had to physically threaten Garth before he finally ordered the team to show me where he'd stashed her. And it wasn't a moment too soon. She was on the verge of heatstroke. She could have died. I want him disciplined, or I'm gone."

He took a step back. "That doesn't sound like Garth..."

I interrupted. "I beg to differ. It sounds *exactly* like Garth. He and the team have been harassing and bullying me since I arrived. You've seen it yourself, and yet you do nothing about it. Do you really expect me to believe you have no idea of the kind of man he is? If you do know, that doesn't say much for the kind of man you are."

He stared at me for a minute. "I know exactly who he is. He was just having a little fun. I'm sure he didn't mean any harm, but I'll talk to him. I promise he'll leave your dog alone from now on."

"Okay," I said flatly. One way or the other Penny would be leaving the island today, so even though it killed me to concede, I let it go because I knew Newton was working on a solution to take care of Penny.

"I stopped by to see if you're ready to talk about the project yet. Any insights you're ready to share?" he said.

"I have a few. Let me get my notes," I said.

"And maybe a cup of coffee for me? Please? It smells great." He smiled what I guess he thought was a winsome smile.

It made my skin crawl. "Sure. Wait here. I'll bring it out to you."

I went back inside the cabin and shoved the project book and all my notes into a large canvas tote. Then I poured coffee into a black travel mug for Brock, said goodbye to Rosalina, and whistled for Penny to come with me. I planned to keep her with me at all times until whoever Newton was sending for her arrived. I wasn't taking any more chances with my sweet little pet's safety.

I handed Brock his coffee and slung the heavy tote bag over my shoulder. He and I trudged slowly toward the outdoor table where we'd been holding our meetings. We were almost there when the familiar roar of an arriving boat broke the stillness. I knew the sound of that boat as well as I knew the sound of *Tranquility*'s engines.

I said a silent thank you to Newton and Dane. They must have gotten the rescue team up at the crack of dawn to get here so early. I kept walking, as though the boat's arrival was of no interest to me, but Brock turned around and craned his neck to see who it was.

"What's he doing back here? I told him I'd call him when we were ready."

I whipped around as though surprised. The recently arrived boat was in fact Liam's *Enviroman* as I'd suspected. Liam would not have been my first choice for a dog sitter, but I was confident he'd take good care of Penny no matter what.

Brock and I watched as Liam pulled his boat into the slip next to *Thundercloud*. I was surprised to see a tall and very familiar figure jump off the boat to help tie her off. I squinted.

Yup. T-8. My husband Rafe's best friend, also known as Tate Crusoe.

And then Rafe himself was there, stepping out from behind T-8 and onto the dock. My heart swelled with the joy of seeing him, and I had to bite down hard on my lip to keep myself from grinning from ear to ear.

Once *Enviroman* was secure, the men walked three abreast down the dock toward where Brock and I stood waiting.

Penny was right next to us, quivering with excitement. The trio was still about fifty yards away when she couldn't wait another second. She tore off to greet Rafe, ears flopping while she ran as fast as her little legs could carry her.

He knelt down to pat her head and rub her belly when she reached him. His face glowed with happiness.

He looked up at me and our eyes met. I had to look away because it hurt so much to see him and not be able to show him how much I love him.

Brock was watching the interaction between Rafe and Penny. "Your dog certainly seems to love that man. Do you know him?"

"No, I don't think so," I replied.

Rafe stood up and took a few steps toward us, Penny following at his heels. I couldn't take my eyes off him.

"That guy looks just like Rafe Cummings," Brock said. "Do you think it could really be him? But what would a big movie star like him be doing hanging out with a nobody like Liam Lawton? And who is that with them?"

Liam wasn't a nobody, and I'd bet Brock knew it as well as I did. But I didn't say anything.

At last, Rafe, Liam, and T-8 reached us. Penny was still jumping around with the ecstasy of seeing Rafe after being apart for so long. I knew just how she felt, but I had to keep a tight rein on my emotions—and my face, which continually threatened to break into a wide grin.

"That's a beautiful dog," said Rafe. "Who does she belong to, and what's her name?" Great actor that he was, you'd have never known that Penny was his dog—or that I was his wife.

"She's mine," I said. "Her name is Penny."

Brock obviously wasn't a dog lover, and he didn't care who Liam had brought with him. He only wanted to know what Liam was doing back here after he'd sent him away.

"Back so soon, Lawton? I thought I told you I'd let you know when and if we needed you."

Liam smiled his most winning smile. "You did. But then I had an idea. I think you might like it. It could be pretty lucrative for you."

Obviously, Liam had said the magic word. Brock's demeanor changed immediately at the idea of money. But he didn't say anything to give away his interest.

Liam pointed to T-8 and Rafe as he introduced them. "What you may not know is that T-8, Rafe, and I have worked together on several very successful and highly profitable documentaries. Our company is T-8/Lawton Productions, and T-8 and I are the producers. Rafe Cummings, world's greatest action superstar, narrates the films for us." Liam winked at me when he said this. "And I have an idea for a documentary about this island and how you've worked tirelessly to bring it back to environmental health. I think it would be worth your while to listen to our proposal."

Brock nodded. "I'm willing to listen. But let's go inside where we can be more comfortable."

Liam nodded. "Sure. Let's go."

"Honey, I won't need you for this. I'll catch up with you later."

Rafe scowled when Brock called me Honey, even though I was pretty sure he knew that was my undercover name. I couldn't blame him. The name grated on me too every time I heard it.

Even though it meant I wouldn't be spending time in the same space as Rafe, I was thrilled that Brock excluded me from the meeting. I tried to keep my sigh of relief silent, but I wasn't totally successful.

Brock narrowed his eyes at me. "Then again, maybe I do need you, if you're going to be my business manager."

I just looked at Brock. "This is the first I've heard of that idea. And I don't think I'd be interested anyway. You know I'm just a diver, not a businessperson."

"So you keep saying, and yet you keep proving otherwise. I'll be very interested in what you think of Lawton's idea."

I scowled. "If I go to the meeting, so does Penny. I'm not letting her out of my sight again as long as Garth and the crew are around. There's no telling what they'll do to her if I'm not there to protect her."

Brock gave an exaggerated sigh. "Very well. Bring her along." The fact that he agreed so easily told me that he knew the truth about what his crew had done to her.

Once we'd settled into the comfy chairs inside Brock's tiny house, Liam and T-8 dominated the meeting. I was impressed, even though I knew how brilliant they were. I wasn't sure they were serious about executing on the idea, but the documentary they were proposing would be a good one.

When they finished their presentation, Brock asked Rafe if he was at the meeting because he would be the narrator on the film.

Rafe nodded. "Yes, I'll narrate, but only on two conditions. My brother Doug writes and produces the score. And I like to have two narrators on my documentaries because I think it makes it more interesting for the viewers and listeners. My contracts always stipulate that I can work with the partner of my choice."

Brock nodded. "I agree to both conditions. If you don't mind my asking, who is the other narrator you have in mind?"

Rafe smiled that glorious smile of his. "I don't want to get your hopes up, so I won't mention her name until I have her okay on the deal. But I promise you won't be disappointed."

Brock rubbed his hands together gleefully. "Probably some gorgeous Hollywood starlet, right? I can't wait to meet her. Can you give me a hint?"

"Well, you're right about that one thing. She is gorgeous, but that's the only hint I'll give you."

The meeting broke up then, and Brock and I walked the movie team back to *Enviroman*. I was waiting for Liam to say something about taking Penny with him. but he jumped aboard *Enviroma*n without a word.

"Excuse me, Liam. Aren't you forgetting something? I thought my friend Nadine had asked you to bring Penny back with you so she could stay with her. She was going to dog sit while I'm here on the island, remember?"

Liam shook his head. "Nadine has an allergy. She can't take Penny."

I flared my nostrils. I couldn't believe Liam really had only come out here to pitch his documentary. What about my dog's safety?

There was a moment of awkward silence. Rafe looked back and forth between Liam and me.

"I can take her if you want," Rafe said. "I love dogs. I'm off work for at least a few weeks so I'll be around full time, and Penny already likes me. She'll be no trouble at all, and it will make me happy to know she's with someone who really wants her to be with them."

Rafe was a terrific actor. He looked at me like he really thought I'd say no when his offer was the best possible answer to my problem. Given his heavy shooting schedule, I didn't know how he'd arrange to have the time off, but I wasn't about to question it.

"Well," I said feigning reluctance, "if you're sure she'll be no trouble, I'd be very grateful. Thank you."

He smiled and handed me a business card. "Here's my personal contact info in case you want to talk about how she's doing. And if you give me your contact info, I'll send you pictures every day so you know she's okay."

It was a brilliant strategy. Now I had a good excuse for contacting Rafe whenever I started to miss him too much. And I could see Penny on my phone at the same time.

First I texted Rafe my—or rather, Honey's—contact info, then I went to *Thundercloud* to gather up Penny's things and carried them back to *Enviroman*. "Thanks again," I said softly as I buckled Penny into her life vest. I was missing them both already, and Liam hadn't even started the engines.

Chapter 27
Two Business Proposals

I SPENT most of the day at that accursed picnic table with Brock, going over the project specs and my productivity ideas. I hated every minute of it, and once again I wondered what I had done to make him think I was good at this sort of thing. I knew full well that I really wasn't very good at it, and since I hated it, I wasn't likely to get any better.

Like me, Honey Hynes was a diver. She only wanted to dive. Brock had originally hired her as a diver.

But it seems Brock had actually wanted a desk jockey when he'd hired Honey Hynes. Or maybe he was lonesome and he just wanted someone to hang out with. I wasn't happy about it either way, although I knew that spending so much time with Brock might make it easier for me to find out whatever it was that Newton and Dane wanted to know.

Unfortunately for me, the change in my status hadn't gone over well with his existing crew. I had been unpopular right from the start, but now every single one of them clearly hated me so much that they would take their hate out on an innocent puppy. I was going to have to wrap this operation up fast before things escalated even further.

Although Honey owned lots of very tiny t-shirts and low-cut shorts that barely cleared her hip bones, she apparently didn't own a hat, so by mid-afternoon my brain was as fried as the skin on my nose. The sun had been beating down on us with relentless fury all day. We'd gone through gallons of lemonade and water, but the liquid sweated out as fast as we could swallow it.

"I'm sorry, Brock. I'm done in. I'm going for a swim, and then I'm going to sit on *Thundercloud* where there's at least a little bit of a breeze."

Brock looked uncomfortable. "You probably shouldn't swim here, Honey. We don't know what's killing the fish, and…"

I held up my hand to stop him. "I'll be fine. I'll wear my dive gear, gloves, a full-face mask. I'll be surprised if I even get wet under all that gear."

I knew that Liam had taken care of the poison Garth and the crew had been using to kill the fish. But so far Garth didn't seem to know that, and whether Brock knew what was going on or not, neither did he. I was sure I'd be fine.

Brock said, "Okay. Far be it from me to try to keep a diver out of the ocean. But maybe when you're done I could join you on your boat and enjoy a little bit of that cool breeze with you. I'll bring the wine."

Ick. His obvious come on made me sick. "No thanks. I really am completely done in for the day. Maybe another time." Of course, I was actually thinking *never*.

I packed up my stuff and slung the bag over my shoulder. I felt Brock's eyes on my back every step of the way to my boat. It was all I could do not to run all the way to *Thundercloud*.

I stepped over the gunwales and gathered up my dive gear. My BCD was still soaking in the rinse tank on the bow of the boat. It had been there since my last dive when I'd brought up the kraken. There'd been so much going on since then that I'd forgotten all about it.

I kept it wrapped in the BCD and went into the cabin. I expected to find Rosalina there, but she wasn't on the boat. I surmised that she must have gotten bored and gone back home to check on her animals.

I hid the kraken in the secret compartment in the head. Although the boat now bore the name *Thundercloud*, it was actually *Sunshine Girl*, the boat belonging to Gus Simmons. He and my late stepfather Ray Russo had been partners in a dive business for many years. It made sense that a boat Gus owned would have a hiding spot in the same location as Ray's boat.

Once I'd hidden the artifact, I geared up and stepped off the stern. Instead of swimming in the direction of the project work, I decided to explore in the other direction again.

I was glad I did. The destruction Brock and his crew had wrought on the other side of the island was nowhere near as pronounced on this side.

Don't get me wrong. The water was still murkier than it should have been, but I knew that thanks to Liam's remediation team, the ashy grey substance blocking the light and visibility was harmless, not the poisonous Tephrosia that the Kraken crew had used to kill every living thing on the other side of the island.

The reef on this side of the island wasn't totally healthy, but at least it wasn't totally dead or dying either. At least, not yet. There were small patches of bleached coral, and many branches of the larger and more delicate sea fans and gorgonians were broken off. Barrel sponges and brain corals had been uprooted and smashed.

In the past, I'd seen similar destruction after a particularly violent storm swept through an area, but the ocean usually began repairs as soon as the storm passed by. From the look of things here, whatever had caused this destruction had happened a while ago, and the reef didn't look to be repairing itself. I could only assume that the island's inability to recuperate from the unknown trauma was the result of the drifting Tephrosia.

As if to prove my conjecture, a small school of brown chromis swooped past me. Rather than swimming in a straight line, most of the chromis were wobbling as they swam. A few were swimming upside down. I pulled my point-and-shoot camera out of my BCD pocket and took a few pictures to send on to Liam and Newton.

Eventually I reached the brackish area where the island's freshwater stream mixed with the ocean's salty brine. There was no current from the freshwater mingling with the sea, and it seemed the flow of fresh water from the spring had completely stopped. I swam into the inlet as far as I could. The water quickly grew shallow and then disappeared, no longer bubbling up from the spring below. With a shock I realized that unless there was another source I didn't know about, fresh water no longer existed on the island.

I waded out of the water and then, still wearing my tank and BCD,

I walked along the course of the inlet until I reached a massive blockage made of rotting garbage and trash. The Kraken crew had been using the freshwater inlet as a garbage dump. Between the Tephrosia, the decaying fish, and the team's putrid garbage, it was no wonder the environment was dying.

Disheartened, I turned around to head back to *Thundercloud*. Try as I might, I couldn't see any reason for the wanton environmental destruction, or for the lack of progress in building the resort. But whatever the reason, or whoever was behind it, the destruction made me sick. Obviously, there was something else going on here, but I still couldn't figure out what it could be. And I really, really wanted to go home, but even more than going home, I wanted these people punished for their despicable actions.

I climbed the *Thundercloud*'s ladder and slid my tank into one of the empty slots in the rack. Then I shrugged out of my BCD and walked over to drop it in the makeshift rinse tank I had set up. By now, the water in the tank was nearly as salty as the sea, so I pulled the plug and let the water run back into the ocean.

Once the rinse tank was empty, I hopped onto the dock to uncoil the freshwater hose to refill it. After placing the end of the hose in the tank, I turned the spigot on. A few drops of water spit out, then nothing.

Unless there was a glitch in the delivery system somewhere, then as I'd feared, the destruction had utterly depleted the island's fresh water supply. Disgusted, I dropped the rest of my gear in the empty rinse tank and went below to send word to Newton and Dane. I hadn't uncovered whatever conspiracy they were hoping to crack, but it was past time for me to go home.

After I'd sent the emails, I came back on deck and noticed a boat approaching. This boat's outline also seemed familiar, but at first, I couldn't place it.

Then it hit me. It was my brother Oliver's boat, the *Flemingo*. He'd chosen the boat's name as a play on our last name, not as a homage to the graceful pink birds. Many people felt compelled to tell him he'd spelled the word incorrectly. Sometimes Oliver explained the joke, other times he'd slap his forehead in a parody of stupidity. But usually, he thanked them solemnly and just ignored the remarks.

But Oliver was supposed to be away on his honeymoon with his new wife, Genevra Blackthorne. What were they doing here?

Oliver expertly piloted his boat into the slip next to *Thundercloud.* I caught the line he tossed me and secured the boat, coiling the excess line in a neat ring next to the cleat.

I was so happy to see Oliver and Genevra that I was sure if anyone was watching, my excitement would give away the fact that I knew them. I tried hard to tone it down.

Oliver's appearance was startling. It had only been a few weeks since I'd seen him last, but to my eyes he looked older, more mature. I realized I'd still been thinking of him as the cocky but insecure teenager I first met. He was obviously no longer that boy. He was now a man.

And Genevra—one of my very best friends—glowed with happiness. I was thrilled for them both, but puzzled as to why they were here.

They obviously knew that I was undercover here, so we didn't go in for the hugs and happy smiles our reunion would ordinarily warrant. Instead, we politely shook hands and introduced ourselves.

I asked why they were here, and Oliver explained that Fleming Environmental Investments was interested in investing in the future resort. Since there was no phone coverage and only intermittent Internet access, he'd decided to take a chance and visit the island in hopes of securing a meeting with the big man himself—Brock Moran of Kraken Industries.

I nearly gagged, but I was still mindful of the potential that Moran had bugged my boat or the dock itself, so I issued them a cool welcome and told them I would check whether Brock was free to take a meeting. In the meantime, I planned to have them sit at the outdoor table where Brock and I usually met each day.

The table had a view of much of the island and whatever its residents were engaged in, so I thought it would be a good place to leave them. They were both very smart and observant, so they might be able to pick up on something obvious the crew was doing that I'd missed.

We walked across the rutted road toward Brock's combo office and home building. The closer we got to the bunkhouse, the more a delightful aroma of barbecuing meat perfumed the air.

"Wow," said Oliver. "Something smells delicious. You islanders will be eating well tonight."

I didn't respond, but I was surprised. Although the food in the bunkhouse mess was more than okay, as you'd expect it was usually heavy on canned goods and short on fresh foods. Maybe the meat had been in a freezer somewhere and Arthur had pulled it out as a special treat. I rarely ate dinner with the crew, although I sometimes dropped in to scoop up a bowl of chili or soup as a change from my usual dinner of peanut butter sandwiches.

Even though my stomach was growling, I walked directly to Brock's door and lifted my hand to knock. Before my knuckles met the wood, Brock opened his door and stepped outside. He caught sight of Oliver and Genevra sitting at his table. "And who are you?"

Oliver and Genevra stood up and walked toward him. Oliver extended his hand. "I'm Oliver Fleming-Russo. I'm VP of market development at Fleming Environmental Investments. And this is Genevra Blackthorne, Editor in chief of *Cayman! Cayman!* magazine. I'm interested in discussing investment options with you, while Genevra is hoping to interest you in a feature article on the resort. We decided to come over together. Maybe kill two birds with one stone.

Brock ignored Oliver. "Ms. Blackthorne—or may I call you Genevra? —I've never heard of *Cayman! Cayman!* magazine. Can you tell me a little about it?"

Genevra smiled, just not with her eyes. "Of course you can call me Genevra. And *Cayman! Cayman!* is a brand new, high-end, lifestyle magazine, owned by Lawton Media. I was hoping to feature your new resort in our inaugural issue."

Brock frowned. "Lawton as in Liam Lawton? That man certainly gets around."

"He is a man of many interests—and many talents. He was impressed by your plans for this island while he was out here, and he suggested I contact you to see if you have any interest in a bit of free publicity."

"Well, Genevra, I'm sorry you had to come all the way out here just to hear me turn you down, but I'm not interested in working with any company Lawton owns. And Mr. Fleming-Russo, I already told the great Newton Fleming himself that I don't need his money. So thank you, but sorry, I'm not interested."

He'd already turned to walk back into his lair when a scream broke the island's placid silence.

Rosalina came running around the corner of Brock's building, carrying a short length of frayed rope in one hand. Tears streamed down her face and she was tearing at her hair. "Mi pollos! Mi cabra! Las mascotas! What have you done?" she sobbed.

Brock looked at her coldly. "What's all your caterwauling about now?"

I gave him a dirty look and hurried over to find out why Rosalina was so upset. I put my arms around her. "Calm down, Rosalina. Tell me what happened."

She gulped and hiccupped a few times, struggling to catch her breath.

Oliver had a travel bottle of water in his backpack, and he uncapped it and handed it to her. "Have a drink. It'll make you feel better. Then you can tell us what's wrong."

She looked at him suspiciously, so I said, "It's alright. You can trust him." Then I whispered in her ear, "It's okay. He's my brother."

She nodded slowly, then reached out for the bottle. She drank like she'd had nothing to drink for days. That was quite possibly true. Since there was no fresh water source on the island, she'd probably had nothing to drink since she left the *Thundercloud*.

When the bottle was empty, she handed it back to Oliver. "Thank you." Then she turned to me. "Those bad men took all my chickens, and Rodrigo, my goat. They killed them, and they are cooking them for their own dinner. Now I have nothing. They've poisoned the well, and my pets were my only source of food. I had nothing to live on except the eggs and milk, since the fish are all dead and they've uprooted all my plants. All my life this island was a paradise, now thanks to them it's hell on earth." She spit on the ground near Brock's feet. "Bad man! I hope your business fails and you rot in hell."

Brock looked bored, examining his fingernails like he'd never seen them before. "It's my island. I own everything on it. And that includes your precious pets."

"Not true," she said vehemently. "Miguel had no right. He didn't own this island. Even his father didn't own it. It's been in my family for generations—I am the rightful owner, and I never agreed to sell it to you. I never would. Not in a million years would I sell to a pig like you." She spat again and started walking away, tears streaming down her face.

I knew beyond a shadow of a doubt that not only had Brock known what his men were up to, he might have even hatched the plan himself to drive her off the island. And I knew that if she stayed here, she was as doomed as her pets had been.

I looked at Oliver and Genevra. They were staring at me, waiting for me to act. It took me only a moment to decide. I whispered in Oliver's ear. "Will you take Rosalina to Grand Cayman on your boat? I don't think she has any money for a hotel, so you can put her up at my house if she needs a place to stay. Ask my roommate to help her get settled."

He nodded.

I turned to Rosalina. "I should be able to wrap this job up in a few days, and I will help you find a job and a permanent place to stay. And a lawyer to straighten out your ownership claim." I hugged her to me and whispered in her ear, "Don't tell anyone here that Oliver is my brother. You'll be in good hands with him."

Her eyes widened but she didn't say anything. She just stepped back and straightened her shoulders. "I'm ready to leave whenever you are, Mr. Oliver."

He smiled at Rosalina. "Just call me Oliver please. No Mr. required." He looked at Brock. "I'll be ready to leave as soon as Mr. Moran and I have a moment to talk."

Brock sneered at him. "No need to talk. I already told Newton I didn't want his money, and I certainly don't need a bunch of do-gooder environmentalists getting in my way. Not interested. Now we've talked. Goodbye." He turned and went back inside his tiny house, slamming the door behind him.

Oliver had a wry smile on his face when he said, "I think that talk went very well. Okay then, we're outta here. Do you need anything before we go, F... I mean, Honey?"

I shook my head. "No thanks. I'm all set. Just take good care of

Rosalina." I turned to her. "Do you need any help packing? I doubt your things will still be here if you leave anything behind."

She shook her head sadly. "I don't have much. Alonzo is gone. Las Mascotas are gone. I just have a single photo album." She turned to Oliver. "Do you have time to wait while I fetch it?"

"Yes, of course, but I think we'll go with you just to make sure nobody gets in your way," he said.

She smiled. "Thank you. Then follow me please."

The three of them walked off in the direction of Rosalina's home, while I returned to the *Thundercloud.*

Since there was no more fresh water on the dock. I packed up my salty BCD and regulator to take to the communal rinse tank. On the way, I passed Oliver, Genevra and Rosalinda heading toward *Flemingo.*

"Bye, Honey," said Oliver, Rosalina, and Genevra almost in unison.

"Stay safe," added Genevra, a worried frown on her face.

"Thanks. You too," I said. I wanted to leave with them so badly it almost made me cry.

Chapter 28
Confrontation

The crew was busy celebrating the fresh meat they'd barbecued, and the raucous sounds of their rambunctious partying carried on the warm breeze. I didn't like or trust anyone on the crew, and I was uneasy being alone in the isolated area behind the tank filling station. I wanted to get back to the relative safety of *Thundercloud* as fast as I could to minimize any opportunities for unwelcome confrontations, so I made short work of putting my gear through the rinse process.

As soon as I finished, I gathered my gear and scurried back to *Thundercloud*. I left my BCD on the gunwale to dry before I climbed to the flying bridge, started her engines, and took off to find some peace and quiet. When I'd gone what I considered a safe distance, I anchored the boat over a sandy patch and then I made myself a peanut butter sandwich with the last of the bread that had been in the boat's tiny freezer. My giant jar of peanut butter was empty now too.

Clearly, whoever had provisioned my boat had not expected my stint undercover to last as long as it had. I certainly hadn't, or I never would have agreed to do it. With a stab of despair, I realized I was no closer now to understanding what was going on with Kraken Industries and this island than I'd been when Newton and Dane had first approached me.

I was ready to quit. I missed my home, my friends, my family, and my job.

Most of all I missed Rafe. I had to find a way to end this.

But on the other hand, I hated to quit with the task unfinished.

It was well after sunset and for the last few hours I'd been stewing over my hatred of this assignment and my longing for home. I grabbed a mug of lemonade and Honey's iPad and went out to sit on the bow, hoping the slight breeze would blow away the cobwebs in my head. I was busily typing up an email to Newton and Dane, when I saw bright lights approaching quickly.

Another boat. Headed my way. Fast.

My heart skipped a beat when I thought it might be the Kraken crew come to pay me a little visit, but after a deep breath and a sip of tart lemonade, I knew that was unlikely. They wouldn't be able to find me with just the few running lights I'd turned on, and I was far enough out to sea that it wouldn't be easy for them to see me even with binoculars—unless they were very good binoculars—and I didn't think anyone in the crew had a pair like that.

If it wasn't someone from Kraken, then who could it be? Not that my ability to sense danger was infallible, but I didn't feel any menace in the boat's approach. The boat's spotlight had homed in on *Thundercloud*, and the unknown boat was heading my way at full speed. I went below to get my own binoculars.

The boat's lights were way too bright for me to see anything beyond them, but when I focused the lenses just a little to the right of the intense light, I could see the outline of the boat in my peripheral vision.

It looked like *Enviroman*. Newton had told me Liam would be monitoring my safety and he'd be able to reach me within minutes if I ever ran into trouble. What was going on?

I turned on some of *Thundercloud*'s additional lights to help guide Liam to me. He made a slight course correction, and then with a mighty roar and a big splash, he pulled *Enviroman* alongside my boat.

He dropped a couple of bumpers over the *Enviroman*'s gunwales and then threw a line over to me. I caught it, pulled my boat close to his, and wrapped it around one of *Thundercloud*'s cleats.

Liam held a flashlight up so I could see his face in the dark and held a finger vertically to his lips in the 'shhh' signal. I nodded, and he motioned for me to join him on his boat.

I stepped over the gunwales and Liam offered me a steadying hand to help me down to his deck. Then he leaned across and unwrapped the rope I'd just fastened. As soon as he disconnected the boats, he climbed to the flying bridge and restarted his engines and slowly pulled away.

When we were about 100 yards from *Thundercloud,* I dropped an anchor into the sand while he shut down his engines.

He jumped down the last few rungs of the ladder to the bridge and turned to face me. His face was pale, and he was biting his lip. "Are you okay?" he asked.

"I'm fine. Why wouldn't I be? And why all the secrecy? Did something happen I don't know about?" His arrival and his question both puzzled me.

He shrugged. "Newton was worried. He asked me to give you this." Liam held out a small bakery box containing a blueberry muffin.

I accepted the box with a smile, remembering all the times Liam had brought me my favorite muffins when we were together.

Liam kept talking, calling me back from the haze of my memories. "Rosalina told him some of what's been going on out here, and Oliver and Genevra corroborated that they felt the same sense of menace she portrayed. Newton sends his apologies and says he'd obviously underestimated how dangerous this assignment would be. He sent me to find you and bring you home."

For one moment, I was thrilled. I was going home. Back to Rafe. Back to Penny. My home. My family. My friends. My job.

Then I remembered how this horrible Kraken Group was destroying the underwater environment and didn't seem to care. They were oblivious to the dead and dying fish who wobbled when they swam or twirled in endless circles until they dropped dead from exhaustion.

The Kraken team was all immune to the horror of the bleached dead coral—in some cases representing years of irreplaceable growth. They didn't care about the juvenile sharks driven out of their safe zone before they were ready or the baby octopuses that choked to death on the black slime they'd unleashed. They'd nearly killed my dog just as a prank, and they had actually killed Rosalina's pets and eaten them for their dinner just for the sheer delight of being cruel.

It was obvious they had a goal that was driving them, and they wouldn't stop their destruction until they'd achieved their purpose. I didn't yet have any idea what their objective was, but I did know that someone had to find out what was going on and bring the group to justice.

That someone was me. There was no one else.

I shook my head regretfully. "I can't go until I know what they're up to. I have to stop them. Every day there's more damage, and soon it won't be reversible no matter what we do. And they're after something. Something big. I just know it."

Liam looked sad. "Think about what this is doing to Rafe. He misses you."

I shook my head again. "He understands."

Liam bit his lip before speaking. "Like you did when I stayed away and never told you why or where I was? Remember how understanding you were back then? As I recall, my behavior made you pretty angry, and it tore us apart."

I shrugged. "We weren't right for each other. Rafe and I will be fine."

He gave a rueful smile. "That's what I always told myself and look how that turned out. You're doing the same thing to Rafe that I did to you. Don't let it destroy your chance for happiness. Get your priorities in order before Rafe gets tired of being at the bottom of your list."

"We'll be fine. It's none of your business, and I don't want to talk about it anymore. Now will you please take me back to my boat?" In truth, I didn't want to admit his words had struck a chord with me. I told myself Rafe and I would be fine. We both had careers that required us to be away from home a lot, and we'd talked about it before we got married. But still, the separation was hard on our relationship, especially when we couldn't communicate at all.

I felt a pang of empathy for what Liam had been going through during the time we were together. But that pang wasn't strong enough to turn me away from what I considered to be my duty. "Rafe understands," I said softly.

Liam didn't say anything, just shrugged and swung up the ladder to the flying bridge. When we were near *Thundercloud,* I threw the bumpers over the side, and Liam carefully maneuvered *Enviroman* close to my boat. I leaned way out over the gunwales and wrapped a line around the cleats. By the time I finished, Liam was beside me.

I thought he was reaching to give me a hand as I climbed aboard *Thundercloud,* but instead, he took my hand and spun me toward him. The kiss was unexpected. It felt familiar, and yet strange.

Liam looked sad. "I'm sorry. I shouldn't have done that."

I stepped away from him, and he easily let me go. "Don't ever do that again. I love Rafe, and I'll never do anything to hurt him.

His shoulders drooped as he turned to walk away, then he straightened up and turned back. "Rafe's a lucky man, but you're lucky too. Don't blow your best chance at happiness by chasing after the bad guys. There are people who love to do that for a living. You're not one of them."

"I don't think my relationship with Rafe is any of your business. You made your choice, and I wasn't it."

"And you're doing the same thing to Rafe that I did to you. If you're not careful, it'll have the same result. I admit our breakup was my fault. I don't want to see you end up alone and lonely."

He left off "like me" at the end, but I could still hear it in the silence.

I watched him cross to the other side of the boat. He leaned forward with his hands on the gunwale and stared up at the stars. I hesitated for a moment. Every line of his body screamed of his aloneness. I wanted to help him.

But I couldn't help him.

After a moment's hesitation, I climbed over the gunwales to *Thundercloud* where I unwrapped the line and tossed it to *Enviroman*'s deck. Then I climbed up to the flying bridge and motored slowly away.

Chapter 29
A Dark Night of the Soul

I HEADED BACK toward the island. I didn't want to get too close to it—I still didn't trust the crew one bit—but I didn't want to be too far away either in case there was anything going on. I anchored at what I thought was a safe distance from the dock.

From what I'd seen of the crew, they were not as comfortable in the water as I would have expected from professional commercial divers. I didn't think they'd chance swimming out to hassle me on *Thundercloud* in the dark. Even so, I turned my lights down low and sat at my galley table, staring out at the sky through the windows until the early morning hours.

I thought about what Liam had said. Could it be true that I was doing to Rafe exactly what Liam had done to me during our relationship? It wasn't exactly the same, but I realized uncomfortably it was very close.

Rafe and I had already talked about the fact that our careers would require us to travel or be in different places some of the time. We'd made commitments about how frequently we would communicate, and the communication methods we would use, and we'd agreed to try to synchronize our schedules as much as we could so that we would be together as often as possible. And Rafe himself was supposed to be away right now, which is one of the reasons I'd agreed to go undercover when Newton asked me to.

So it was with a sinking heart that I realized that Liam had been right. I'd taken on this undercover assignment without discussing it with Rafe. He'd had no idea I might be in danger. No idea I wasn't on Grand Cayman, working at RIO, and taking care of our pets. No idea why I wasn't keeping to our agreed upon communication protocol.

I'd even screwed up taking care of Penny, although I still wasn't sure what had caused Dane to go back on his word to dog sit for her whenever Rafe and I were both traveling.

But that was beside the point. This was my screw up, and Rafe must be feeling as betrayed and left out by my behavior as I'd always felt when Liam had taken off with no warning.

I was gambling with a relationship that meant the world to me, and for what?

A quick adventure? The ego boost of being asked to take on this dangerous assignment? Was I trying to curry favor with Newton and Dane, the two most important father figures in my life since Ray Russo's death? I had no idea why I'd agreed to do it, and I couldn't believe that I'd been willing to jeopardize my relationship with Rafe for this or any other reason.

When I realized how similar my behavior was to the way Liam had been when we were together, I knew then that he'd never meant to hurt me. He'd been caught up in the same emotional turmoil I was feeling now. The newfound awareness allowed me to understand his actions and forgive him when I'd never been able to before.

Forgiveness didn't mean I magically fell back in love with Liam. That was over. Completely over. My relationship with Rafe was absolutely the most important part of my life.

But my new-found compassion and understanding did mean that Liam and I could be friends and maybe even work together again. But not until I was able to talk to Rafe and ask him for his forgiveness. I resolved to go back tonight to track him down and tell him how sorry I was. I'd make a solemn promise that I'd never do something like this again.

Newton and Dane and their committee would just have to find

another way to figure out what Brock Moran was up to. I was going home. Right now. I stood up to go to the flying bridge and start the engines.

But when I turned around to head out of the galley, I stopped short. Bert was tying a small dingy to one of the cleats on *Thundercloud*'s stern. Garth, Ken, and Arthur were already standing on the deck leering at me.

"Going somewhere?" Garth said. "We thought you might be lonely after your boyfriend left, so we brought the party to you." He brandished an open bottle of rum and smiled an evil looking smile.

I was scared, but I threw my head back disdainfully. "Not interested. Get off my boat."

He took a step forward. "You looked pretty interested when you were kissing your boyfriend. Too bad he had to leave so fast…"

I broke in. "He's not my boyfriend, and he left quickly because I told him the same thing I'm telling you. Not interested."

He held out the rum. "After a few sips of this you might find you're a lot more interested."

Shaking my head, I said, "I don't drink alcohol anymore. And I told you I'm not interested. Now get off my boat."

He licked his lips lasciviously and leered at me. "We're just here to show you a good time. I promise you'll enjoy it…"

"No thanks."

Ken, Bert, and Arthur had stepped forward while Garth was talking, and now the three of them lined up and blocked my way to the bridge. I couldn't get to the bridge on the bow, and I knew I'd never be able to climb up to the flying bridge fast enough to prevent them from catching me. Retreating to the cabin was a dead end. The flying bridge was a dead end, and so was the cabin

I was trapped. I couldn't win against the whole crew in a fight.

Unless I went overboard, into the dark, deep water. The ocean is my happy place, but this slimy, smelly poisoned ocean was not the sea I loved. There was no other way out except to go overboard.

Looking around desperately for a way out, I spied my dive gear tucked under the gunwale where I'd left it after coming back from the rinse tank. My mask was hanging from the valve of a nearby empty tank, and conveniently, my BCD's carry strap was facing out. My fins were on the bench, but several feet away from the BCD and mask. It was unlikely I'd be able to grab everything before they caught me.

But if I could reach the mask and BCD and go overboard before they got to me, I knew I'd be fine. I could quickly gear up underwater, and either swim to shore or wait them out. I quickly averted my eyes from the gear so they wouldn't wonder what I was looking at and catch on to my plan.

Garth was still holding out the bottle of rum in his left hand. "Just take a few sips. If you don't like it and you still want us to leave, then we'll leave."

I knew he was lying. They would never leave until they'd done what they came to do.

But thanks to training with Rafe, I also knew enough about fighting to know he expected me to reach for the bottle with my right hand, which would put me in a position where it would be easy for him to grab me with his own right hand. Of course, no matter what I did, Bert, Ken, and Arthur still flanked him and could easily jump into the fray. I had to do something unexpected, and I had to do it quickly.

So I reached out low and fast with my left hand, raising my hand from below his arm and chopping him on his funny bone. The bottle flew out of his hand, distracting the other men. I took advantage of the moment and scurried over to the gunwale. I grabbed my mask and the handle of my BCD as I jumped from the deck to the bench to the gunwale and then into the sea.

As soon as I hit the water, I purposely sank down a few feet to put my mask on. Then I donned my BCD and stuck my snorkel in my mouth. I swam several strokes underwater before surfacing.

The night was dark, and I'd only turned on a few of the *Thundercloud*'s lights, so the area around the boat was shadowy. I could see them standing on the deck, peering into the water to see if they could see me. I wanted to get far enough away that they wouldn't have a prayer of locating me, so I took a deep breath and ducked under a few feet, swimming toward shore.

My progress would have been a lot faster if I'd had my fins, but I'd recognized I wouldn't have enough time to get off the boat before they caught me if I'd paused long enough to grab the fins, and I needed the snorkel and maybe some of the other stuff I keep in my BCD pocket for emergencies. And the much despised dive knife should be in one of the pockets if I needed it for protection.

I was a couple of hundred feet away when they gave up peering over the boat's sides to see me. I could hear them discussing what to do until they finally decided to leave me to my fate and head back to shore. Garth, Ken, and Arthur climbed into their dinghy while Bert untied it. Then he jumped aboard. Bert and Arthur rowed the boat back to the island while Ken and Garth sat in the bow and drank from a new bottle of rum.

I blew some air into my BCD so I could stay on the surface without exerting any effort. I turned and watched their progress toward shore. When they landed on the beach, they dragged the dinghy up on the sand and hid it behind a huge pile of dirt and rocks near the remains of the road.

No wonder I hadn't seen if before. If I'd known they had access to a boat I'd have taken *Thundercloud* a lot further out before anchoring.

I kicked my way over to the dock and followed its line toward shore, hiding in the shadows as I observed their actions. Once they'd finished covering the dinghy with dead palm fronds, they walked down the road to the bunkhouse.

I considered just going back to *Thundercloud* and heading home, but I wanted to do one more dive before I left.

I didn't want to have any more unwelcome visitors, so I crawled up on the sand. Crouching low to the ground, I ran behind the rock pile where they'd dragged their boat. I wanted to disable it so they wouldn't be able to come after me, but when I looked at it, I realized I didn't have anything heavy enough to punch a hole in the thick hull.

I tiptoed over to the tool crib and felt along the top of the doorjamb for the key Ken had told me was always there. Once I found it, I unlocked the door and went inside. I'd noticed a large pickax nestled in a rear corner when Ken had shown me around on my first day, and luckily, it was still there in the same spot.

I grabbed it and hurried back to the dinghy. A few blows to the hull rendered the boat unseaworthy, and I hoped, unrepairable. I returned the axe to its assigned location and locked the tool crib door behind me. Then I swam back to *Thundercloud*.

I moved the boat out far enough from the island that I didn't think anyone would decide to make the swim, but just in case, I set the perimeter alarm that Newton had given me. Satisfied that short of leaving I'd done all I could to ensure my own safety, I lay down on the daybed and fell into a fitful sleep.

Chapter 30
Early Morning

THE SUN WAS BARELY UP when I rose the next day and made coffee with the last of my stash—and worse yet—the last of my fresh water supply. My vital provisions were beyond running low. Nearly everything was completely gone. I'd have to skip breakfast today or eat in the bunkhouse with the crew—and after what happened last night, no way was I up for that. I was angry and afraid—and lonesome.

No one, least of all me, had expected my stint undercover to go on so long. I'd been here for nearly a month—a month of days that blended seamlessly one into the next—except for those days when bad things happened or someone from home visited. Those days stood out from the rest, and usually not in a good way.

I weighed last night's epiphany about what I was doing to Rafe against my obligation to Newton and my own self-image. I had to admit that the balance tilted strongly toward making things right with Rafe—but I felt sure I could make it up to him when I did finally return.

And after the bad experience of last night, it seemed like no matter how long I stayed here, I'd never figure out what was going on. Maybe I really should just call it quits and go home.

Except I'm not a quitter.

So I sat on the deck listening to my stomach growl and remembering the luscious warm blueberry muffins from RIO's café that I usually ate for breakfast. I saw a small boat appear on the horizon. It was moving at a brisk clip and headed my way. At first, I didn't recognize it.

As it came nearer, I realized it was Vincent Pollilo's old wooden dory. Sitting on the bench beside him was Gus Simmons, the owner of *Thundercloud,* which was known as *Sunshine Girl* when she wasn't in disguise.

Vincent, captain of RIO's primary research vessel the *Omega,* waved his baseball cap in the air as he made a quick turn and came alongside of me. "We brought you some fresh provisions. Newton thought you'd be running low by now. There's a blueberry muffin for your breakfast."

Gus was already unloading crates containing water, fresh veggies, frozen meats, jars of peanut butter and jelly, and bread, cookies, and other baked goods. "Eat your muffin while it's warm," he said.

Gus had a heart condition, so I didn't want him to over-exert himself. I rushed over. "Let me do that," I said.

"Thanks, but we all need to pitch in. We have to get in and out of here before we're noticed." He smiled. "Theresa said to say hi and hurry home. She and Angel both miss you." He was referring to his wife, Theresa, who was my best friend, and their daughter, Angel. My heart cracked with the need to see them.

I grabbed a case of provisions and hurried below. Meanwhile, Vincent had put out a couple of bumpers and tied his boat to *Thundercloud.* As soon as he finished, he began unloading crates of food too. We had everything transferred from their boat in less than ten minutes. It would take me a while to get everything sorted out and put away, but I didn't think anyone had spotted us

At least, I didn't think so until I came out of the galley and saw Brock Moran striding angrily along the dock. "You there. This dock is private property. Get away from there. No outside docking allowed."

I noticed Vincent had already managed to untether his boat from *Thundercloud.* He took off his ballcap and raised it respectfully toward Brock. "Sorry. Our GPS is on the blink. We were headed for Little Cayman. This nice young lady was kind enough to provide some navigational assistance. We'll be on our way now."

While Vincent was talking to Brock, Gus had nimbly reboarded the fishing boat and pushed it away from *Thundercloud*. He kept his head down and began to row away.

Vincent seemed slightly startled when he felt the boat start to move, but he went along with it, knowing Gus would have had a good reason for wanting to make a quick escape.

Vincent touched the bill of his ball cap again. "Thank you, young lady. I'm really happy we bumped into you."

And then they were gone, leaving nothing visible behind them but a sparkle on the surface. I knew they hadn't rowed all the way out here from Grand Cayman, so I assumed Vincent had anchored his much larger fishing boat nearby, just out of sight.

Brock glowered as he watched them leave. "More friends of yours?" he said nastily.

I shrugged. "I don't know them. They were just lost. Stupid to be wandering around strange waters without knowing proper navigation. And way out here, too. No way they'll make it to Little Cayman. Crazy."

"You seemed to know them pretty well. That tall guy was even on your boat. In the cabin. How do you explain that?"

I smiled. "He needed to use the head. They don't have one on that old boat."

Brock looked incredulous. "There's a whole ocean out there he could have used if he had to go so bad."

I shrugged. "Maybe he's shy."

Then I smiled at Brock, hoping to distract him from my friends' visit. "You're up pretty early. What's on the agenda for today? Must be pretty special to get you out and about this early."

He looked embarrassed for a minute. "Arthur told me he saw you smashing a hole in the hull of his dinghy. He said you were wielding a pickax like a crazy person, so he was too scared to try to stop you. He wanted me to tell you that you'll have to pay to have the boat repaired."

I crossed my arms. "I see. Well, I won't be doing that."

Now he looked annoyed. "Did you or did you not punch a hole through his boat?"

I shrugged. "I did punch a hole through a boat. I didn't know it was his. But to be fair, it wouldn't have made any difference in my actions after what went on right before I did it."

He frowned. "Arthur didn't mention that anything happened before you hacked his boat to pieces. What went on?"

"I've told you before that your crew is harassing and bullying me. They had obviously decided to take their vile actions way too far last night. They made their intentions very clear, and I have every right to protect myself from them since you won't put a stop to it—the way any decent human being would. Or any responsible manager or business owner who didn't want a huge lawsuit headed his way if you're so lacking in morals that the only thing that would get your attention is a huge monetary loss. You should have put a stop to their behavior immediately—the very first time I told you about it. Haven't you ever heard of the #metoo movement?"

I took a deep breath trying to regain my cool. "Last night was the final straw. I don't feel safe here if your men have the means to reach my boat. Since you refused to put a stop to their unacceptable behavior, I solved the problem in the only way I could—short of me physically hurting them." Then I gave him all the details of my unexpected visit from the rowdy crew.

He listened without saying a word until I finished. He chewed his lip for a moment, then he snorted derisively. "That's it? They came out to your boat and offered you a drink?"

My mouth fell open with shock. Somehow, even though I'd been as clear as I know how to be, it hadn't penetrated his smug brain that his men were aggressively threatening me.

"No, that's not all they did. They tried to corner me in my cabin. Garth grabbed my arm and told me he was there to 'show me a good time.' Surely you understand what he was implying? I was afraid for my life and personal safety," I said.

He shrugged. "No, I don't really understand your point. I think you're overreacting. They just wanted to blow off a little steam, and make sure you felt like a valued part of the team. I'm sure they didn't mean you any harm."

"You weren't there. You didn't see them or hear them. None of them told you I had to jump in the water at night, with no light and no gear, just to keep them away from me, did they?"

He stared at me for a long minute before he shrugged again. "I still think you're over-reacting."

"Okay," I said. "How's this for overreacting? I quit."

He smiled, almost as though my resignation had been his objective all along. But he still wasn't through playing cat and mouse with me.

"Have you read your contract? I mean, really read it. Because you can't quit—or actually, you can, but you'll owe me a pretty substantial sum of money for the privilege. Definitely more than you've earned while you've been here. I think it amounts to five years of your salary/"

I smiled. Five years of my salary at Kraken was a pittance to me, and not even pocket change compared to Newton's fortune. But it didn't matter. I know contract law pretty well since I've been negotiating multi-million dollar agreements on RIO's behalf for more than ten years. "You can't force someone to fulfill a contract for personal services. It's against the law."

He nodded. "Which is why there's a penalty clause."

I could almost see the word "gotcha" floating through his head.

I didn't really care. I knew I'd either solve the mystery today or I was going home to tell my husband how much I love him and to beg his forgiveness for ever even taking on this undercover role.

"Fine. Have it your way. Right now I'm going for a dive. I'll be in your office by ten AM."

He couldn't keep the triumphant smile off his face. "See that you are." He strode away, every line of his body showing me that he thought he'd won.

We'd just have to wait and see who ended up the real winner when this was over.

Chapter 31
Breakthrough

As soon as Brock was off the dock, I donned my dive gear and stepped off *Thundercloud*'s transom to start my dive, hoping this would be the last dive I needed to make on this assignment. Once away from the dock, I sank down to about sixty feet and headed toward the area where the team had been working.

I swam past the pinnacle that concealed the cavern entrance and arrived at the line of those weird towers the crew had been working on. I could see that they'd added several more of the towers since I'd last been on the site. Including the new ones, I counted twelve completed units, and the beginnings of half a dozen more.

Three more of the original towers now seemed to be in an operating status. The large plate at the top of the tower still looked like a satellite dish to me, but now they were all slowly oscillating, turning in a wide arc like a hungry mouth seeking food. I still couldn't figure out what they were for.

I swam right up to one to see if its purpose would be more apparent from up close, but even hovering right next to one, I still couldn't determine what it was for, although its oscillations gave me vertigo and made my head ache. I pulled the compact camera out of my BCD pocket and took a quick video clip. If I could manage to email this to Newton, maybe someone on his team would know what they were.

As I lowered my arms to put the camera back in my pocket, I noticed the hands of my dive watch pulsating, moving backward in time when the tower turned toward me and switching back to forward as the tower turned away. The towers were obviously emitting some sort of intense electromagnetic current. No wonder they made my head hurt and caused the fish to swim upside down.

My best guess was that they were using QKD, otherwise known as Quantum Key Distribution, to communicate with a satellite or other land based platform using photon laser technologies. T

his method of communication is extremely secure, although still highly experimental. In my reading on the topic, I'd learned that QKD is under consideration for fast complex communications with submarines and for generating unbreakable secure keys for highly sensitive data transfers.

So now I understood—or thought I understood—what Kraken Industries was actually trying to build on and under this island, and it had nothing to do with a luxury resort. Its ultimate goal appeared to be secure communications that could cross land, sea, or air. Although I knew this technology was theoretically possible, I hadn't been aware it had progressed to the level where an actual working installation might exist. And if such a thing did exist, what was the purpose of the communication it was built for?

Deciphering the project's purpose was definitely above my pay grade, so I concentrated on taking as many photographs as I could of the installation so the people who actually had a shot at figuring this out would have as much information as possible to work with.

When I'd taken pictures from every possible angle and distance I could, I turned and headed back toward the dock. As soon as I climbed the *Thundercloud*'s ladder and doffed my

gear, I uploaded the pictures to my cloud account and sent an email to "Nadine"—actually Newton—gushing about the gorgeous fish and coral I'd seen on my latest dive and raving about the photos I'd taken. I'd already given my father access to a new file in my cloud account where I'd sent the pictures. With any luck, he'd have his team trying to unravel the mystery before breakfast.

I sighed with relief. Now I could go home with a clear conscience, although there was one more thing I wanted to do before I quit this accursed island. I planned to make another trip to the cavern to pick up as many of the golden figurines as I could carry. Although I felt sure they were extremely valuable, I wasn't interested in them for their monetary value. I wanted to understand their history, and let the world see their artistry. But before I could make that final dive, I had to get through one last workday with Brock Moran.

https: / / www.naval-technology.com / features / featuredeep-secret-secure-submarine-communication-on-a-quantum-level / ?cf-view

Chapter 32
Monster Dive

THE DAY DRAGGED on worse than usual. I wasn't sure about Brock, who was even less engaged than usual, but my thoughts were definitely not on the make-believe hotel project. We spent long minutes ostensibly thinking about solutions to whatever problem or procedure we were working on, only to agree to table the issue for later review every time. We didn't make any progress at all, and I began to think he was extending the meeting just to aggravate me.

Thank the universe that Brock ended the day slightly earlier than usual. I couldn't wait to get out of his office. All I wanted to do was make my last dive to retrieve a few more of the gold relics, and then turn the *Thundercloud* toward home. My heart sang whenever I thought about my upcoming reunion with Rafe.

Brock was already poring himself a drink while I gathered my notes and papers, stuffing them in a canvas tote along with my copy of the project plans. "What time do you want to meet tomorrow?" I asked, still acting as though I intended to return.

He turned his palms out and raised his shoulders. "It doesn't matter to me. Come by whenever you're ready. I have a lot of other business to attend to, so I'll be here. We'll probably need to cut the meeting short, so you'll have more time to work on your own too."

Brock was usually more precise about our times. His words were out of character unless he was tired of pretending he was here to build a fabulous resort for wealthy adventurers.

The sudden change in his attitude should have made me more suspicious, but I was just so happy to be out of there I didn't think twice about the dramatic change from his usual behavior. I just wanted to accomplish my last task and then get off this island.

I raced out of Brock's tiny office building and scurried down the dock to *Thundercloud,* where I dumped my tote on the daybed in the cabin, and quickly donned my dive gear. I was in the water no more than ten minutes after Brock had dismissed me.

Once submerged, I went straight for the pinnacle that concealed the entrance to the cavern. I swam at a downward angle, so I was both descending and making progress toward my destination as I moved. I was so intent on my goal that I didn't pause for even a moment to contemplate the scenery or the sea life.

That was my second mistake.

I quickly ducked behind the outcropping on the pinnacle and picked up the reel and the large flashlight I'd left stowed just inside the mouth of the cavern. Usually I made a point of staying close to the cavern wall until I'd gone about halfway around the circumference before I made my way to the small rise where the gold sculptures waited, but today, I made straight for the small jumble of artifacts.

I'd brought a large mesh catch bag with me to hold the figurines, but it was filled to capacity before I'd managed to claim even a third of the treasure. I stuffed a couple of small manta ray statuettes in my BCD pockets and wedged a large sea dragon into the BCD's cummerbund.

I sorely regretted that I'd have to leave the rest of the treasures behind, not because I coveted the treasure themselves but because they were such extraordinary artistic specimens that the world deserved the chance to see them all. I comforted myself with the thought that I could come back later once Dane and Newton had busted the Kraken gang for whatever it was they were up to here.

I turned toward the exit but stopped short when I saw flashlight beams zigzagging across the coral outside the cavern mouth. I ducked down behind the mound and shut off my flashlight. The darkness was intense.

Despite my nerves, I breathed as slowly as I could to minimize my telltale bubbles as well as to minimize my air consumption. My pressure readout was nearing 1000 PSI, but I knew I still had 500 PSI in reserve that wouldn't show on the gauge.

Still, I didn't want to push it if I didn't have to. This was a deep dive, and I'd need to make a safety stop. If I had to stay here in the cave more than another minute or two, I might possibly even need to make a deco stop on the way back to my boat.

Anxiously, I peered around the mound toward the cavern entrance. Luckily, within a minute the lights moved away, and I assumed it was safe to make my exit and then a hurried retreat back to my boat.

As soon as I exited the mouth of the cavern, I felt a heavy blow to my head that left me dazed and disoriented. I was too out of it to fight back when three divers wearing black neoprene full face masks grabbed me. I didn't need to look through the lenses to identify them. I already knew who they were.

A pair of rough hands pushed me onto a rocky outcropping barely large enough to support my body and held me down until another diver flipped me over onto my back, wedging the tank valve and the first stage of my regulator into a tiny crevice under a small coral ledge.

My vision was blurry, so I still couldn't see their faces clearly. But I didn't need to. One would be Garth. I didn't think the identity of the other two would matter. Everyone on the team was a monster.

Now that they'd stunned and at least partially restrained me, one of them detached the heavily laden catch bag containing the gold artifacts from the d-ring on my BCD. Then a very heavy weight settled over my body, covering my entire length from neck to knees.

I was still too weak and dizzy from the blow to my head to defend myself effectively. But anyway, I knew I didn't have a prayer of escaping alive if they thought I was alert enough to fight back. I wanted to be sure I fully understood my situation before I gave myself away. I closed my eyes so they wouldn't realize I was awake and becoming more aware by the second of what was going on around me.

The communication module in my full face mask was still part of the Kraken team's communication band, and it was broadcasting everything they said to each other. I recognized their voices as I listened to their conversation. They were pretty careless now that they thought they'd gotten the drop on me.

Actually, let's face it. They definitely had taken me by surprise, and now I was in a very precarious position. But I wasn't about to panic, at least not until I was sure about what was going on. I kept my eyes closed and stayed quiet.

"That should keep her down," said Garth. "She'll never get out from under that heavy steel plate."

"Check her air. If it's low enough, we'll take off and leave her here. I don't want to just hover over her watching her die."

Although I'd thought from the start that he was one of the divers attacking me, hearing Brock's voice stunned me. I should have accepted a lot sooner that he knew exactly what his crew of monsters was up to.

I kept my eyes closed as the other diver approached. The diver picked up my left wrist and turned it over. "750 PSI," said Arthur.

"Good," said Brock. "Even if she regains consciousness right away, that steel plate must weigh a ton even underwater. She'll never manage to get out from under it before she runs out of air. She's done for. Let's go."

I waited through several breaths to be sure they were gone before I opened my eyes. Because they'd jammed my tank valve into in a very small slot under something very rigid, I couldn't turn my head very far in either direction, but I did what I could to take stock of my status.

I knew I was in trouble, but as soon as I thought about it I started panting in fear. I couldn't afford over-breathing in this situation—I didn't have enough air to waste it like that, and I couldn't afford to panic. I made a very deliberate effort to control my breathing.

Slow deep inhalations; slow easy exhalations. Not only would that help conserve my remaining air, but it would also help to keep me calm.

Now that I had my breathing under control, I needed to come up with a plan to save myself. And that meant addressing first things first —my air supply was crucial to my survival.

Arthur had said I had 750 PSI of air left, which because of the specially configured gauge meant I really had 1250 PSI.

Not great, but not so terrible. No need to panic about air just yet.

Now it was time to take stock of my body. They'd wedged my tank valve into a crevice under the ledge, so I couldn't lift or even turn my head. My right arm was free from just below my shoulder down, but the weight of the steel plate trapped both of my legs under it. Worse yet, my left arm, where I wore the watch with the emergency beacon that Newton had given me, was completely under the plate, without so much as a finger sticking out.

I pushed up with my right hand, my left shoulder, my knees, and my abs, hoping to dislodge the steel plate, but I couldn't get enough traction. I tried to twist my left hand far enough around my wrist that I could push the emergency beacon to call Liam, but the angle was impossible. The steel plate had me almost completely immobilized.

Next I tried to snake my right arm under the steel plate to see if I could reach the emergency button on my left wrist with my right hand, but there wasn't enough space between my body and the steel plate for me to reach the button.

My heart sank, even as the fingers on my right hand kept scrabbling at my BCD looking for a way to reach my left hand. I touched the figurine I'd stuffed into my BCD cummerbund and struggled to lift it out of the confined space. I finally pulled the Velcro apart and grasped the statue. Slowly and carefully, I slid it across my body.

The statue was small and made of gold, so I knew it wouldn't be strong enough to use as a lever to raise the plate, but it was something. I wracked my brain, but I couldn't come up with any way I could use it to help free myself.

I was about to give up when I realized I had that gigantic and much despised dive knife Velcroed onto my right thigh. In this situation, it just might save my life.

Carefully, I stretched down to see if I could free it. I wasn't sure how I'd use it yet, but at least I'd have another tool. Millimeter by millimeter, I pulled back the thin Velcro straps until I felt the knife's sheath come loose. I grabbed it quickly and holding on tight, I slid the whole thing out from under the steel plate.

First I tried to use the knife to lever the steel plate up, but it wasn't long enough to be an effective lever.

Think, Fin. Think.

With my tank valve wedged under the rock ledge, my neck was stuck at an uncomfortable angle. It was getting tired, and I endured a painful spasm. Biting my lip, I thought *What else can go wrong*?

Then I nearly shouted with joy. The spasm had shown me the way.

I grasped the knife's hilt and slid it out of the sheath. Then carefully, I raised it up over my head and brought it down hard on the coral ledge. I had to be careful not to hit myself with the knife, which slowed me down a little bit. Luckily the small outcrop I was trapped by was not much bigger than my fist, and the coral was already weakened by bleaching. Even so, it took a lot of awkward pounding before I managed to break off enough of the coral that I could raise my shoulders and neck.

I placed the knife on the ledge beside me. Now I could use my shoulders along with my right hand, my abs, and my legs to move the steel plate.

If I'd had a free hand I'd have used it to slap my head at my own stupidity. I'd never needed to lift the plate up to get it off me. I could simply slide it to the side, a few inches at a time. Eventually, its own weight would send it to the bottom. I blamed my fuzzy thinking on the blow to my head and set about pushing that plate sideways with everything I had.

Slowly, so very slowly, I managed to shift the plate a scant few inches. Then a few more. By now I was sucking down my air like an enraged bull from all the effort, but I knew if I didn't get the plate off me soon I'd was doomed anyway.

So I made another awkward push. Then another.

With a shudder, the plate finally slipped off the edge of the rocky outcrop where I'd been marooned and plunged along the wall to the bottom, taking large swaths of coral and rock along with it.

I sent a mental apology to the coral for all the damage I'd done, but the damage couldn't be helped. I'd had to get free. I removed the watch Newton had given me, and pushed the button that controlled the emergency beacon. Then I placed it carefully near the fold in the pinnacle that hid the entrance to the cavern.

A quick glance at my tank pressure told me I still had almost enough air to make it back to *Thundercloud*. I decided to conserve as much as I could in case an emergency arose, so I started swimming slowly to the surface at an angle that I hoped would allow my body to take care of enough off-gassing that I could skip my safety stop because I knew I didn't have any margin of safety in my air supply for that. I might make it to the surface if I went straight up, but there certainly wasn't enough air to cover the required safety stop even if I sucked the tank completely dry.

When I reached the surface, I barely lifted my eyes above the water to take a look around. It would be stupid to pop out of the water right in front of the Kraken team after all I'd done to make my escape. With my eyes barely above the surface, I made a 360 degree turn, but I saw no sign of them.

I took a quick breath through my snorkel and began swimming toward my boat, carefully staying a few feet under the surface as I swam and only letting the very tip of my snorkel stick out when I needed to breathe.

I ducked under the dock for the last bit of my journey to *Thundercloud* and swam underwater under its boards for added concealment. When I reached my boat, I cautiously poked my head up and looked around. I didn't see or hear anyone, and *Thundercloud* looked undisturbed. I decided it would be safe to climb aboard.

Chapter 33
More Monsters

I DROPPED my gear on the stern, sliding my tank into an empty rack and stowing my fins and mask under the bench near my gear bag. Then I headed into the cabin to grab the *Thundercloud*'s keys. I flipped on the light switch as I entered and nearly jumped out of my skin.

Liam was sitting in one of the captain's chairs, his head lolling to one side. His left eye was swollen shut, adding a nasty purple punctuation to the mess they'd made of his battered and bruised face. His right shoulder had obviously been dislocated—again. A trickle of blood had dried near the corner of his mouth. Next to the seahorse figurine on the table, a bloody hammer lay in front of him, and I realized Garth had used it to break some of the fingers on Liam's right hand.

Not the first time he'd suffered that particular injury either. Mercifully, it looked like he was unconscious.

I rushed forward to help him, and as I did, Brock and Garth stepped out of the shadows at the back of the galley. Garth stepped forward and held a gun to Liam's head. Brock pointed another gun at me. The red dot was steady on my mid-chest, letting me know he was serious about using his weapon if he felt the need. I stopped short.

Brock smiled an evil looking smile. "Welcome home, Honey. Or since we all know that's your real name, should I call you Fin?"

I figured my best shot at getting both Liam and me out of this without further injury was to stall for time. "I'm Honey Hynes, as you know. You checked my references and verified every item on my resume. I don't know who you think I am or why you think I'd want to scam you."

He snorted. "Nice try. We've known your real identity since before you arrived. And the steady stream of visitors connected to RIO did nothing to preserve your cover story. We just had to find out why you were here. And of course, we hoped you'd find the gold sea monster chess set for us."

I gestured at the table where my catch bag lay glittering in the dim light. "You've got them. You took them all away from me before you hit me in the head and dropped that steel plate over me. Remember?"

Garth glared at me. "How the heck did you get out from under that plate anyway? Nobody else has been able to."

"Oh, you've done this before?" I asked coolly. "Then I can only assume Miguel and Alonzo both met their fate that way. Anyone else?"

Garth opened his mouth to speak, but Brock held up his hand. "Shut up, Garth."

Brock took a step closer to me. "Where are the rest of the sea monster pieces? There's supposed to be thirty-two of them. We only found eight in your catch bag. One we know you sent back to Grand Cayman with your boyfriend here. We'll get that one back from Newton before we're done, don't you worry. And there's that one," he said, gesturing toward the figurine on the table with his gun. The golden seahorse glowed softly in the fading sunlight.

I shook my head. "I have no idea where the rest of them are. That's all I found."

"We'll see about that. Garth, you do the honors. I know how much you enjoy it."

Garth placed Liam's hand on the table and picked up the hammer. Liam didn't wake up until Garth hit his right thumb as hard as he could.

Liam's scream was the stuff of nightmares. I couldn't let them keep on hurting him. He was tough, but not invincible, and he'd obviously been through so much pain already.

I held up my hands, palms out. "Okay. You win. I'll show you where I found them. But you have to promise to let us both go if I do."

Brock laughed. "Sure. We'll do that."

Everybody in the room knew he had no intention of keeping his word. Liam and I—and maybe even Newton, since Brock obviously knew he was involved—were doomed unless I could find a way out of this. But I smiled like he'd set my mind at ease with his lie.

"We'll have to dive pretty deep to bring the rest of them to the surface. Are you up for that?" I asked to buy time.

"Don't worry about me. Worry about you," he said snidely.

"There are a lot of these statues down there," I said. "We should get a crate and a couple of lift bags. That way we'll only need to dive once, and then you can be on your way." I paused. "I assume you'll be leaving once you've gathered the treasure, right?"

"Wrong. You saw the communication towers down there. This place will be a gold mine, even without those statues.

I tried to look confused, which wasn't that hard, since I really had no idea who Brock wanted to communicate with. "I don't understand," I said. "How will the towers become a gold mine?"

He gave me a pitying look. "I thought you were sharper than that. There are so many ways. First, we're very close to Grand Cayman, one of the financial capitals of the world. If I can intercept transaction data, I can access some of the fattest bank accounts in the world. Easy enough to move some of that cash into accounts I own. Small amounts that nobody will miss, but I can move enough of them that they'll add up fast."

His sharkish smile made me sick as he continued. "But the really big money comes from passing communications to others. Drug cartels need secure communication with their mule subs. Terrorists need to communicate with cell members. Governments want to connect with their embedded assets. Really, who in the world doesn't need a secure communications channel today? And I can supply it. Land or sea or satellite, bidirectional across unfathomable distances, and it withstands any kind of interference. I'm using a brand new technology called QKD."

"Quantum Key Distribution. Untraceable. Security ensured by the very laws of physics. It's so secure it makes Blockchain look like passing handwritten notes in class. Once it's up and running, I'll be the information clearinghouse for the entire world, and that's a very lucrative place to be."

I nodded. "I've heard of it, and I can see that it would be lucrative for your purposes. So then what's up with the hotel project? Was that just a smoke screen?"

"Of course," he said. "Just an excuse to be doing construction out here. As soon as we're finished, we'll scrap the resort plans. I'll think of some excuse to give the investors."

I thought about this for a moment. "So that's why you poisoned the water. You needed to make sure nobody would ever want to come here so you can be sure your QKD network stays safe and undiscovered.."

He nodded. "Yep. And I have to get all those figurines from wherever they're hidden and make sure the world knows they're gone. Otherwise, as soon as the first few hit the market, treasure hunters will be constantly lurking around this place."

"Funny. I never heard of the statues before I came here, and my stepfather Ray Russo was a renowned global treasure hunter. If there'd been so much as a whisper of their existence, I'm sure he'd have known about them."

Garth gave me a sour look. "You people at RIO don't know everything there is to know. You just think you do."

I smiled sweetly at him. "Sounds like somebody had some sour grapes with lunch. What's the matter? Wouldn't Maddy hire you?" I paused. "Of course, she only hires the best. Maybe that's why you didn't make the cut."

Garth walked over and raised his fist like he was about to punch me in the face. I stood my ground. Liam was struggling to get free of his bindings, but after his beatings he was too weak and too hurt to be much help anyway.

I gave him a small shake of my head, warning him to stay where he was. I wasn't sure he could withstand another round with Garth and his hammer.

I stood up straight, defiantly looking Garth right in the eyes. I hoped he didn't have the courage to hit me, but I braced for the impact just in case he did.

So it was a surprise when Brock grabbed Garth's wrist and stopped him before he could wallop me. "After she shows us where the figurines are, I promise you can smack her around as much as you want. But not yet."

Nice guy that Brock Moran.

But since he'd just admitted that he needed me, I figured I might as well push my luck a little further while I was at it. "So, Brock. What gave me away? When did you catch on to my true identity?"

He laughed. "During your interview, of course. I bet you didn't know they were showing old RIO documentaries on the TV over the bar the whole time you were talking to me, did you? I couldn't believe you were sitting there trying to pretend you were someone else while the TV right behind you was showing your image big as life-size. It was a real hoot. Garth and I laughed for hours afterward."

I almost groaned aloud. Stefan Gibb, who owns Nelson's bar where I'd done the interview, usually shows old Sea Hunt episodes full time on the bar's big-screen TVs. Except when I come in, he invariably switches over to RIO documentaries. I believe he thinks he's being nice, but I hate it. This time his habit might have cost me my life. And Liam's.

I nodded. "Yes, that must have been pretty amusing."

"Not nearly as amusing as all your visitors—every one of them well-known for their association with RIO. Did you really think I wouldn't recognize Stewie Belcher, Gus Simmons, or Vincent Pollilo? Or even your fiancé, Liam Lawton?"

"He's not my fiancé," I said, hoping that would buy Liam's safety. "I dumped him and married someone else."

Liam winced, but the bad guys didn't notice. Or they didn't care. Either way, they didn't react.

"Great. Then I guess we don't have to worry about keeping him alive anymore." He gestured with his chin at Garth, who aimed his gun at Liam.

"Stop," I shouted. "We may not be engaged any longer, but Liam's a very good friend. You harm another hair on his head and you can search for the figurines on your own. His safety is the price of my cooperation."

"That's a great deal for us since we won't need your cooperation for very long. You do realize that once we have the chess pieces you're both expendable. But no problem. We can wait until then to take care of Mr. Lawton."

Of course I knew that was the case, but at least my bargain bought Liam some more time. I'd think of some way to get him to safety when the dive was over. And I hoped Newton was receiving the beacon's signal. He should already be on his way with the calvary.

Garth lowered his gun. "C'mon. We're wasting time. Let's get going."

Brock smiled coldly. "I agree we should get started." He turned to me. "You're a charming conversationalist, my dear, but I've had more than enough time to chit chat with you while you were posing as my assistant. You've grown tedious. Now show me your famous diving skills and take me straight to the rest of those chess pieces."

Chapter 34
Tech and Tricks

"WE'LL NEED to stop by the tank shack for fresh tanks." I gestured at the row of used tanks on *Thundercloud*'s stern. "All these are empty. And we'll need a large crate, some lift bags, and a couple of CO^2 capsules."

"No problem. We can get whatever we need from the tank shack and the tool crib. Let's go." Garth pointed down the dock with his chin.

I stepped off my boat onto the dock and starting walking slowly toward the tank shack. I hoped Ken might be in the tool crib, and that he wasn't part of Moran's gang. There was a slim chance that might be the case, since he'd never seemed to really be an integral part of the Kraken team.

Under the watchful eyes of Garth and his gun, I stopped outside the tank shack and picked up the cart I'd made. I grabbed three fresh tanks and piled them into the cart. Then we all walked over to the tool crib.

As I'd hoped, Ken was there, quietly working on rebuilding the first stage of someone's regulator.

"Hi, Ken." I said. "We're going for a dive, and we'll need lift bags and cartridges too. Oh yeah, and a crate. About this big." I held my arms out wide to the side.

My hopes that Ken wasn't part of the gang were dashed when he looked up and eyed Garth's gun. "Put down the pop gun, Dude. Honey, this isn't Chicken Delight. I don't deliver, and you know where everything is."

Brock and Garth both threw back their heads and roared with laughter.

I didn't say anything, just went behind the counter and picked out a collapsible crate, a few lift bags, and some CO^2 cartridges to use to inflate the bags. I placed everything in the cart, piled the gear bags on top, and stood beside it to wait.

I was staring out at *Thundercloud,* hoping to catch a glimpse of Liam. I nearly jumped out of my skin when I saw him leaning against the cabin on the bow, staring back at me. I don't know exactly how he got free, but I suspected he had used his easily dislocated shoulder to help him escape the bonds.

He'd done it before, and I knew it was excruciatingly painful for him. I hoped he'd use his freedom to escape instead of coming after me, but I knew him too well to think that was a likely scenario. The best I could do for him—for us both, really—was to keep Brock and Garth distracted.

I started pushing the heavy cart toward the usual entry point which was about halfway around the tiny island. The cart bogged down in the sand every few feet, even with the runners I'd made for it. I sighed with relief. I really didn't want to arrive too quickly.

To make sure Brock and Garth focused on me instead of possibly looking back toward *Thundercloud,* I let out a stream of profanity and repeatedly kicked the cart's tires and runners. Garth, Brock, and Ken came running, and they burst out laughing watching my imitation of an angry and frustrated diver.

Actually, it wasn't an act at all. The only difference was that the men watching me would think I was angry because of the cart, but the reality was that I was angry at myself for letting these buffoons catch me. I should have been more careful through this whole assignment, starting right from the interview set up. I prayed that my carelessness didn't get Liam killed.

In the middle of my tantrum, I noticed a substantial pile of sand in the middle of the beach. I didn't look directly at it, but I did grab the cart's handles and aimed for it, shouting and cursing the whole way as I pushed.

Brock, Garth, and Ken were having a big laugh at my expense. Their hoots of laughter followed me, but it didn't sound like they were getting any closer.

I didn't want them nearby when I executed my plan, which might be my best and only shot at saving Liam and escaping from this island of madmen.

When we reached the pile of sand, I quickly pushed the cart over, falling to the ground beside it and letting everything spill out around and on top of me.

Exactly as I'd planned. My gear bag hit the ground first, and my BCD fell on top of it, hiding the unzipped top.

While kicking my legs like I was trying to get up, I reached into the gear bag's opening and rummaged around for the gun I'd placed inside. I thought it was very near the top of the bag, but the fall must have dislodged it. I groped frantically, and almost gasped with relief when my seeking hand touched the hard metal encased in a waterproof LDPE plastic bag.

Carefully, I withdrew the weapon, still under the cover of my BCD. I slid the gun and its bag into one of my BCD's voluminous pockets and then made a great show of my faux struggle to get up again.

Once back on two feet, I unloaded the cart so I could turn it upright, and then reloaded everything, taking care to zip my gear bag closed so Brock and Garth wouldn't get suspicious. I resumed my plodding pace toward the entry point.

They still hadn't joined me by the time I arrived, so I unloaded the cart and set up everyone's gear. I carefully turned on their tanks to fill the hoses and then turned them almost all the way off. The air pressure on their integrated computers would show full tanks, but soon after they got underwater the air flow would be so minimal as to leave the diver air starved. I felt sure neither of the men would bother checking their tanks or the setups before they went in, so they wouldn't know I hadn't turned on their air completely until they were well underwater. And with any luck, they wouldn't know how to rectify the problem.

Now I had two hidden weapons at my disposal, and I was sure they'd work well together, allowing me to get the upper hand on my captors.

Chapter 35
A Very Bad Dive

I'D JUST FINISHED SETTING everything up when Garth, Ken, and Brock strolled up. Garth waved his gun at me. "In the water. Now. Swim out a few feet then wait for us."

I nodded, geared up, and put on my fins. Then I waded backward into the water, dragging the folded crate and the lift bags while keeping a close eye on Garth and his gun. When I was about twenty feet from shore and near the edge of the drop off, Brock raised a hand. "Far enough. Stay there and wait for us before you descend. Garth, give Ken your gun. Ken, if she comes out of the water, shoot her."

Ken took the gun and nodded. He handled the gun with assurance, so I knew he was an experienced shooter. I'd have to think of a way to avoid him when I emerged from the water. That is, if I managed to emerge at all. I blew some air into my BCD so I could stay on the surface without effort until Brock and Garth finally joined me.

I watched as Garth pulled a very large wicked looking dive knife out of his gear bag and strapped it to his right thigh. One more thing to worry about. After I'd escaped from their trap, I'd left my knife on the ledge far below.

"Take us directly to the figurines. Don't try any tricks or we'll kill you and leave your body for the sharks," Brock said. I was pretty sure that was the plan either way, but to gain some time I had to pretend I hadn't guessed.

Garth gave the signal to descend, and we sank down to eighty-five feet. I noticed Brock having some trouble clearing his ears. Garth swam over, grabbed Brock's ankles, and pulled him down to eighty feet. Brock's eardrums must have hurt like crazy from the unrelieved pressure, and his screams reverberated through the comms unit in my mask the whole way down. Garth's ignorance and cold-bloodedness appalled me.

I swam away from the fold in the pinnacle that hid the cavern entrance and stayed close to the wall. I made a point of studying the wall as though I were looking for landmarks, but I was actually checking out the sea life. I knew I was safe as long as they thought I was looking for the cavern entrance.

There were still a lot of fish swimming upside down, wobbling as they swam, or swimming in circles. I'd noticed a slight improvement in the health of the sea life after Liam's team had replaced the poison with a harmless substance, but now they seemed worse off than ever. I couldn't figure out why they were regressing so quickly now.

Until I came around the edge of the pinnacle to where the communication devices were now operating. I could feel the vibrations rattling my brain, and the tiny hairs in my ears went flat. Suddenly I was dizzy, and I couldn't tell which way was up.

Brock and Garth didn't seem affected by the emanations, so I surmised they had taken something to prevent the disorientation I was dealing with. At first I was scared that I was at a further disadvantage since my sense of balance was off, but then I realized that if they thought I was a little more out of it than I was, it might actually be an advantage.

I peered at the fish, analyzing their motions. I flipped over onto my back and twisted my body in random directions as I swam. I heard Brock's sigh of disgust through the comms link. "I knew we should have given her the Zoloft."

"Nah," said Garth. "It's more fun this way, and it'll make the end easier if she's not aware of what's coming."

"Oh, Garth," I thought. *"I'm very aware of what you have planned."*

I swam in a few looping circles, moving away from the pinnacle as

I did. In case they grew tired of waiting and managed to take me unawares somehow, I wanted them as far away from the cavern entrance as possible.

I put a dreamy smile on my face and wobbled my head around. I gazed up at my bubbles, trying to look amazed. This act would have been fun if it hadn't had the potential to be life-ending.

Out of the corner of my eye, I saw two juvenile lemon sharks frolicking out in the blue. They must have felt my random vibrations and mistaken me for a fish in distress. I needed to stop my act or take some action to distract them before they became too interested in me. I thought about how I could use them.

I already knew Garth was afraid of sharks, and as a marine biologist, I also knew that lemon shark bites are rare and rarely fatal to humans.

I had my gun.

I had some sharks.

Now I had my plan.

Under cover of my random contortions, I reached into my BCD pocket and found the gun in its waterproof bag. I knew I could fire it through the BCD pocket, but the bag would very likely flood after that so I probably only had one shot. I had to make it count.

Garth or Brock?

Brock or Garth?

Which would give me the most 'bang' for my one shot?

I chose Brock. I was pretty sure that Garth would do anything to get away from the sharks, especially if I hit Brock and he started leaking blood into the water. But if I hit Garth, Brock would come after me, sharks or no sharks. And any second now, they'd both discover their air wasn't flowing.

Putting a dreamy smile on my face, I wobble-swam toward Brock. I couldn't afford to miss with my one shot, and I didn't know what effect the water and the heavy BCD would have on the bullet's trajectory. I'd have to be up close or risk missing him completely.

As I drew close to Garth, he spoke to Brock through the comm's link. "I thought she had more mental stamina than this, but she's totally out of..." Bang!

Or more like glug.

Either way, the sound immediately following was Garth's scream of shock and pain.

Drat. The water had altered the bullet's trajectory.

The water around him filled with blood, and the sharks were on us within nanoseconds. I backpedaled out of their way, but not before Garth headed for the surface as fast as he could swim.

He had several good reasons to hurry. In addition to the bullet wound and the sharks following him, he must have used up the residual air in his hose. I shot up after him.

I hoped the heat of the bullet piercing the LDPE bag would have reformed the bonds of the plastic bag's surface so that it resealed and wouldn't leak. If it had, my gun might fire again. If it hadn't resealed, the gun would very likely not fire at all, and I had no other weapon.

I was a few feet below and to Brock's right when Garth shot past us. Instead of heading directly for the surface, he was swimming toward our original entry point. He was flailing and jerking around, inadvertently begging the sharks to follow him. And although I could see he was sucking heavily on his mouthpiece and working hard, there were no bubbles coming from his regulator, and he was too panicky to stop and check that the valve was turned on.

Good. At least one of my adversaries wasn't thinking clearly. I could only hope Brock was having the same problem.

I gave a mighty kick and rose to the same level as Brock, but he was on my left and the gun was in my right BCD pocket. I started to turn so I'd have a clear shot when he reached out and knocked my full-face mask off. It floated behind me, still attached to my tank by my air hose, but I couldn't spare the time to attempt a recovery. I had to incapacitate Brock before he could come after me.

But he was too quick. He reached for my neck, wrapping his big hands around my throat and squeezing. I kept my lips sealed to hold in my air and reached into my BCD pocket, shutting my eyes so I could concentrate. I needed to be absolutely certain that the gun was pointing at Brock. I couldn't afford to miss. If I did, it would seal my doom.

I saw bright spots dancing behind my closed eyelids. The emanations from the communication devices' were disorienting and making me dizzy.

I was rapidly losing my ability to think.

I had to do something, and I had to do it fast.

I tried to swallow. Couldn't.

Well, if I shot the gun, either I'd hit Brock and be able to save myself or I'd miss and he'd kill me. Or maybe the gun wouldn't fire at all, or if it did, the bullet would go off to the side instead of straight into Brock.

Almost every possible scenario ended with my death, but I couldn't let myself think about that. I had to act.

I pulled the trigger. The glug sound was loud.

I felt no pain, but I didn't see any blood in the water either.

Then, mercifully, Brock let go of my throat and placed his hands on his belly, trying to hold back the flow of blood. His mouth was open in a surprised 'O.'

Two more juvenile lemon sharks came to investigate.

I swam away from the sharks and recovered my regulator, which was now floating behind me. Then I headed slowly and gently toward the surface, where I crawled out onto the sand.

"Get up," I heard.

It was only then that I remembered Ken and Arthur were still free and on the island.

Slowly, I stood up, thinking as hard and as fast as I could. I shook my head, trying to shake off the last of the confusion I'd felt underwater.

Laughter. I heard two people laughing.

"It's disorienting, isn't it?" said Ken. "Don't worry. It'll wear off in a couple of hours.' He snickered again. "Oh, right. I forgot. You'll be dead in a couple of hours." He cocked his gun.

I deliberately took a few staggering steps to hide the search for my gun in my BCD pocket. It was extremely unlikely it would still work. But it was all I had.

I couldn't believe it when I pulled the zip lock bag open and no water gushed out. The magic heat bonding properties of the low density polyethylene polymer had worked not once, but twice.

My lucky day.

I dropped to the ground, pulled out my gun and shot first Ken, then Arthur.

Perfect. Both shots in center mass.

I thanked the universe that Rafe and I had spent hours over the last year practicing at the range. He was practicing because he needed to be good at it for his movie roles.

I'd only been practicing because I loved hanging out with Rafe. I'd never thought I'd have to use the skill to save my life.

I needed to check on the people I'd shot and administer what first aid I could. I didn't want them dead. I'd only wanted to stop them from hurting me. Still shaking with the aftereffects of adrenaline and the submerged tower-induced confusion, I stood up to go to Ken and Arthur.

I heard shouting and looked up. Several men were running across the beach toward me. I let go of my gun, closed my eyes, dropped back to my knees, and raised my hands over my head.

There was no fight left in me. I was finished.

Chapter 36
Failure

I HAD FAILED. I'd failed Newton and Rosalina and Dane. I'd failed Liam. Worst of all, I'd failed Rafe and cheated us out of the long and happy life we'd planned.

I could taste the salt of my tears when gentle hands touched my arms and helped me to my feet. Soft lips kissed the tears away.

"You are amazing, my love. I may play a superhero in the movies, but you're one in real life. No wonder I love you so much."

I thought I must be dreaming, but when I opened my eyes, Rafe was right there. I flung my arms around my husband and sobbed with joy and relief. "Did you get them all?" I asked.

"No, actually we didn't get any of them. You got them all before we even got here." He grinned at me.

I shook my head. The underwater communication towers plus the blows to my head had left me confused. "That's not possible. There were four of them. Only one of me."

"Then it's no wonder you got them. Those were definitely not fair odds. They didn't stand a chance," he said laughing.

Rafe was holding me steady so I wouldn't fall down, close enough that I could rest my head on his shoulder. I still thought I must be hallucinating his presence, but his hand smoothing my wet hair felt so real that I relaxed into him.

"It's okay. I'm here now. Everything will be fine," he said.

Except it wasn't.

It happened so fast.

Rafe had barely finished speaking when the sound of a shot rang out.

He spun away from me and fell to the ground.

I screamed. I wanted nothing more than to go to him and make sure he was okay, but I knew if I did that, we were all lost. We'd taken our eyes off the bad guys, and they took advantage of our lack of attention.

I looked around.

Ken was a few feet away, kneeling on the sand. Blood seeped from a wound in his belly, but he was ignoring the pain. His hard eyes focused on me with a white hot hatred. He held a pistol in both hands, trying to keep it steady. Only his anger and hate sustained his determination.

Ken stood up, walking toward me with the gun trained on me.

I took a quick step to the side and dropped to the ground to search for my discarded gun. I didn't think the gun would still work, but it was my only hope. My hands were shaking so badly I couldn't keep them steady. My one thought was for Rafe and his safety.

At last my hand touched my gun half buried in the sand. I grabbed it, stood up, and took aim.

I pulled the trigger. The revolver didn't fire.

I tried again. Nothing.

Ken laughed.

He took a triangle stance and aimed at me. He was only a few feet away, and even though his hands were shaking, there was no way he could miss. I knew my life was over. I bowed my head and thanked the universe for Rafe and all the other good things I'd had in this life.

There was a loud bang.

I felt nothing.

Peeking through slitted eyelids, I looked down along my body for visible blood. I had a few scratches and scrapes, but no bullet wounds.

I opened my eyes fully. Ken was lying in the sand, a few feet away. I didn't have any idea what had happened, but whatever it was, it had saved my life.

A gun landed in the sand beside me just before strong warm hands grasped my arms and tugged me to my feet. "You're okay, Fin. I've got you."

Stewie patted my back as he held me upright. "First time I ever fired a gun. Thank God I actually managed to hit him. Ray would never have forgiven me if I'd let that scum hurt you."

I turned my head to rest on his shoulder, but I took a quick step back when I saw Rafe lying motionless in the sand.

"Rafe. We need to save Rafe." I was crazed with grief and terror. "Where's Doc?"

He patted my shoulder. "She's helping Liam. He's pretty bad off…"

"Not as bad as Rafe. We need her here. NOW!" I was practically screaming in his ear. "NOW!" I stepped back and waved my arms over my head. "Doc! Doc! Rafe's been shot. We need you here. Hurry."

I saw Doc look at Liam and then back at me. She was too far away for me to hear what she said to him, but I saw him nod. She grabbed her medical bag and took off toward us at a run.

Chapter 37
Raid

I KNEW it was annoying her, but I couldn't stop hovering over Doc's shoulder. "Will he be okay?" I asked for at least the tenth time.

She sighed with exasperation. "Yes, nothing has changed since I told you he'd be fine"—she looked at her watch— "a minute and a half ago. He'll probably have a little scar, but that will only add to his action hero image. Relax and let me do my work."

"But he's unconscious. Are you sure…"

She turned back toward me, and I could tell from the expression on her face that she was about to send me very far away when at the last minute we were both saved from our first ever fight by a faint moan from her patient.

I threw myself to the sand next to him. "It's okay. You'll be fine. I'm here with you and so is Doc. You're in good hands."

Doc frowned. "He'd have a better chance of a full recovery if you'd get out of my way and let me do my work."

Reluctantly, I stood up and backed off a few paces. Blinking back grateful tears, I lifted my head and looked around, hoping to take my mind off Rafe's condition. My gaze landed on Stewie, standing off to one side, tears streaming down his face. He was shaking as badly as a person can shake and still remain upright. I hadn't seen him this bad off since someone had cruelly set up a smorgasbord of drugs and alcohol in the dive shop to tempt him off the wagon.

Stewie tried to seem tough, but I knew underneath he could be as fragile as glass sometimes. His relationship with Doc meant the world to him, and he was well aware it was utterly dependent on him maintaining his sobriety. So far the knowledge kept him on an even keel, but right now, he looked ready to pack it in and dive into the nearest bottle.

I realized he'd focused his eyes on Ken's body, lying untended in the sand. He'd never killed a man before. Stewie wouldn't stay sane and sober for much longer if he didn't know for sure that Ken would recover.

The look of guilt and horror on Stewie's face was profound. He was a good man and he needed help and reassurance that he'd done the right thing by shooting another human being. I didn't want to go near Ken either, but after all the times Stewie had saved my bacon, I owed it to him.

I looked around, hoping somebody was on the way to help, but there was no one else here on the beach. Our own casualties consumed the entire attention of the crowd from RIO, and it seemed that Ken's teammates were either dead or had fled the scene, leaving him behind.

But then again, what would you expect? They were the bad guys, and he was as bad as any one of them.

Even so, that didn't excuse the good guys for ignoring him. Someone from our side should have checked on him by now. Yes, he was a bad guy, but he was a human being and if he was still alive, he deserved whatever medical treatment we could provide before we hauled him off to jail.

In our defense, we had limited resources here on the island. It was only because of our concern for Liam and Rafe that nobody had bothered to check on Ken yet. I didn't know for sure, but I assumed Ken was probably just in shock and would be okay.

The idea of touching Ken was utterly repugnant, but someone had to do it. I gave Stewie a hug. "It's alright. I'll take care of him."

Stewie shuddered. "I think he's dead. I killed him."

I patted his back. It was gut-wrenching to see the self-loathing on his face. "I'm sure he's fine. Why don't you head over to *Thundercloud* and send Newton or Dane here to help me out?"

He nodded and began walking slowly toward the dock. His feet dragged in the sand and his head hung low. I watched him until I was sure he'd make it to the dock on his own, then I stepped reluctantly across the sand to Ken's body. Unlike what I'd told Stewie, I was certain the man was dead because of the growing splotch of blood staining the sand under his torso. That, and the fact that he hadn't moved a muscle in all the time I'd been watching him.

I knelt near his head to test for a pulse. I'd just touched my fingers to his neck when Arthur rose from behind a nearby pile of sand. The pistol in his hand looked enormous, and he aimed it right at my head. For a split second, I froze.

An evil smile spread across Arthur's face, and that was all the warning I needed. I threw myself backward just before I heard the bang and felt a pain like fire spread along my ribs. I touched my hand to the spot, and my fingers came away red.

Arthur stood atop the pile of sand and aimed at me again. I didn't want to become an easy target by standing up, so I scrambled backward toward the ocean waves, moving as quickly as I could.

Because of his fear of sharks, I knew Arthur wouldn't enter the water if I was bleeding—and I was definitely bleeding—so reaching the water was my only hope. I could swim underwater until I was far enough away that I'd be safe. Except I couldn't leave Doc and Rafe alone and undefended on the beach.

And anyway, crabbing along on my back wasn't a very fast mode of escape, and Arthur was walking toward me. I had to move faster without making myself a target. So I rolled. I kept rolling until I hit the water and was out far enough that the water was deep enough for me to swim. The salt in my wound stung like crazy.

I heard a high pitched whizzing sound and a nano-second later, a bang. I was sure I was a goner. But I kept rolling anyway, and I was face up just in time to see Arthur spin in a half circle and fall to the ground.

Oliver ran across the beach toward me, and Genevra followed, holding a wicked looking rifle in the ready position. Oliver plunged into the surf toward me. He lifted me to my feet and together, we waded back to the beach. Both Oliver and I watched as a grim-faced Genevra poked first Arthur, then Ken, with the tip of her rifle, checking to be sure they were dead.

Neither Oliver nor I had ever seen her like this, but once I did, so much about her that had never made sense fell into place. Her martial arts expertise. Her willingness to work for peanuts at RIO when she was obviously qualified for so much more. Her easy acceptance of Liam's frequent unexplained disappearances. Her timely arrival on that other occasion when one of the bad guys had threatened my life.

Obviously, she must be part of the mysterious international peacekeeping force that both Newton and Liam belonged to. She was one of my best friends. She could easily have set my mind at ease about Liam's absences. She'd never said a word about it to me, even when I was complaining about Liam disappearing for weeks and months at a time.

I was struggling to grasp this new vision of my friend Genevra and wondering if Oliver knew, when the bullet wound in my side made itself known once again. Oliver helped me sit down on the sand, and Doc came over and gave me a shot. I shut my eyes against the sun and the pain. That shot was the last thing I remember until the next morning.

Chapter 38
Hospital

I WOKE up with the sun in my eyes, and when I opened them, I recognized RIO's infirmary. As soon as I realized where I was, yesterday's events came rushing back. I gave a start. Where was Rafe? Was he okay?

Genevra was sitting beside my bed. She reached out and patted my hand. "Relax. Everything is fine."

"Where's Rafe? Is he okay?"

She pointed behind me. "Right there in the next bed. Alive and well, although he's sleeping. It's still pretty early."

The curtains between the two cubicles were open, and when I turned my head I saw Rafe's blond hair on the pillow of the bed next to mine. A soft snore provided even more reassurance that he was doing well. "Liam?" I asked.

"Also fine. He's in the cubicle on the other side of Rafe."

I nodded. "You're with the international police consortium, same as Newton and Liam, right?"

She nodded.

"But you don't disappear all the time like they do. Why not?"

She shrugged. "My assignment is different."

The light dawned. "I'm you're assignment?"

She nodded, and my heart cracked. "You were, but I have a different assignment now."

I took a deep breath to steady my voice. "I thought we were friends, but you never said anything. I guess I was always just an assignment to you."

Genevra looked sad. "I admit you were an assignment before we got to know each other, but we are friends. True friends. Nothing will change that."

I stared at her. "That's where you're wrong. Something already did."

She bit her lip. "Please don't say that. I value our friendship, and it doesn't matter how it started. What matters is that we are friends. It would be sad if something as meaningless as a job ruined it."

"If you call years of lies and a relationship built on subterfuge meaningless—yeah, I guess it would be sad." I inhaled deeply. "I don't see it that way."

She brushed a tear from her eye.

I looked away. "Why me? Why was I chosen by this stupid association to have a babysitter?"

She looked startled. "You can't figure that out? Newton is very high up in the organization. You and Maddy are his greatest weaknesses. You both have agents assigned to keep you safe, because the best and easiest way to get to Newton is through one of you."

I thought this over for a minute. "Newton loves Oliver too. Is Oliver your new assignment?"

She nodded.

"Did you only marry him because he was your assignment?"

She shook her head. "No. He became my assignment when we got married. They'll give you a new protector soon."

"I'll turn down whoever it is. By the way, who is Maddy's guardian?" I asked after running through and rejecting all the possibilities.

She shook her head, "I'm not at liberty to tell you, and I'm pretty sure you wouldn't believe me even if I did."

"But it's not Dane?" Maddy would be devastated if she thought the only man she'd cared about since her beloved Ray had died actually thought of her as an assignment.

Genevra shook her head. "Not Dane."

Another thought struck me. "Does Oliver know about you?"

"No, and I'd like to keep it that way if we can," she said.

"Why? Is he just another assignment too?" I couldn't keep the snark out of my voice.

She sighed. "No. I truly love Oliver. I wouldn't have married him otherwise. Please don't tell him."

I rolled my eyes. "You don't think he'll have questions about how and why his new wife went strutting daintily down a beach carrying an assault rifle and blowing away a bunch of bad guys? Without even batting an eyelash? As far as he knows, you're just an overqualified executive assistant."

That remark was slightly unfair. Genevra had always been much more than an assistant, but I wanted to emphasize how different the two roles she played actually were.

She shrugged. "I'll find some way to explain it to him."

I was very protective of my adopted brother. He'd had a difficult life, and I always tried to smooth his path. I folded my arms stubbornly. "Good. You'd better find a way pretty quickly, because if you don't tell him soon, I will."

"He's my husband. I'll tell him when I'm ready," she snapped back.

"Tell him what?" said Oliver, who had just entered the infirmary and was standing at the edge of my cubicle.

Genevra glared at me. "This isn't how I wanted to tell you. Maybe we can talk about it later when we get home."

He smiled his goofy smile. "Since Fin already knows, I don't see why you can't tell me now."

Her nostrils flared. "Okay. If that's how you want to play it." She stepped toward him and took his hand. "I'm pregnant."

My mouth fell open. I didn't know if this was the real truth or if she'd just made a story up on the spot to get out of telling Oliver about her involvement in the consortium, but at this point, there was nothing I could—or would—do.

Oliver's face was glowing, and the biggest smile I'd ever seen was spreading across his face. "That's amazing!"

He stepped forward and picked up Genevra. He swung her around in a happy dance for a few seconds, then he put her down as carefully as though she were made of glass.

"Oh, I'm so sorry. I wasn't thinking. I hope I didn't hurt you or the baby."

She smiled at him. "Don't worry. We're both fine." She took his hand. "Let's go home and celebrate—just us two…er…three."

Oliver nodded. "Great idea," he said. He turned back to me. "We'll be back later after you've had a little more time to recover."

He winked at me, and we both knew his return was not at all dependent on my recovery.

I was fuming at Genevra, but what could I say? Her secrets truly were hers to share.

I glanced over at Rafe, but he was still sleeping soundly. I was certain he'd have questions about what had gone on while I'd been on that accursed island, and why I'd been there in the first place. I was trying to figure out what I could tell him without compromising Newton's or Liam's safety when Doc walked in.

"How's my favorite patient this morning?" she asked.

"Never better," I said. "A more important question would be when can I get out of here. And I'll want to take my husband with me, of course."

She smiled. "You can both go home later today, as long as you're still feeling up to it after lunch. And the meeting, of course."

"What meeting?"

"Newton and Dane want a 'lessons learned' meeting later today, including a recap of everybody's part in the operation. Apparently, they've never had so many casualties in any prior assignments."

"You know?" I asked.

She nodded but answered with a question. "Know what?"

Her response was startling, but I filed it away to contemplate at some future date. I had more important things on my mind right now. "Why hasn't Rafe waked up yet?"

Smiling, she said, "I'd guess it's because he didn't sleep a wink the whole time you were alone on that island. He had no idea what was going on and why he couldn't join you. Or even call you."

I shrugged. "That makes at least two of us. I'm not cut out for that kind of activity, and neither is he. I don't know how Newton and Liam do it."

"No names, please," she said pleasantly.

I looked at her sharply. Was she telling me something? Could she be Maddy's protector?

No way. They'd been friends since college. But…could it be? It made a certain kind of sense.

I knew she'd never tell me, so I changed the subject. "How is Stewie? He looked like he was going to have a breakdown after he killed Ken."

"Genevra killed Ken, remember?" She looked pointedly at me.

I was pretty sure Ken had been dead before Genevra and her rifle came on the scene, but I understood why Doc would want to let Stewie think he hadn't killed a man, no matter how bad that man had been while alive.

I nodded. "Sorry. I guess my brain is still a little addled from all the trauma."

She nodded, and I could see in her eyes she was glad I'd agreed to go along with the story that might save the man she loved from drinking himself to death.

The silence lasted until Rafe broke in. "What do I have to do to get some breakfast around here? A patient could starve in this place."

I was so happy he was awake. I jumped up and threw myself across the aisle between our beds. "Thank the universe you're alright," I said, kissing him. "I was worried sick when you didn't wake up."

He smiled and kissed me back. "I was just as worried when I came back from the production meetings and Newton told me you were out there all alone, hobnobbing with a bunch of bad guys. Please don't ever do that again, or at least if you must, let me come with you."

"I promise," I said, nestling as close to him as I could get. I ignored the pain in my own hip, but Rafe groaned when I bumped against his injury.

"I'm a wounded man. Could you take it easy on me?" He smiled to take the sting out of his words.

Horrified that I might have accidentally hurt him, I jumped away. Then after thinking about it for a second or two, I laughed. "We just have to change sides. Then neither of us will be poking at the other's sore spots." I hopped out of the narrow bed and walked around to the other side where I nestled my uninjured side against Rafe's uninjured side.

"Better?" I asked.

"Much," he said. "Brilliant thinking, as usual."

Doc rolled her eyes. "Breakfast will be here in a few minutes. The meeting's at ten. See you there." She started to walk away, but as she passed Liam's cubicle, she must have noticed he was awake. "

You too, Liam. But I'll bring you in a wheelchair myself. Will you need help with breakfast or a shower? Are you in pain? Your shoulder? Your hands…?"

Liam's familiar chuckle filled the room. "It's mainly my head that hurts. Lucky it's so hard or they might have done me some real damage. My shoulder's fine. Thanks for popping it back in. I usually do it myself, but this time I couldn't manage it on my own with all the fingers on both of my hands broken."

There was a pause. "Not too sure about the hands," he said softly.

I was shamelessly eavesdropping.

"We'll talk later," Doc said. "You'll need physical therapy. And I think your adventuring days should end. I don't know how many more times you can come back from all the damage to your hands. The bad guys do seem to love breaking your fingers."

"They do, don't they?" he said, and the sadness in his voice nearly broke my heart.

Chapter 39
Final Report

RAFE and I scarfed down our breakfasts and then took turns in the infirmary's showers. I went second, and I have to say that I felt one hundred percent better when I emerged from the shower area, dressed in a clean set of RIO scrubs.

I could hear laughter when I approached the cubicles, and it surprised me to see Rafe sitting in the chair at the foot of Liam's bed when I came out. They were both wearing scrubs like mine, and they were laughing uproariously at something Liam had said that I hadn't heard.

I was happy that they seemed to be on friendly terms. I hadn't been sure we'd ever get to this point after Rafe and I eloped, but I guess Liam was an even bigger man than I'd given him credit for. Plus Rafe is so charming that he's very hard to dislike.

Or at least, that's my opinion.

I was about to pull up a chair to join them when Newton poked his head into the infirmary. "I hate to rush you, but the rest of the crew is waiting. Any idea how long you'll be?"

We all looked at each other and shrugged.

"I think we're ready now," I said. We all stood and followed Newton to RIO's glass-walled conference room.

They'd left three seats along one side of the polished mahogany table open for us. Dane, his brother Marvin Scott of the Department of the Environment, and Captain Peter Roberts of the Coast Guard, sat together along the opposite side. Vincent Pollilo, the captain of RIO's research vessel the *Omega,* and Genevra each sat at an end of the table. Gus Simmons was in a chair against the wall next to T-8.

We took our seats. Newton stood in front of the screen. He gave a two minute recap of the reasons the consortium targeted Kraken's island project for investigation. Then he talked about why he'd opted to bring me in, even though I wasn't an actual operative. His justification centered mainly around my dive skills and my ability to emulate a commercial diver. Finally, he looked at me.

"Can you give us an overview of the events on the island? What you saw, and any lessons learned that would help in future operations."

I glared at him for a second. He'd caught me unprepared and put me on the spot. I wasn't ready for a presentation. "You'll have to excuse me if my recap is a bit disjointed. I haven't had time to wrap my arms around the whole thing yet."

Rafe reached over and squeezed my hand. I smiled at him.

"First off," I said, "don't give a woman operative a stripper name and a sexy wardrobe, and then send her alone to an island where she's the only woman among a group of very bad men. Fending off their hazing and advances made my job a lot harder than it needed to be, and I believe it led to the Kraken guys deciding I was fair game right from the start."

"Second, it would have helped if I'd had more time to prep for the operation. Maybe then I wouldn't have been sitting in front of a TV that I didn't know was showing RIO documentaries while I was trying to convince the bad guys that I was Honey Hynes, not the woman on the screen. You should have been more open and given me more information on the project, more time to prepare, and set up a sanitized location for the interview that was in character. Or even better yet, you should have sent in someone with actual undercover experience. My dive skills were not essential after the first couple of dives, and if I'd had more insight into what you were after, I probably could have avoided even those few dives. So my dive skills were absolutely non-essential. It would have helped a lot if you'd told me what I was supposed to be looking for. Even a hint would have helped."

"While I appreciated the visits when you sent people by to check on me, the bad guys were laughing at us because it made it even more obvious who I was and why I was there. And you should have removed Rosalina off the island right up front." I paused a moment. "By the way, what's going to happen to Rosalina? She can't live on the island now. It's poisoned, and there's no fresh water."

Newton smiled. "Rosalina has accepted a job as my housekeeper, which she'll only need until her ownership of the sea monster chess set is certified. It turns out that, as you suspected, the sea monster figurines are solid gold, but the value of the items as antiquities substantially overshadows by their value as metal. We estimate their worth will ultimately exceed the value of the entire treasure from the San José galleon, sunk near Cartagena in 1708.

"They are superb examples of Columbian art, and we assume they came from one of San Jose's sister ships. Legend has it they were commissioned as a gift for King Filipe, but we have no way of identifying their authenticity or which ship they might have been on until we've done more research. Rosalina thinks there might be some records in her family papers, so she's working with a historian to see what they can figure out. Once they've established the chess set's authenticity and provenance, she'll be a very rich woman. She can go anywhere she wants and do whatever she wants. But in the meantime, she's safe with me."

I nodded. "Good. Thanks for seeing to her safety."

Newton nodded and motioned for me to continue my story.

"Last, if I'd known what I was looking for and how Alonzo and Miguel died, I would have been a lot safer and I might have been able to shut down the investigation a lot faster. I certainly wouldn't have let Brock and Garth get the drop on me with their steel plate routine."

Newton shuddered. "You have no idea how scared I was when we realized your rescue beacon was broadcasting from underwater. I was terrified we'd arrive too late." He bit back a smile of pride. "I should have known you had the whole operation well in hand. You really are amazing."

"Thanks, but I didn't have any hope at that point. I wanted to reach the surface as fast as I could so I could help Liam. Both objectives were long shots. I left the beacon on the ledge outside the cavern because I didn't expect to survive, and I wanted to give you a clue that there was something in the area you needed to seek out."

I glanced over at Marvin Scott, who had been frantically taking notes as I talked. "The entire operation plan was flawed. Those flaws resulted in unnecessary casualties and injuries; disruption to civilian lives; and extensive environmental damage, the very thing you were supposed to be trying to halt. Not to mention that you dropped me in with a bunch of predators without even a heads up."

Newton's face paled, but he recovered quickly. "I apologize that we put you in unnecessary danger, but your performance exceeded our expectations. Not only did you discover how and why the Kraken team was creating the environmental damage that was our primary concern, but you also discovered a cache of invaluable and historically important artifacts."

I was still angry at Newton for sending me into danger in the first place, but I put that aside for now. We'd discuss it later.

"And the communication towers? What will you do with them?" I said.

Newton and Marvin Scott exchanged pointed glances before Newton finally spoke. "We'll dismantle and remove the towers. We'll set the system up in a secure location to test it out. The Kraken team had a very advanced technology going, and we'll need to understand it better before we decide what to do with it. The commercial opportunities are limitless, but so are the criminal applications. We'll be very careful about letting that technology loose in the world."

I sighed. "Technology doesn't stay hidden. If one group of bad guys figured it out, the next group won't be very far behind. You have your work cut out for you, and I'm glad I won't be involved. This was a terrible experience for me, and I'm very happy it's over."

"And I have a question. Whatever happened to Bert?"

The room froze and nobody spoke for a few seconds.

"We're on it," Captain Roberts said finally.

Newton nodded and reached over and touched my hand. "You did an amazing job. Not many people could have done what you did.

Despite our screwups, we picked the right person for the job. But I have a question. Why didn't you leave when we tried to recall you?"

I was puzzled by his remark. "Recall me? I don't remember any recall. I was begging to come home."

"How many times and how many ways did we have to deliver the code word before you remembered that muffin meant to get out of there fast?"

I slapped my forehead. "Right! I thought you guys were just being nice and making sure I had something to eat. It never occurred to me you wanted me out of there."

The four team leaders stared at me, surprised by my confession of utter stupidity. Rafe put a hand on my shoulder, showing me he was with me no matter what.

After a moment of silence, Newton resumed speaking. "You were very brave to stay there. You helped us get to the bottom of the mystery, and you saved the island and the reef from even more environmental damage. Well done, Fin."

I looked at him with sadness. "Thanks, but I quit. Don't ever ask me to get involved in another one of your investigations. The human cost is just too high for me to deal with." I stood up and headed toward the door.

Behind me, I heard several chairs sliding back from the table. Rafe caught up to me and took my hand as we walked out of the conference room. Liam and Genevra followed behind us, and T-8 brought up the rear.

Chapter 40
Final Dive

IT WAS A WEEK LATER, and I hadn't seen or spoken to Newton since the meeting. I wasn't quite sure how I felt about our estrangement. On the one hand, I felt completely justified for cutting him off. He had knowingly sent me into danger, all alone and unprepared for what I'd be facing. Granted, he'd given me some high tech tools, one of which had saved my life on multiple occasions. But that shouldn't have been necessary in the first place.

On the other hand, he was my father, and I loved him. He hadn't been in my life while I was growing up, and I'd felt the ache of missing him every single day. It had taken me a while to learn to trust that he'd be there for me when he'd finally returned to my life, but almost right from the start, I was overjoyed to know him and happy to know that we'd built a strong relationship.

Except I couldn't help but realize that since he'd been back in my life, RIO had been at the center of a lot more crime than I ever remembered in prior years.

Granted, Newton's presence wasn't to blame for all of it. Maybe he wasn't to blame for any of it, except possibly this last episode. Or maybe I just hadn't been aware of any earlier crime because I was young and oblivious.

It was hard to know what to do or how I should feel. The stress of my ordeal and this latest estrangement from my father had been keeping me awake at night, and it was even keeping me from eating.

Like now, when I sighed and pushed my uneaten breakfast away.

Rafe looked from the plate of fresh fruit and whole wheat toast he'd prepared for me and frowned. "You're eating even less than I do, and that's not good for you. You're so active, you need to keep your strength up." He pushed the plate back toward me. "Just a few more bites," he wheedled. "For me? Please."

Reluctantly, I picked up a grape and popped it in my mouth. "There. Happy now?"

He smiled sadly. "I'm only happy when you're happy. You know that. What can I do to make this better?"

I saw the shadow in his eyes, so I smiled to make it go away. I popped another grape in my mouth. "Let's go on our honeymoon. Because we thought someone had stolen the *Tranquility*, we never got to finish everything we'd planned. That's no way to start a marriage."

I rose to walk over to his seat at the kitchen table. He reached up to wrap me in his arms, and I plunked myself down on his lap. "It's the perfect time. Filming on your movie's been delayed. Our latest documentary is coming along well, and we're slightly ahead of schedule. If you want to, we can work on it while we're away. Or not. We can do whatever you want. And we can dive Bloody Bay Wall again. Take long walks on the beach with Penny." I whispered some additional suggestions in his ear and he laughed.

"I'm sold. Let's do it." His grin was a thing of beauty.

"Yay! We can leave right away." I stood up to go pack my bag.

"Not until you finish your breakfast," he said sternly. "You'll need a lot of energy to withstand what I have in mind for you. I can't have you fainting from hunger while we're on our second honeymoon."

He laughed, and I could see he was delighted by the idea of actually resuming our honeymoon.

Forty-five minutes later, we were on our way. I'd called ahead, and we were able to reserve the same cabin we'd stayed in before when we were at Paradise Villas on Little Cayman. I checked the tide tables, and if we hurried, we'd be able to make the crossing on *Tranquility* without worrying about currents. We'd just gotten a fresh supply of Penny's food, so we didn't have to worry about going shopping for her. Even all the laundry was done. It's like the universe had conspired to make sure we could go at a moment's notice.

Rafe and I were both giddy with excitement. Even though we'd returned from our original honeymoon just a few short weeks ago, we'd been apart almost continuously since then. The idea of spending long lazy days together was intoxicating, and diving Little Cayman was always a joy.

We arrived at our hotel shortly after sunset, and by that time we were both pretty beat. We decided to have dinner in our cabin, and then take Penny for a long walk on the beach before heading to bed early. That way we'd be able to get in our first dive tomorrow morning, right after sunrise.

The next morning, as soon as we'd fed and walked Penny, we dropped her off with the management team at Paradise Villas. They'd agreed to watch her while we were diving. She'd loved hanging out with them when we were here before, so she was excited to be back in the land of endless belly rubs and almost unlimited treats. We laughed at her excitement, and then hurried off to the *Tranquility*, grabbing our gear bags on our way out.

We'd decided to make our first dive at Mixing Bowl, because finding the *Tranquility* missing when we surfaced the last time we'd been there had ruined the good feelings from that amazing dive. We hoped that making it our first dive on this trip would reset the vibes.

Mixing Bowl is a fantastic dive site, offering the opportunity to explore all the best that Little Cayman has to offer. The site includes a sheer vertical wall, a vast area of hardpan, and an abundance of swim throughs. The sea life is equally diverse, and divers frequently see pelagic creatures, sharks, mantas, typical reef fish like parrot fish, assorted angelfish, blennies, spotted drums, tiny shrimp, schooling jacks, and colorful chromis, as well as stingrays, eagle rays, moray eels, and octopus—all on the same dive. Whatever it is a diver enjoys seeing, sooner or later they will it find at Mixing Bowl.

Rafe and I had decided to start our dive by going through one of the many swim throughs the site offers, since that's how we'd started our last dive on the site. But we didn't want to totally duplicate that dive, because it hadn't ended well, so we chose a different nearby swim through to start.

As before, the coral on the site was incredible, vibrant and healthy. As we swam, we noticed several shy specimens hiding in the crevices, including a couple of spiny lobster, a tiny juvenile spotted drum, and an octopus. We almost missed the octopus because he had done such an amazing job of matching his surroundings.

We emerged from the swim through onto the wall at right around one hundred feet, and we spent a moment hovering over the drop off that plunged to unimaginable depths. While we hung there, we peered out into the blue. Our patience was rewarded with the sight of a Hawksbill turtle, a spotted eagle ray, and a Caribbean reef shark. None of the creatures showed any interest in us, but they hung around long enough for us to get a good look at them.

We headed back up the wall, and as we approached the ledge, we saw several large Nassau groupers. A spotted moray eel waited in line at a cleaning station, with his mouth opened wide for his dental checkup.

As we started swimming over the sand, a large group of garden eels ducked into their burrows at our approach. A female southern stingray buried herself in the sand, and two more stingrays glided past us on their way out to the blue.

Huge schools of jacks and grunts hovered over the coral heads, swooping and swirling in some rhythm only they could understand. A trumpet fish hid in the seclusion of a giant gorgonian, obviously hoping to catch his next meal unawares. Several anemones swayed gracefully in the mild current, and a queen conch sheltered under a nearby overhang waiting for sunset.

Fairy basslets, rock beauties, and chromis swirled about, adding brilliant color to the landscape. Queen angelfish swam sedately in a figure eight near a large orange barrel sponge, and a jaunty filefish passed right in front of Rafe's mask, making him laugh out loud. On our way back to the *Tranquility*, we stopped to peer under a secluded coral ledge and found a nurse shark snoozing the morning away.

All in all, it was an amazing dive. It felt almost like the sea creatures had turned out in force to welcome us back and to provide solace for the troubles we'd endured since we were here last.

Of course, I knew that wasn't the case. This rich site teems with abundant sea life all the time.

For every diver, on every dive.

I'd never heard any diver complain about this site. It was universally and enthusiastically loved.

Rafe and I took turns climbing the *Tranquility*'s ladder and stowed our gear for our surface interval. I changed over our BCDs and regulators to fresh tanks while Rafe sliced up some fresh fruit in the galley for a quick snack. We sat together on the bow, sipping water and licking mango juice off our fingers, laughing the whole time. The surface interval flew by.

We decided to do Lea Lea's Lookout for our second dive, so I started up the *Tranquility*'s engines and motored over to the mooring there. The wall at this site starts at about thirty-five to forty feet before dropping to immeasurable depths, but we planned to stay in the shallower areas, exploring the coral along the sand chutes.

We geared up and made our entries. It wasn't long before we reached the reef and were traveling along the hardpan looking for interesting sea life. We were admiring a group of Pederson shrimp when several reef sharks passed over us on their way out to the blue. We were thrilled to see them, but they took no notice of us.

We grinned at each other and continued our dive. We found a flamingo tongue munching away and clinging to a sea fan. Careful not to let the slight surge push us into the nearby black coral, we hovered near him for a while before continuing the journey along the sandy path that led toward the wall. Several nearly invisible sand tilefish flitted around below us, and we saw a massive peacock flounder.

Too soon, we reached the turnaround point on our air, so we headed back toward the *Tranquility*. We did our safety stop hovering over the coral and hardpan to see what we could see. Our payoff was the sight of two stingrays burying themselves side by side under the sand.

Rafe climbed up the ladder first. I handed up my fins when it was my turn to reboard. We sat on the benches on the *Tranquility*'s port side and slotted our empty tanks into the racks that lined the gunwales behind us. It had been an amazing morning, but we were eager to get back for lunch.

We couldn't wait to pick up Penny and take her for a long walk on the beach and an extended session of catch using her favorite raggedy old tennis ball. She might even agree to go wading with us, although we always made her wear her life vest, and we kept a tight grip on her leash when she was in the water, even if it was only an inch or two deep

When we arrived back at the hotel dock, Rafe secured *Tranquility* to a cleat on the boards. I shut down the engines. As soon as I jumped off the last step of the ladder from the flying bridge, Rafe said "I'll race you to the office to pick up Penny. First one to touch the check in desk wins. Loser has to clean the gear after every dive for a week." His eyes sparkled at his challenge.

"You're on," I said. Without warning, I ran quickly across the deck and hurdled the *Tranquility*'s gunwales, maybe a half-step before Rafe landed behind me. Together, we raced along the wooden pier to reclaim our puppy and restart our interrupted life together.

While I ran, I contemplated how lucky I was to have found Rafe, and how compatible we were. Just being with him made me happy.

We ran neck-and-neck across the beach to the office building, neither of us going all out until we were a few steps from the open door. Knowing that Rafe's best pace was a little bit faster than mine, I needed to do something if I were going to win the competition, so I put on a burst of speed and pulled ahead for a step or two.

Rafe was laughing, but he caught up within a few paces, and our hands landed on the check-in desk at the same time. We were glowing with the exhilaration of the run and our love for each other.

I called Penny's name, and knowing she would try to leap into our arms when she heard us, we crouched low so we could easily catch her. She'd been asleep behind the desk, and she rushed toward us and jumped. We caught her into a three way hug, complete with kisses and licks.

I caught Rafe's gaze with mine, and we beamed at each other. I'd never felt such joy and contentment as I did when I was with him, and I could see on his face that he was feeling the same deep-seated connection. We walked out of the resort's lobby hand in hand. I made a quick promise to myself that I would never again do anything that might jeopardize the blissful life we'd found together.

Famous last words.

Also by Sharon Ward

In Deep

Sunken Death

Dark Tide

Killer Storm

Hidden Depths

Sea Stars

Rip Current

Or see the entire series Fin Fleming series by following the link or use the QR code on the next page.

If you enjoyed Rip Current, you can continue reading about the adventures of Fin and the gang by following the links above.

Also, nothing (except actually buying the book) helps an author more than a positive review, so please give Hidden Depths (and me!) a boost by leaving a review. Here's the link:

Rip Current or use the QR code

Link to the Sea Monsters Review Site

And if you'd like to subscribe to my totally random and very rarely published newsletter, you can sign up here. or use the QR code

Link to SharonWard.com

Links to my Books

Shop my online store

Shop the Series Page on Amazon

Acknowledgments

So many people help out, and many of them don't even know how much help they really are. Thank you all. I hope I don't forget anyone, but here goes:

Kate, Mary Beth, Stephanie, and Andrea, my writing/drinking group. Can't do one without the other. Definitely can't do it without you.

Michele Dorsey, my friend. So glad we took the self-publishing journey together.

The entire Tropical Authors group, a continuing source of inspiration and a fine example of writers supporting each other. Special thanks to Nick and Chris for always cheerfully fixing it when I flub the newsletter.

Additional special thanks to David Berens for the astonishingly beautiful covers.

And Wayne Stinnett, thanks for inspiration and encouragement. (Betcha didn't know you inspire me, didja?)

And Hallie Ephron, a continuing example of class, charm and great writing. Best writing teacher ever. Thank you for everything.

Teri Hoitt, another line all your own!! 😎

And always:

Erin, Scott, Cam, Taylor, and Milan Lambrinos.

Erin, Pat, Colin, and Anthony Rogers.

Josh, Jenn, Parker, and Isaac Ward.

Ed, Bob, and Dave Hoitt. Good brothers all. With great wives Teri and Trish, plus Patti who is greatly missed

Molly for the snout pokes. She never gives up, even when I do.

And Jack, who continues to be the best husband in the universe.

Check out the link below if you're interested in learning about Quantum communication

https://www.naval-technology.com/features/featuredeep-secret-secure-submarine-communication-on-a-quantum-level/?cf-view

About the Author

Sharon Ward is the author of the Fin Fleming Scuba Diving Mystery Series, which includes *In Deep, Sunken Death, Dark Tide, Killer Storm, Hidden Depths, Sea Stars and Rip Current, as well as this book, Sea Monsters*. The ninth book in the series, *Ice Water* is coming in early 2025.

Sharon was a marketing executive at prominent software companies Oracle and Microsoft before becoming a writer. She was a PADI certified divemaster who has hundreds of dives under her weight belt. Sharon is a member of Sisters in Crime, MWA, ITW, Grub Street, the Authors Guild, and the Cape Cod Writers Center. She lives in Massachusetts with her husband Jack and their miniature long-haired dachshund Molly, who is the actual head of the Ward household.

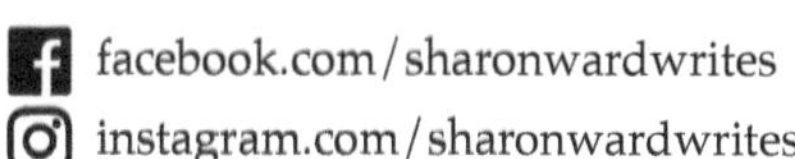

www.ingramcontent.com/pod-product-compliance
Lightning Source LLC
Chambersburg PA
CBHW030358310726
48979CB00001B/352
* 9 7 8 1 9 5 8 4 7 8 4 3 1 *